T0107302

MISSION TO PHANTERICA

BY

Charles E. Miller

iUniverse, Inc.
New York   Bloomington

Mission to Phanterica

iUniverse books may be ordered through booksellers or by contacting:

iUniverse
1663 Liberty Drive
Bloomington, IN 47403
www.iuniverse.com
1-800-Authors (1-800-288-4677)

Because of the dynamic nature of the Internet, any Web addresses or links contained in this book may have changed since publication and may no longer be valid. The views expressed in this work are solely those of the author and do not necessarily reflect the views of the publisher, and the publisher hereby disclaims any responsibility for them.

ISBN: 978-1-4401-0590-6 (pbk)

Printed in the United States of America

iUniverse rev. date: 12/20/2008

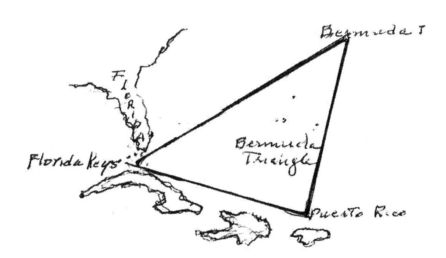

The Search

Chapter 1

The Plan Revealed

One of my closest friends, Dr. Igmar Barodin, and I were discussing the mysterious colony said to be anchored somewhere in the Bermuda Triangle of Mystery in the Caribbean Sea, a colony that had borrowed so widely from cultures all over the world that it can not truly said to be a colony of any nation but, instead, is pan-national. I had first read about such a colony, not an Atlantis but an actual island in the Caribbean Sea that was perhaps once attacherd to the mainland of North America. I was perplexed as to which island, since they are numerous, some with numbers only in a vast area of open sea bounded roughly by Bermuda, Costa Rica and the Florida Keys.. Many geologic and scientific mysteries—other than mysterious diappearances—lay hidden, like sunken treasure, within the alleged boundaries of the Triangle..

Dr. Barodin was a very cutured and refined man, and a superb fisherman for blue marlin, and we had gone on this cruise, the two of us, to test his newly invented fishing reel, designed to change the gear ratio in such a way as to make fishing almost effortless, a sort of hydromatic shifting mechanism built into the reel gears. We had caught none of his prize filsh on our second day out. On the third day we brought in one apiece, neither weighing over 800 pounds but magnificent specimens none the less. As the day was just setting we decided to defer our return to harbor until early the next morning. We had iced the fish on deck as best we could, guessing at their weight, and we were sitting in the cabin enjoying a gin and tonic—rather, he was, since I am a tetotaler and have been all my life, but I enjoy watching others relax and lift the lids of their thoughts in my direction. An old expressioin of mine.

"These are not a warlike people—very peaceful, I am told, and they are way beyond us scientifically."

"Who?" I enquired, half listening as I watched a school of dolphins play.

"Why, Doctor Kennison, of course."

"But Dr.. Kennison could in no way have fallen into their hands—or could he? I mean, what scientific knowledge he possessed … what information they could haved gotten from him …"

"He was an amazing man—is, I should say, since we don't know if he is still alive."

"Missing since—last—August, I believe, on a similar cruise such as this—either dead, a captive or a willing … citizen of the colony."

"The lack of evidence—that's what causes me to believe his boat did not sink—no junk, no debris, nothing amiss. The Coast Guard reported no findings … just the one word—*gateway."* Barodin's mind was at work on possibilities, none of which included the Bermuda Triangle theory.

"Mysterious," I said. *"Gateway."*

"As if he had found *a—gateway"* said Igmar.

"Precisely. I'm something of an amateur mariner, myself," I said with some pride. "And I've come across old charts of this so-called Mystery Triangle. They exist, you know."

"Charts of the Mysterious Bermuda Triangle?"

"Yes—I could give you the coordinates if I had my charts with me It lies roughly 30 degrees North Latitude, extending a line down through the Tropic of Cancer at 20 degrees North Latitude, then eastward to 70.5 degrees West Longitude by 28 or so degrees ssuthern Latitude. We both know that the triangle bisects the Tropic of Cancer—the northernmost lattitude attained by the sun, Capricorn being the Southern. But these, it seemes to me, are insignficant, Doctor Galway. Yet this Triangle is just such a phenomenon as most mariners take for granted—merely another area in the vast Atlantic."

"Then that's why the Caribbean area is called a—*Mystery? … or* why even a *Triangle?"*

"Because ships, airplanes, small boats like this—yes, even pleasure craft—have suddenly disappeared, as if they had never existed," I replied.

"Impossible!!" Barodin said with a gusty emphasis.

"Not at all, not at all. In fact—remember, I am drinking strong coffee and it is you, Doctor, my friend, who are enjoying your euphoria … pardon me." He nodded sagaciously and smiled.

"In the back of my mind is *this plan*—to go there."

"To where? To no place … a chimera that does not even exist in reality but only as coordinates on a map."

"Oh, it exists," I insisted. "*Gateway*—that was Kennison's last communication with shore. A medico ham radio operator in Tampa picked it up, sent it to his laboratory for voice analysis and the communication fell into my hands. He has no wife, you know, no family—this … Kennison."

"No, I didn't know that."

"And therefore he could travel to—I shall call it-*Phanterica*. How's that sound to you, Doctor Barodin?

"Mysterious enough. That was a heavy one" He looked around the cabin. "Wind is up, I guess." He stepped up topside momentarihy then returned. "Strange—sea's like glass, obsidion black. Felt like an rogue wave created by an undersea disturbance struck us broadside—like a fist. We get these things occasionally. Seismatic disturbances, hardly big enough to cause a sunami tidal, but significant to the marine geophysicist. But do go on, Doctor. Galway. You say you would go to—"

"Phanterica—to search for Mory Kennison."

"Tomorrow, if I could," I said "Phanterica exists, I'm quite certain. By narrowing the area of my search, 1 just might find—*Gateway*"

"Good try, good try, doctor," said my friend with some slight envy and a tinge of disdain. "Fantasy is not my indulgence," he said.

"Nor mine, but as a scientist, I must claim my right to curiosity …"

"And a very lively imagination—"

The night passed without further discussion of the subject of a mission of rescue. As things will, fatigue took over, and I turned in, slept soundly until early pre-dawn, when I heard my friend crank up the fine big diesel engine and we started in toward harbor, still with our running lights on, it yet being dark. The shore line rose up as if submerged, a broken string of glimmering lights aeparating the dawn's dark waters from the gunmetal sky. My skipper friend had pulled in his sea anchor when I came from my bunk forward.

The return trip was uneventful, my mind now being filled with a new resolve, and his with the weight of our two catches, the docking of his boat and other utilitarian matters, which I'm certain included his own lab work on a project in sea urchins, floating colonies of anemone that he was investigating—life that charted the sea currents through their cycle of propagation. Outside the gulf they became food for the

Blue Fin whale. He was wrapt up in his study, a man of great patience, dedication and independence. He had at least listened to my plan in which I detailed what would seem to many of my Sunday-sailor friends an implausible dramatic dream in its telling and, ultimately, in its unfolding... Instead, I had, with my bravo rescue plan I had unintnetionally revealed my personal presupposition: that Man lived in the ultimate stages of his decaying civilization which outwardly was clever and brilliant, but was inwardly corrupt. Yet I was being too judgemental, I suppose. As did many of my colleagues, I simply turned personal conjectures over in my mind. Parts of the the account I am about to relate were incorporated into a scientific paper, which I read for a symposium of scientists at a much later date than when the present events transpired.

It was my intention to explore, to invade, not to disturb or to interrogate too closely but simply to go ashore, if and when I did find this Phanterica. I would be an alien in their land. I wanted to confirm that *Gateway*, the doctor's last word before his disappearance in August of last year, was a visible and tangible reality. Two months had elapsed when I had hired a small Cuban-type fishing vessel of unknown registry, unlicensed, a smuggler's craft if ever there was one. It had always seemed to me that ships missing in the area carried with them either persons with scientific knowledge and background, or navigators, seamen, boat and ship personnel whose knowledge was so specialized that they could not but increment the learning of alien colonists who were not a part of our own scientific community. Call it professional pride, I call it rational deduction. I had to start someplace.

And so with little more than my own charts, a reliable mariner's compass, my own sextant from academy days, I started out—I was about to say, *set sail—on* this Cuban smuggler's craft for three days of searching. I guessed it to require no longer than that, since *Gateway* had rough coordinates, supplied to the ham radio operator at Latitude 70 degrees, 10 minutes North, Longitude 30 degrees 17 minutes West. But they were not accurate and therefore undependable for the purpose of navigation. On my second day out—I could speak some Spanish—I had my pilot stear our small, troublesome craft with its constant engine problems into an unsearched area within sight of the low forage and sinister black line of a distant island off our port bow. It rose and stretche like a green snake sunning itself along the horizon with mists attempting to shroud it and only a dark area, perhaps a lagoon, breaking its green line length Mists hung like a canopy shroud of death and nascent revelation over the distant island. The almost pellucid sea between our boat and the shoreline floated thereon what appeared to be flakes of flesh or silver, like the manna cast into a fish tank. The water rippled with conflicting small tides as if stirred by some Grendelian monster breathing from below. I had never seen calm off-shore water that appeared quite like that disturbance.

I was a vagabond, an explorer of caverns unlighted by the brave torches of other men, one who had traveled to distant countries to learn how their people live, what foods they ate, how they worked, the ways in whichs they amused and governed themselves. I am a Cultural Anthropologist, as one may by now have guessed, and my friend Dr. Barodin, a man involved in the physical side of the study of foreign and ancient peoples—a Geologist—began his exploration generally with rocks. I sometimes chided him on this crude start.

"And why not rocks?" he had once time asked me, since they are where civilization' history truly starts?" he had answered with acerbity and wisdom.

Good answer. Well, this trip was a part of my hobby-work combined, although geology had once been my real craft and preoccupation. But so dead, and the inverted end of human life on this planet.. One must, I had always believed, investigate life even to start to understand the elemental rocks.. It was a given that the four states of matter were coexistent—liquid, solid, gas and plasma, almost like the ancient Platonic elements of fire, water, earth and air.

This philosophical presuppossition set my course intellectually. All my life I have found no total darkness but only a clear and molten incadescence where I did in fact understood life's origins, as if looking through a glass, darkly, a phrase that springs to mind from somewhere. 1 had set out to bring back a physicist, if I could—kidnapped, I could not say—from a place, I imagined, where the Nabobs of speculation fought the Willowwitches of jesting. He was gone, vanished, and none of his friends or colleagues had heard from him since last summer. This was for me, therefore, a rescue mission. Many possible answers had occurred to me:: that he had drowned in his overturned sailboad when struck by a rogue wave, that he had taken his life to conceal from his associates his personal misery or, most rationally, that he was being held as a captive in exile from his known world, to be indoctrinated and used by an alien culture.

As a secondary objective, I wanted to determine why mariners; needles for at least two hundred years had deflected when vessels approached a certain intersection of grid lines—I posessed no reasosn to suspect that they had not done so for thousands of years, since the days of Columbus. Did the line of the sun's closrest proximity exert some strange magnetic force on ships' compasses, or cause airplane engines to stall by an induced desynchronization? Those theories are far more plausible than that a subterranean force had drawn down to sink under the waves forever huge vesses weighing hundreds of thousands of tons. I had confessed to Dr. Barodin that one of my first efforts would be, as I laughingly put it, to look for some Vault of the Heads where I might confer with proper authority over the life of this said-to-be pan national colony. The good doctor did not think me at all clever, but forgave my temerity providing I should bring back some artifact, some token of my search, if nothing more than a skull fragment or vial of wine of-the rock, the fermentation of lichens I promised to do so, providing I could locate what I imagined to be an incredible race, strangely mutated by scientific processes the which I had yet to discover. Thereupon, I tender to all who will listen and read the experiences in this, my personal journal, of the adventure. It was, indeed, a mystery that provided many offshoot venues for investigation.

Looking once more beyond the port bow, I observed that the hovering mists which had shrouded the sequestered island were evaporated, leaving in their wake, a column of reflected light from the piercing whte sands and glistening vegitation that resembled, to my overactive imagination, a column of fire, as were the similar symbols from God that had led the Israelites in the wilderness. I was astounded, but said nothing to Barodin, being yet content to record what I had seen as perhaps an optical illusion. I was tired and fell asleep on deck; Barodin had curled up like a cat at the stern of the boat, by the warmth of the cranky engine. The Cuban was nowhere to be seen.

Chapter 2

The Landing

On the day following my first sighting of the island I was perplexed as to why Marco, our intrepid boatman, navigator and guide, should so abruptly fell asleep on the roof of the cabin. Fear, fear in his eyes, has prompted his strange aberrant behavior, I thought. I woke him up. I urged him to throw out what he called his anchor, the exhaust manifold of a diesel engine. I would have preferred a chunk of volcanic rock as more appropriate to our mission. Lamentably, we wasted an entire day, just floating offshore about two miles and watching the island as if it were, indeed, a species of tropical snake sunning itself on the rim of the ocean. I used the time to sketch what I expected to find compared to what I would actually find on the island, for so it was, an island. That fact established no mystery for me or for Dr. Barodin. The island, Marco was quick to inform us, was Number 5467—a fact that held little meaning for us, except that there must accountably be 5,466 islands ahead of it, lying somewhere nearby, perhaps more as discernable shoals and so-marked to deter close investigation by captains of deep-draft vessels.

The night was lonely and muggy and lay upon us an oppressive air, saturated with humidity under virtually cloudless skies. I scanned the wilderness and the cascading surf through my binoculars. I thought I heard the thunderous echo of the surf dashing against shore rocks. I paced the five-foot deck, as mariners have done for centuries. There appeared to be a high mountain on the island with its ridges shaved off. I dashed into my makeshift chart room, an old landsman's table in the cabin, and locating the transection of compass coordinates, I marked our position. Dr. Barodin watched me me in these stratagems, saying scarcely a word, secretly admiring my ability to orient our little scallop on the immensity of the ocean, so accustomed was he of the presence of modern navigational instruments. But he was bound to be disappointed in that regard from here on. Lo, we now seemed to be drifting with a current. Could this island be Dr. Kennison's Gateway? I wondered. I exclaimed aloud, "There she be!" like any greenhorn deckhand on a a 18th century whaler who had screamed aloft, "Thar she blows!" I urged Marco to bring us in closer, and so he weighed our exhaust-manifold anchor and cranking up directed our nameless little craft toward the shore.

I again focused my binoculars on the island where, to my great astonishment and inner satisfaction, I thought I glimpsed the portal of a great stone gate that breeched the dark shore cliff like an immense maw. All the while we moved cautiously, and under a south easterly breeze, so that we were brought by our small vessel to the sound of beach combers dashing themselves on the rocks. Just as I expected! Thunder followed by silence then the repetition, the familiar sounds of the surf, like the pulse and sweep of wind through the sheets of a fully rigged sailing vessel. I wished that we had a wind gauge, an anenometer the better to judge the convective winds that buffeted our frail craft. I had packed with me the mariner's compass and sextant and my climbing gear required for spelunking, and not much more. Dr. Barodin had similarly outfitted himself. I carried a holstered pistol; Barodin brought with him no firearm. Both of us bore with confidence our machete-like knives Anyone but ourselves would call us foolhardy and ill prepared for our rescue mission on a strange island inhabited by heaven only knows what predatory life.

At last it was time to take our chances, to make our landing. I was ready to pay off Marco with Cuban currency, and that done we should, the two of us, be virtually alone on the island, self-marooned. I heard the ruffle of the seas wash past the sides of our boat. As if emerging from the grayblack fog that had closed in steadily since our sighting the island, dripping shreds from the skies as if an early nightfall, yet it was mid-morning. As we closed in, I observed a wall rising up out of the water. Each ground swell thundered up into white irridescence at its base. My chief concern now was to keep our frail boat headed toward shore; for to broach would certainly spill us into unfamiliar waters., with the prospect of drowning before we had even landed. Marco was extraordinary; he managed with a long great oar and his tiller to direct the craft through the waves I had heard but now felt the power of. There came a moment of tumultous, rapid sweeping motion shoreward whereupon I heard the feint rasp of wood on sand as we beached her—temporarily.

"Where are we?" Dr. Barodin asked, having scarcely uttering a word until that moment

"Somewhere in the Caribbean Sea, I cam't say exactly," I replied disingenuously, my mind playing upon this sea wall, a breakwater like a great offshore levee, maybe only the top of one innundated by the ocean, sunken, to hold back hurricane forces of wind and water from life within its confines. Yet it appeared to be of nature's making.

"It is a fortress, Senor Doctor." Marco stood behind me. On his face I observed the wrapt expression of instant recognition on his brown face.

"You know this place?"

"Se, Senor Doctor. The natives, we call them—pardon, Senor, I do not remember."

"Go into the cabin, get a pencil, a lapiz. Write it down, please!" I urged him with hand motions.

If this was made by human hands, this had to be one of the wonders of a past world—a sea wall which I estimated, by our position, extended above a low tide of some 250 meters, downs to ocean bedrock, and that another twenty fathoms. Rock placed on the sea bottom by human hands, human ingenuity. I marveled at the magnitude of the task. As they were protecting what lay beyond, exotic species of sea scorpions and salt water worms writhed and crawled about on the structure, the bites of which I was certain were poisonous and could be fatal. The moss, the barnacles and the stench of the slime repulsed me. Barodin and I looked at each other.

Marco came rushing out of the cabin with a piece of paper in his hand, "You will be able to push your boat back into the water." He assured me it would be a simple effort when the tide came in again. In his hand for the moment he held a paper on which he had scribbled one word—sichofantiasmas. Sychophants! I exclaimed in a phonetic translation of his sacred word-worshippers of other gods, pluralistic, possibly pygmies or giants in size, ingratiating and persuasive as toadies are, of phenomenal brain power, and harboring who knew what weapons, but all the same— toadies. I could not imagine such creatures to exist. Yet how was it, if what this simple Cuban sailor was telling me in his half-articulate way, how was it that I had never heard of these Sycophants? Incredible as it seemed, they must be a people who have banished themselves from the rest of the world, and if they were ever known to the pre-modern world, we have mostly forgotten them. Impossible! Impossible!

"Si, Senor Doctor—imposible!" Marco whistled under his breath.

As a doctor I sought in my mind for an analogy. If I were to tie off the circulation of blood to any one of ny limbs and were to sever the nerves, the operation would pain and embarass and inconvenience me for a while. But in time, if no other coomplications set in, such as gangrene, an incredible medical impossibility since the cause of gangrene is death of living tissue, the limb would atrophy, die and finally drop off, much as lepers lose ears and noses and fingers to the disease. I would learn to get along without it until the day came when I would no longer ask questions about its death and would assume that it had never been a part of me—which would be the case. Self-amputation would have occurred. So with the world on the other side of that seawall crawling with odious and abysmsal sea creatures. Perhaps the Sychophants are a forgotten people. I had yet to discover this to be so. The amazing conclusion to me was that they were responsible for their own kind of social amnesia, extrapolated into their global amnesia.

My own knowledge in the science of Anthropology had equipped me to understand the physical societal phenomena of humankind on this planet in terms of human endeavors, mores and cultural hopes, but I was ill-equipped to comprehend the precarious and dangerous thrust-faults of a people's wholesale abdication from the human race and from planet life. That was the way of suicide or of monastic alienation from this world's human travail. Confronting this colossal challenge, I was determined to learn all I could while completing my mission to find and to rescue Mory Kennison, the reknowned geophysicist.

I could see that Marco was in a hurry to return to his home port of Gibara. It was while contemplating his return journey that I espied—great scott! an opening, a portal—the gateway—in the wall, hung round as if in memorium to the past with the repulsive creatures I have just described. I saw the fear on Marco's face, as I pointed to the breech in the great wall. Streaks of green, brackish slime extended down over the wall's bronze and white surface. Sea birds had made their nests in its cracks. I sensed our boatman's impatience. I took a wad of pesos from my sea jacket to persuade him to enter. He was fearful of moving any closer. I added another wad from Barodin's hand. These overtures persuaded the leathery young Cuban to move his craft up to the wall, where the creatures, hissed and twined and charttered, scratching the stones with their clawlike beaks upon our approach. We all kept deathly silent as the little craft slid through the shallows of the moat and into the confines of the new land. By reversing and forwarding his engine repeatedly, Marco was able to swing his boat about, by this means turning its prow seaward again. He had an emergency dinghy aboard which we inflated with a foot pump and lowered by two ropes over the side and then we dropped down into it our survival gear, that of myself and Barodin, cOonsisting of backpack essentials canteels, compass, inadequate topographic maps, flashlights, stoves and the like, all that well-equipped backpackers carry with them, We had little for food in our rucksacks.

Marco had faithfolly launched us onto that primitive terrain. He feared to be trapped, himself, when the tide should go out he wanted to go with lit. I tried to make it clear that I would pay him much dinero if he returned in one year. He stood mute at the cabin of his gently rocking boat. I was alerted to our precarious situation when a wild and furious screeching broke out and the incoming tide ran like a horse through the portal and into the sluce where we idled. I thought of a similar tide at Mont St. Michael, France. My eyes suddenly caught a horrible sight, a combat between the giant scorpions and an ocean eel at feeding time. Green water squirted out from the eel as the scorpion seized the giant worm, severed it with its claw and partook of its meal at the base of the rock sea wall.

Marco reached out his hand to me and I thrust into it three thousand pesos. He grinned broadly. Chunks of the dissevered eel fell into the moat where we floated. He kissed my hand like a good diplomat—it embarassed me to accept such gratitude. With a wave of his hand, as I clambered down the short rope ladder, he bid me goodbye. We and Gorodin were now alone in our inflated boat. I paddled the dinghy away from Marco's boat. He cranked up its diesel engine and without further delay headed straightway for the opening in the wall, the Gateway While I was occupied in my thoughts with beaching ourdinghy, our Cuban friend had threaded the gap and was gone from sight. We were left with mingled emotions of wonder, loneliness and dread. We were now the castaway scientists. "What lovers of nature these people must be!" I thought, pushing to the back of my mind all thoughts about danger that lay ahead of lus fierce beasts, predatory birds, a veritable replica of pre-dawn life on this planet. But the people, the Sycophants-how could we deal with them, ever? An enormous rogue ground swell swept through the Gate and almost upset our dinghy. We promptly beached it. As soon as I stepped out I searched the sparse narby woods for any sign of huyman life; but there were none.

Spread out before us in the growing sunlight were low hills covered with thorn trees and the brown verdure of mid-autumn, while leading my eye away into the distance lay grassy meadows that shimmered beneaths blue haze rose and undulated like billowing blankets. They seemed at once inviting and desolate and foreboding. I was anxious to proceed with Barodin, against all calamities considered, even death, cannibals and monsters of a prehistoric age. We had beached our dinghy on the sands of dread.

To our utter astonishment a voice as of a thousand megadecibels thundered from the clouds—but there were no clouds. It filled the sentient airlike a giant invisible speaker from the heavens, an invisible ingredient of what we used to call airwaves. Yet these sound waves emitted tendrils of smoke, like translucent snakes that swept the ground in sweeping, searching motions, trying to locate us and envelop us in their net, just as wraiths of smoke will sometimes follow air currents. We both stood still, enthralled by the strange threatening phenomenon.

"You are invaders in our land!"
"We've come to explore," Barodin ventured in a quavering voice.
"You speak lies. You are marauders. You have come to ravage our land with words. Words are your bullets. We are a peace-loving people here."

"Actually, we're here to find our friend, a geophysicist, a doctor named Mory Kennison."

"You will not find him by invading our sacred land."

"This island has been around for a long time. What makes it sacred?" I asked.

"Its puriity—constantly we're threatened and twice in our history we have been ravaged by interlopers like yourselves."

"We don't come to fight—but to discover," I said,

"Baah! Always the same answer, always, and always." All while this dialogue was going on I searched the woods, the top of the sea wall and round about us to determine the source of the words. But only the enclosure of the area cast back as an echo the words of the interrogator. The thunderous voice faded and there followed the clatter from the wall. As if they were the wings of a thousand risisng birds, there came the flapping resonating, ear-piercing sounds of a great flock of pterodactyl-like birds.

"Look, Barodin!" Open-mouthed, I watched them fly over, headed seaward. Several hundred of them, I estimated. Their black winds overlapped shutting out the blue sky above, their long beaks and cfanelike necks were extended, and they flew in a single direction as if to oppose an invading force.

"The Great Venger birds are our food providers. They fish the seas for us. They provide us with the most succulent meals. You Conquerors know nothing about the good life."

"I suppose they catch fish."

"They catch porpoise, a whale now and then, but often they come back with dead fishermen and the lost. You are fortunate. They could have swooped down and seized you."

"Do not threaten us. We can learn more about your exotic land—if you do not threaten our lives. We are scientists."

There came no reply. We heard only the fading flap of the longwkiged Pterodactyl Venger birds. I had seen condors with fourteen foot wingspans, but these wings were more like 25 to 30 feet, from tip to tip.

We stood there our mouths open in wrapt wonder, watching the thunderous flight of the fisher birds head for the open ocean, to bring back food for the Colony. And a Colony I shall call these people and their ways. Yet I had not located the voice. It came as if from the woods, like that of an outpose sentry.

We pulled our dinghy up the sand, deflated it, stached it beneath some bushes. I secured my revolver in its holster adjusted my cork hat and, slhouldering our backpacks, we set off together along what appeared to be a trail. If a trail, then what animal or what creature, human or sub-human, had walked along it before us? I ponered this question, inspecting indentations in the dirt.. The tangled and thorny vines slashed at my boots and tore the flesh beneath my breeches. Where were they? I continued to ask myself. I wondered half aloud, that these were people who had banished themselves from the world. A phrase kept returning me me—banishment from the world. The phrase seemed mythological, maybe similar the lost Slir Walter Raleigh's Roanoke colony of Englishmen in Virginia. They too were lost to time, in a word, decimated . Was Kennison among them? I had no clue in the first place as to whether or not he was here only a premonition warned me of that possibility and my intuition reinforced my will to procede. His little plane Discovery had gone down within the coordinates of the Bermuda Triangle. He, too, lhad been looking for hidden islands.

The primitive flora around me, the thick underbrush and tall, gnarled and twisted pines on the pallisades above amazed me by the swirling, interlacing of the vines, a veritable wall of foliage. Were they prisoners of that nature, like Abramic rams caught in thorns, or, say … like the Azetecian peoples of Mexico and kindred tribes in Central America, whose land had been reconquered … overrun by nature … or like the Anasazi Indians of New Mexico, its people either mysteriously vanished or assimilated by neighboring tribes? As a cultural anthropologist I could only wonder. Would these Sycophants furnish me with a clue as to where Kennison had disappeared to, if he had not drowned in a plane crash. Would we … suddenly and mysteriously disappear? My God, I've got work to finish …!

I did not have long to wait for an answer. As we both walked over the crest of a sandy tower, formed by an immense ant colony such as one finds in the Serhenghetti of Africa, three humanoid looking creatures, giants by any measure, approached me. I say creatures, for they shared aspects of human appearances—two legs and arms, a human like head, a prehistoric thumb for holding onto trees, three dexterous fingers—deigned simply to eat with, labor of any sort, I was later to learn, being done by robots. Their feet were designed to walk. They too resembled lost voyagers, who had adapted to an alien environment—lean, gangly, though seven feet and taller, their backs sloped, no tails thank God!-small ears and very beautiful tender, limpid eyes. Their mouths were small and puckered, as if formed by a life-long of sucking on tree roots or exotic fruit, which included the fisher-bird catch as their nourishment. I came to learn that they both drank and distilled for its liquor the milk of the Cocoanansus tree, whose fruit was larger than an ordinary cocoanut and was shaped like an hourglass, one of nature's useless mutations.

I remark about their unusual clothing: for most of these Sycophants—that is who they were indeed—were attired in a similar dress. One had clothed himself in a wolfs fur, showing it off with a virile pride, while the female—there was a trio of them, these greeters—curried his collar. This attentive grooming was distantly simian, related to the manner in which monkeys lovingly curried their family members for fleas. Pieces of bone tied the ends together, and paws of monekys and racoons were imbedded in the hairs of the fur. Their feet were shod with leather and sinews of plant roots for thongs, although one of the three walked barefooted. Altogther they were amazine, though of their natures I had yet to learn. Their faces were extremely bearded so as to obscure the natural features, except thoe large, limpid eyes.

"Don't I resemble the Magnificent Orb?" he asked me. I had no idea of just who the Magnificent Orb was, probably one of their gods. "That coat gives you strength, Pastich," the woman said.

They joined us to walk with us along the trail. Should I attack these barbarians? My revolver was loaded. As I look back upon my question, it was admittedly an indefensible arrogance on my part. I was glad I had said nothing. Pastich took off his wolfs coat, waved it frantically thrice in the air, one in each direction of the compass. I had yet to learn that the Sycophant compass points correspond to the space-time-mass continuum, so man's actions are never out of synchronization with the universe. I would subsequently learn that D(distance) and (T) time to the fourth power, multiplied by (M), representing mass were the points of that ancient Einsteinian equation. The waving of the wolfs for was thereefore merely symbolic.

"Your country—what is its name" I enquired.

"You have come to … Phantericfa." the woman replied.

Fair enough, I thought. Phantreriea, Phanterica, I kept repeating in my mind. Not too far from fantasy.

The third of these inhabitants who had come ostensibly to greet us stood nearby and watched the duo perform their rite of passage for us. In my own Veblenesque terms, the waving of the coat constituted a form of conspicuous consumption, toward which the others members of the party were obliged to show reverence and envy. I made my first professional note—that clothes in Phanterica contained the power to bewitch the senses and to produce a euphoria of contentment quite unknown to more sophisticated people like the Americans. Ecstasy was their accompaniment, an almost frenzied piranna-like behavior which to the woman in the reception party seemed commonplace. What a solid scientific find I had stumbled upon! while the search for the missing Kenniston continued. I fell into conversation with Barodin as we walked along.

"Surely these people who could introduce mob amnesia and personal oblivion must know more than I, than either of us, about the human brain," I ventured to opine to Dr. Barodin. He merely shook his head and smiled a wan smile of doubt and anxiety.

"Stop and think, Galway, what do they know about the world of normal human beings?"

"They must be great engineers who can build so immense a breakwater structure. Just look at it back there-like the wall of Sennacherib or King Hezekiah."

"Let me suggest, my good friend, that the wall serves a dual purpose and maybe, just maybe the creatures on that wall are the— pantry for the Phantericans?"

"What! You're out of your mind."

"Wait and see. Just a thought, a possibility. Sea worms and scorpion-like creatures."

"That's … that's a mere wager, Barodin."

"Why not—we eat clams and I'm told snake meat is delicious."

I could say no more. I did not want to alarm these creatures or frighten them and have to abort my mission, so I kept my pistol holstered, my mind as open as I possily could. I thought of plunging into the brush and losing them, but thorns as long as darning needles poked out at me along the trailside. Besides, these Phantericans would rush on ahead of me, they were so familiar with their environment. I knew, however, that at one point we would have to confront them. I anticipated resistance to ourentry—or worse yet, absorption, brainwashing. Enculturation, as we called that merging, could spell disaster for all of us. I anticpated a threat to our safety and did not have long to wait. Our arrival had been communicated to the Axoepion Priest, whom, we were to learn, had borrowed the habits of the scorpion—to seize its prey with its pincer claws, innnervate it with a poisonous sting and then consume its victim for food . We were to satisfy a scavenger's appetite. The juxtaposition of science and primitivism were soon to become evident.

I had begun to dwell on this idea of doing battle with these creatures, when there arose in front of us a pair of growling interceptors that were encased in furs, like our greeters, and waving their long arms at us brought us to a halt. At this point, Pastsiche grunted inintelligible sounds to indicate that we were to go on past the sentries—upon one condition.

"Condition!" I exclaimed. "Why, I thought that because we are friendly, that was enough."

"No—You must first acquaint yourselves with the dopier effect."

"Oh, great scott, and what was the dopier effect way out here in this wilderness?

Our ... host explained. "You speak these words, Alamadilsh ven catorbliet, and then you wait for the sound to diminish before you continue on."

"Did you get that, Barodin. We say something then wait for the sound to come and then fade, like the dopier effect. I and Barodin both suspected, that that was a ruse to try the level of our scientific knowledge." I just supposed the test might have been better conducted in a sound chamber, but ... here goes.

The woman explained that the dopier effect transmits speed, direction and distance—and that it also informs molecular density and internal activity.

What does all that tell you. I Imean, we're here to find a friend—that only.:

"We discover your thoughts, we can control where you go, how long you stay, whether your intentions are honest."

"Why do you have to have all that information?" Barodin asked.

"We must preserve our purity in Phanterica—interruptive thoughts, bad motives, all these are considrered by our government— Oh, holy, beneficient, righteous government! in allowing you to stay."

"That's all perfctly clear to me," I said. "Is it to you, Igmar?"

"Oh, perfectly clear."

"Say dopier these words," a sentry ordered us . "Alamandilish ven Catorbiliet."

We both uttered the nonsensical words, at which the two sentries and our greeters looked much relieved. Another waved his fur directionally and with great vigor. They all laughed uproarously and appeared mollified that we were friendly invaders. But caution ruled my thinking.

We would accede to our hosts request. I shouted the nonsense words, waited for their echo to appear and then fade, and Gordin did likewise. But neither I nor Barodin heard any echo, as we had expected. The smiles on the faces of our trio of welcomers showed, however, that we had complied and been found approved by their test. And so we walked onup the trail, wondering what other experimental tests and challenges we would have to undergo to insure our safety here in Phanterica, land of the Sycophants.

Chapter 3

Quick Justice

These citizens of Phanteriea walked neither like the race of *homo sapiens* that I belonged to nor entirely like any of the lower four-legged animals. They exhiited a clumsy, ambling sort of gait, as if their legs were longer than in human gait. Yet, in truth, their arms did not resemble arms so much as wiry appendages fashioned not for labor or artisan work but for encircling, for embracing their kind or for crude games sor exercises in climbing. . It occurred to me that they might be replicas of prehistoric man, retarded into the 21st century, or then again, they might be a species of *sapiens* who, deprived of struggle, stress, competition and pain, those forces which develop the physical aspect of the human race in my world, had returned to a sapienic past unmindful of the universe beyond their domain. I was enthralled.

The Greeters, 1 shall call then, were draped in furs, other Phantericvans in dried skins of goats, in old fabric from driftwood sails, in shrouds of sea coffins and, most amazing, in clothes without hooks, all the garb of primitiv ecastaways tied toegther with ships rope or vines aplenty along ourtrail; bent nails, pieces of wood, bone and leathern thong completed their accourtrement. Not a creature of them was attired in the same, catch as catch can. Whatever they could find, they put to useas apparrel

As to their manner of walking, they were perpetually bent, grappling-like at the elbows, their four fingers moving as if saying the rosary or counting money or knitting an afghan, or, indeed, cleaning a carcass. Of course these were a small number of the day to day activities of my world, not of theirs. As they walked, surrounding us, I observed that their legs reminded me of human legs yet with knees jointed so as to swing forward, like the hocks of giant hounds. There was considerable hair on their bodies that protruded from openings around their scavenged attire. Their women ocasionally wore blazing jewels of carmine, sapphire and topaz. I immediately recognized their robotic manner of speech, and for some, the craftsmanship in white capes whose generous amplitudes ballooned in the wind that constantly swept over the landsape. They were, in short, la motley bunch if ever I saw one.

Theirs was apparently the proper costume for the daily life of leisure enjoyed by these Utopians, for so I had fashioned my opinion about them. They had constructed this entire world as their Utopia, without interference or influence from any other known civilization. How masterful, how exotic, how brilliant, putting me to mind of the Greeks who also created, as from nothing, a phenomenal civilization of science, art and government. We would see if there was a parallel.

Small of head, none of which I would judge to have exceeded ten cubic centemeters in volume, they regarded me with staring yet beautiful dark eyes through shaggy black beards. Their full stature was about 150 centimeters, putting them in the class of giants. One was carrying a pail, another a pair of scales and the last a rod about one yard long, fabricated of some sort of metal . By their manner they seemed neiter surprised nor fearful, as if they had comne purposely to welcome me. I was to learn that these *Greeters,* I shall call them, were the Mutants of the Kingdom of Phanterica, evolutionary products of time-space-energy adaptation over eons of time. On their feet they wore crude slippery like moccasins, stitched from animal skins, as I was to learn using the ligaments of their deceased, for they thought it a criminal to let any item created by man or by nature go to waste. Another example of this penchant for recycling was that the human blood of the deceased was used to fertilize their fields. Such humanoid features as teeth and nails they readily used to stud their crucifix-like idols of worship, and their cynnbaBne-like stringed instruments as well as the flute, whilest among the apparent elite, as in Hitler's day, the skin of the desceased amply supplied his own family members with lampshades and fine four-fingered skin gloves for the widow and her mourning friends..

But I am getting awlay from our present circumstances. One of our *Greeters* spoke, he with the rod poised delicately in his four-fingered hand, the smallest of the five digits missing apparently not by accident, for there showed no scar of amputation—and, besides, such dangers that were incidental to my and Borodin's lifestyles, fighting, contending, feuding, slandering and wilful endangering were all but eliminated by the Phanterican codes of safety. Matches were forbidden as they are causes of arson. Firearms were disposed of long ago as dangerous to civilized men. Lightlbulbs, our necessity, were an abandoned hilatrity many moons ago, for these Utopians had successfully magnified the night stars to illuminate as day heir everyday existence. The concept of night had not occrrred to them as a result of this Fresnel—my closest parallel, this Fresnel-like focus of available light into their dwellings and onto their very windy, narrow streets—a matter I shall come to later.. And such things as grease, gunpowder, caustic soaps and cleansers, and pesticides had gone out within menory. Why, these Phantericans believed there ought not to to be any sound reason for retaining these useless producets of life-threatening danger made me think of how civilization casts off many things at an alarming rate of disposal, like washboards, tricycles and unwanted babies, the last of which it considers obsolete or inconvenient. There exilsted, for example, no combs or brushes in Phanterica for the people there all allowed their hair to grow wild, with a magic residing in a magnificent shock of hair. The most respectsed of these folk possessed hair that draped his shoulders.

"We knew you were coming," said te *Greeter* who carried the scales,.showing a mouth without human fangs, as he laughed, since hunting and flesh-eating by humans had disappeared when Mars, Saturn, the sun, moon and earth were lined up in 32, BC.

"And who told you this?" Barodin asked. "Only just now have we arrived.." Ail three of our Greeter giants, like guardian agels, I call then, burst out in a high-pitch laughter of the most devilish and raucous sort.

"We captured your voice from the airwaves—like radio does in your world. It's out ears. And when you talked with your friend Marco on his fishing boat, we heard every word, even heard you tralk about your alarm."

"We had no radio on board."

"Radio? What is that—radio? We hear like the bat that hears the insect. Your words are translated from our radar," said the giant carryring the scales. I did not take offense but only mused."

"Were we that close—as insects?" Dr. Barodin asked.

"When your voice disturbs the molecules of the air, it is that disturbance created by soundless audio waves that travels forever but which we can hear and translate. Even long Russian physicists posited the molecular insubstantktion of physical objects. The energy is never lost, only changed into percievable sound which can go on forever if not blocked."

I decided that I, as a scientist Anthropologist, would make a intentional and energetic attempt to understand these Phantericans' concepts of science, of which both I and Barodin were familiar. Their explanations stunned me, coming from figures that seemed to incompetent, so wierd and unnatural of speech and appearance. Their aural capacity exposed a rare understanding of energy exchange, transposition of waves into auricular phonemes, involving the laws of conservation of energy coming into play here, and perhaps even the quantum mechanics of light transmission by photons—based, of course, on the theory that all identifiable waves, and others yet hidden, are of the same composition, including the waves of heat, but that of a different and more primordial status of moledular disturbance. I had been led to consider that radio waves, heat, electromagnetic and sound waves were of a similar status, their medium being the air, but unidentical *perse.* Then I began to think further—was it the vehicle of air that transmitted the waves, or was it the unique character of waves that differed according to their source. The ionosphere altered light's colors by refraction but the converted heat from a burning log remained of the same content only to dissipate ... I stumbled over a tree root as I pondered these questions/

Our *Greeters* began to lead us into the jungle overgrowth, the trail delineated by exotic flowers shaped like fragile fingers, dainty stalks of colorful daffodils, snarled vines of a *genus* I could not identify and the most unbelievable *wine flower.* It dripped, like an insipient spring, dripped a red wine, which one of our Greeters invited us to try. He had seen my drinking cup hanging from my belt. I did so, and found its taste full, exciting, rather dry according to my wine judgement, but completely heddy and refreshing to travelers like ourselves.

"The Wine flower is our basic drink—instead of water, which does not cleanse and purge like this wine," one of our guides remarked. He clattered his scales with an awful clashing of metal.

"*Tahw si ti eh sraef?* said one to the other. *Ewllahsees.*"

I let a small amount fell, drip into my cup and held it to my lips to taste. 1 was elated. We had hit upon a common ground. I had failed to notice one thing—that the wine flower grew from within a wild gossimer and moss that draped downward from overhanging branches of a thorn tree. Was not the wine flower then a parasite, since I could not find that the blossom belonged to any root system. I thought so.

Again our Greeters started off into the gloom of the Phanterican forest. "Where are you taking us?" I asked

"You are going to see our cultured leader We take you to the dias of our High Priest, the Great Neolite, Overlord of the whole of Phanterica."

"I am honored, I suppose, but I do not like dictators."

"The three of them discussed my words; they seemed offended that I should deem their vaunted leader a tyrant,.

"Our great leader will orient you."

Again that inverted dialogue: said the scales bearer, "*Od uoy kiniht eh si ot eb detsurt?*

"*Ew nac ylno epoh os.*" said the rod bearer.

"What the devil are they saying?" I asked Barodin. "Breats me—ancient Gaelic, a sheer invented language. Take a linguist to figure it out."

They began to chatter voluably among theselves, and I could see that talk was for them the birthmark of their peculiar wisdom. All of the sudden, they fell silent while I stood in the center of the clearing, glossy-leopard-patched tree trunks, some with thorns others with moss and lichens, slimy with the perpetual wetness of the forest that surrounded us. Strange, I reflected, that I had not heard any of the familiar forest sounds, chattering squirrels, scolding crows, the rapid hammering of a rednecked woodpecker. Where were they? I listened, meanwhile waited for them to enact some sort of ritual. I could feel my revolver pressing against my thigh, yet, it would have shown poor judgement for me to frighten them with harm. Also, they carried no arms—one would have expected a bow and arrow at least. Blut they had more subtle protections, as I was to learn.

The Sycophant holding the scales intercepted my thought. "We do not fear you. One of us is adequate to handle your civilizations evil modes of violence. But, as you see, we travel in threes to prove to aliens our Truth of Secession."

The ambassador with the scales, the smallest of the trio, he with splayed filsngers and the same wide, tender eyes, dropped an ordinary iron weight, of several ounces, such as those one found in candy stores across America, onto one of the balance platforms. On the other ploatform, with fingers so slender they looked too fragile for strength, he placed a wafer of gold and waited for the balance arrow to settle. His enraptured companions watched like scientists grouped around a laboratory retort, waiting intently for the results of an experiment. When the pointer finally came to rest and the platforms ceased moving, these Phantericans as of one mind, turned to me and gazed intently into my face.

"Would you mind telling me what this is all about?" I asked with no small exasperation.

"We have just weighed your words … and we find them equal to one wafer. That wafer represents an ounce of truth. Take that down, GAB." GAB—the Government Appraisal Bureaucrat—wrote down the weight in a small book, hidebound with snake skin. "They are lost—that is Truth." He slipped his log into a ragged coat pocket. Apparently he was their diarist and secretary, I mused.

"And now—" He suddenly lashed out at a snake that had coiled down onto us and almost struck my face. His rod converted the snake into a forest monkey. The vision of that chattering monkey suddenly swinging off into the top ranches of the tree still baffles my imagination. What a strange power of magic, 1 thought, to be able to change one species of life into another with the mere thrash of a magic rod!

"Come with us," said the Phanterican who carried the pail.

"Why the pail—are you collecting specimens,?" Barodin queried. "Ah, after my own heart—collectors of artifacts." I smiled; but my intuition told me otherwise.

In this pail we gather rhinestones from along the trail—to show the honesty of our mission to the Master when we return. Without these tokens of grace, we would, I fear, not be believed."

"Then you were not sent to meet us? I asked

"Oh, of course, but since our Phanterica thrives on dishonesty. We cannot be expected to tell the truth. As a consequence of that social ...."

"*More,* we call it."

"Exactly. As a consequence of that more, we have to return with this pail full of evidence to convince *The Great One* of our Honesty."

"I was flabbergasted. "Don't they believe you—take you at your word?" Barodin asked.

"Without proof of our honesty—banishment!" exclaimed the Greeter with the scales. He thumped his chest repeatedly with one long arm as if in an act self-chastening.

Looking about me, I realized that the rhinestones grew like hardened berries from bushes that steetched out into the path, milky agate, blue topz, green sapphire, deepest red ruby. Even in the deep forest light they dazzled the eyes.

"These natural jewels must make you fabuloudly wealthy," I ventured to state.

"They are—well, they stand for ... for promises. When we give *The Great One* our pail full of gems, we give him a pail full of our promises." Well, I thought, their form of materialism was in a way much like ours—*dollar guarantees* we still call them

"Have you ever heard of anything so ridiculous, so flantastic?" Dr. Barodin remarked.

"Never—except if you think of how Indians accepted bribes from the Dutch of New York as promises for Manhattan Island...."

"Bribes—I've got it!" I shouted so aloud the three giants turned and stared at ;me. "Money talks—yes, yes, that was it—only jewels—from bushes!"

What, however, if it lay within their power as quasi-workers of magic to change elemental nuclei into molecular crystals of the natural stones? Had not the Alchemist of old hoped to transmute lead into gold? By golly, that's it! Still, I did not comprehend the energy transfer of heat to aid in their fabrication. Nuclei of atoms contain incipient, ready heat-energy. What amazed me was the quantity of these stones of—evidence discovered along the trail. Like kernels of energy waiting to be released. It was the energy quotient of the jewel crystals that enticed research into that atomic energy entrapment—molecules and their atomis aligned in such a manner as to reflect selected colors from white fight. What a discovery I had made for my personal enrichment!

The Phantericans jabbered wildly in their language of inverted English, using such phrases as:
"Meht hitw od ew dluolhs tahw?" "Mih ot on taht ees sutel taesl ta."

I never ocurred to me that—until I put their words down in my diary-that they were speaking English words, although they turned the words on their heads, backwards. How absurd of me not to perceive that from the very start. What at first I assumed was illiteracy turrned out to be, in fact, a brilliant command of inverted English, even though some of thewords bore triple meanings. <;u ;Greeting cohorts appeared to be well-gratified that 1 understood, and they continued to jabber amongst themselves.

We then received some daunting news, a warning from the rod-bearer, who appeared to be the leader of the trio.

"You must cross a wild and raging river, filled with death, poison to fish, a river that comes from out of the red stones of the mountains to the north. This river divides your world from that of Phanterica, yours of corruption and ours of pristine cleanliness. Do you you dare to make this crossing of the Tanges River?"
"I thought the ocean separated our worlds."
"A common fiction," the scales bearer replied. The ocean is a mere barrier, not a separating current of death."

Barodin and I discussed the crossing, all the while observing the smirks on the faces of they who were becoming our captors. We could not summon Marco to return. We had come too far; we were captives of our own curiosity, of our eagerness to explore and to learn, and to play ther role of rescuing heroes.

"We will dare to go," said Barodin before I had given my assent I said not a word to reject his choice.

"The river velocity of the flow has a vector of 238 to 605 to compensate for variant direction."

"These figures mean nothing to me," I replied,

"Impossible." said the Leader with the divining rod. More jabbering followed. They could not comprehend my antiquated challenge to their deductive methodology. As a scientist, as was Barodin, our intellectual lapproach had to be inductive. I had to begin with a premise; these curious folk began with a conclusion.

"Three hundred and sixty degrees is our circle," I interjected.

"Then you stay—or go back to your boat if you refuse to accept our circle."

"Our only mission here is to search for my friend, Doctor Kennison. I, for one, will not change my mind!"

"Sey, Sey, Sey," he replied, and they yawked, and gaggled and chittered away amongst themselves in the tongue I have just described.

The Phanterican with the scales set them carefully on a wide red stone. "The velocity we know—triple zero, zero thirty five with factors for ... and in the narrows.... The current is too strong for you and your friend to cross without us. Besides if you tried to swim the Tanges River its water would poison you,"

"Then I suppose I won't to swim," I said. They laughed. They found this remark hilarious. Their small black obsidion teeth shone like glass in the forest light. "Listen—listen—hear with your eyes, taste with your ears."

What a confusion! I hear nothing. The tallest of the trio, fully 260 centimeters in height and resembling the ancient apparition "Bigfoot", took me by the arm and walked me along the trail another 1000 meters all the while saying nothing to either of us.

"Do you hear the music of the waters—the greater tones give hearing, the greater the turbulence ... why ... death."

I did not think 1 had heard the waters; yet I had, although I was having problems of discovering, of distinguishing betweem autosuggestive remarks amd hallucinatory impulses, the realty sound of rubbish being beatem out by angry activists. These Phantericans—who really were they and where did my professional observations fit into their synchotropic perceptions?

Before I could take another step one of these Sychophants placed about me what appeare to be an old fashioned life jacket. I did not know them that it contained an antibiotic to protect me from the river's poison. I had become acquainted with these rings when as a soldier I had made the Atlantic crossing long ago. Cork had filled them then.

"You will not sink and the water will buoy up your inertia and cany you along. We will cast a spell on you so that the poisonous waters will not affect you."

"Well, thanks," I said. "But what if I drown, who will rescue me?"

Pity appeared to be a feeling that was alien to these Phantericans. 1 had asked a question that was to them absurd and they reacted accordingly with laughter again. Almost as if it were against their better judgement—or was I decripting their message wrongly?-they led me to the foaming, spraysing edge of the overlooking rocks of a river the wildness of which I had never seen but on the ancient Colorado River. Like boys pushsing one another about, one of them gave me a hard shove and I found myself gulping wafer and gasping for breath, entrapped in the river's current. They continued to laugh atop the rocks, as I glanced backward, and to play amongst theselves. My death, of course, meant not a whistler's bargain..

Then a most spectacular thing occurred. The first of the trio, whom I shall call the Wizard, resenbled an Indian shaman witch doctor praying for rain. He lifted his magic metal rod high into the air and thrust it into a cloud, just as a bolt and of brilliant green lightning smote the river, The entire Tanges River instantly converted from water into vapor, revealing to our eyes the contents of the river bottom, saturated logs of ancient trees, mulfti-colored smooth boulders, the diggings of former river badgers, the remains of a Phanterican's wheeled gig and a conglomeration of debris that represented the discards of this strange colony, some of which were glistening bones and remnants of old musical instruments, their stilled strings dripping with river moss, their players hands removed by time, Lumiscent balls lay u; pon the mucky bottom, within which were tiny effigies of political (I suppose) leaders, like the crystalises of gods lost or destroyed. Doubtless these were toys to Phantericans; visibly distinct to my eyes. I perceived the remains of palacial goldfretwork that had either been cast aside or washed away. Strangely I saw no broken urns, pots or the like, usually the shattered discards of bygone civilizations. But we were ineed dealing with a current life, a society of humanoid beings, by our calendar, contemporaneous with our own.. There, to our utter astonishment stretched from bank to blank, over this debfris in the river, was a footbridge which the magician invited us to cross. I suddenly found myself standing in riverbotton mud. I grabbed for the bridge and climbed up onto it with Barodin's hep.

As soon as I and Dr. Borodin had put our feet to its respendent planks a dense and soupy fog settled over us, instantly returning to its liquid state, and we could again hear nothing but the roar of the rapids. Our voices were muted, while, meantime, the three Greeters—Wizard, The Scaleman and their Royal pontificator with the pailfull of collected gems clambered across with Barodin—I had manged to catch the walkway bridge, below where the *creeps* had pusherd me into the river, to their great glee and excitement.

Going through my mind in the midst of my peril was my wonder how, without heat or change of temperature of any sort of intrusive, the Wizard had been able to change river water into fog, that shrounded its course as far as we could see, and then instantaneously condense the fog into water.

Back at the river, while the rapids boiled around Borodin's feet, I had focused my attention on the one cyrpress close to the waters edge, and on the cluster of smooth fog-drenched boulders nearby; I stepped throudh overhanging ferns, springs flowing copiously from them into the river. I looked behind and saw his struggle as tips of iridescent green water lapped at his trousersed legs. Since 1 am a confessed agnostic, I dismised the absurd notion of praying. And then, as if by intention, I fell again into the river. Within my arms reach there floatsed a log, a piece of huge tree branch, half submerged. I seized it, rested a moment, and as I floated down-current with great rapdity, I watched as animals came to the poisonous water and turn away. Instinct. I found myself spinning around in an eddy of immense power. I struggled against it, this time to reach the shore. I refused to accept drowning as an option. Dr. Barodin had successfully crossed the bridge and with the Phantericans was headed down river to meet me. My head struck stones glancing blows several times; my scalp was bleeding.

I smelled the moist green ferns gigantic ferns and the moist, bland, dry smell of river water mingled with forest scents. I could hear only the roar of the river rapids and feel the cool of the river forest on my face.

As I was now flushing close to shore when, rounding a spur in the bank, the water turned strangely quiet, calm, almost placid because the energy of the river ran away from the embankment where I sought sanctuary. Heartily trying to convince myself that I was enjoying this impediment to my life, I felt my energies quicken. I swam toward the shore and presently was able to plant my feet there. Once ashore I fell not into sleep but into unconsciousness from the blows to the head. I remained in that state for how long I do not know, but when I came to I saw bony fingers pointing at me, jestling, mawkmg my situation and taking delight in my injury, my circumnstances and my escape from deatfh. They were the Greeters, and beside them stood doctor Barodin. He broke the verbal silence. with a shout.

"I see you had great momentum, 90 kilos at approximately 30 knots.

"I can't say how fast but its good to be on solid ground again. And damn it all, Barodin, you needn't make fun of my nearly drowning."

"Yes, I dare say … and we thought, or rather, I assumed you were lost, a goner … drowned. These … these creeps never give me a bit of help."

"We do not oppose drowning," said the Scaleman, rattling the scales on its stand. You are a stranger in another dimension of time where the event of drowning is acceptable. The Great One approves. Besides, that could not have happened should not have occlurred, and events that did happen are so transient as to be non-existent."

"Do you understand what he's saying,?" I asked Borordin.

"Perfectly—he is stating the theory that a quantillion odds for an event ever transpsiring mean or *imply* that it never did happen."

"You/re getting to be as vague and abfiiscatng that these guys," I said.

"To put it bluntly, my friend, your intertia while in the water disqualified you for assistance of any kind."

The interpreter Rodman then spoke for the trio: "Molecular rearrangement," was all he said to explainl the Scaleman/s words. GAB took then down—the supposed explanation for a physiological phenomenon reposed in those two words. Couldn't be my platelets, naturally not. 1 scoffed inwardly at the Phanterican's attitude and words, bedraggled and exhausted as I was. Our giant Greeters led usaway from the river. At least I still had my shoes on my feet and 1 could complement myself for sustained courage.

And so no longer dwelling on the phenomenn we discussed the day's events that night as we lay upon pine toughs, pulling tent tarps from our backacks and sharijng instant trail food to appease our craving for food. The Greeters bedded down amongst the brush, wrapping torn bundles of leaves about their feet for warmth. Our campmates did not come near to us for the night.

"Have you ever seen such a thing?" I asked, referring to the transition, by voice command, of water into vapor and back into fog. "But who in the world, my friend, can deny the existence of such an interchange of energy? We saw it with our very eyes."

"I know, I know Galway. It happened … but … yes … river water contains condensed molecules of vapor—like in a laboratory retort."

"You've hit it, my friend—the sudden release of ionic-magnetic power that holds H2O electrons in orbit …"

"By …? Yes, by what intervening force, Galway?

"Let me venture a guess—a powerfull magnetic flash force that converted the water into droplets by dispersion … the principle that with the introduction of a powerful ionic-magnetic field that separates molecules from eath other, divides their electron rings, splits them in an instant—*voila,* you have the existence of a fog with all the propertties of water but with the molecules rendered separate and distinct as mist."

"I think 1 understand, Shawn. But I … we saw no lightning due to the release of ionic energy. Nevertheless,instant ionic separation is a brilliant concept these folk have evidently mastered. But the rod …"

"Don't ask me now. Ask Moses who conjured water out of a rock in the desert with his rod. Was God in on that? Maybe we'll discover its power, the quantum power of some … an ionic-magnetic power that divides molecule from molecule—as does heat, but in the absence of heat … a force that delivers just enough energy to split molecules yet does not split atoms."

As we made out way intend our trail led beneath pendulous rock stalactites that hung from outcropped ledges, dripping a poison that ringed the ground with amber, orange and green rings like colored fiimeroles. It occurred to me that we might use the drippings for medicine, much as Indians in our country used herbs, plants and trees for their medicine. The scene reminded me of a cavern turned inside out. The geology of the lanscape defied common knowldge. Our Sycophant companions loped alongside my self and Dr. Barodin. like giant native runners, simple, amiable and full of mischief. Indeed our escorts appeared to have dispensed with every worldly care. They also found no end of mirth in pulling each other's legs.

The Scalebearer was the IMghtweight of the trio. He kept repeating the mantra: *O, holy, benevolent, kindly government.* He punctuated each remark with this same phrase of adoration and submission. Because he seemed the wisest of the three, I would question him about the mysterious missing airplanes and ships whose disappearance had occurred within the vecinity of his colony.

I digress a moment to explain the Phanterican system of *weightlifting.* The Sycophants indeed have a way by which they beg grace of the government They record the weight of the eitize's words in a ledger known as "Cruel Sharps." It was thereby possible for a citizen, by the sheer weight of his words in golden wagers, to lift himself to Olympan heights of success in any endeavor. Each Phanterican was also expected to calculate the wortth of his neigbor's ideas in this manner, and to submit the total to the government office where it was recorded in a government ledger, whether directly or by evesdropping—carried out to a great science and art. That is to say, interloping and spying earned premiums or tickets that were good in exchange for food, clothing and goods. His security from cradle to grave was thus assured to him by the Phanterican governemt. A Sycophant had only to talk much or to listen to his neighbor speak often for him to be well suipplied with the necessities of life. Work, as dull and demeaning labor, had been banned long ago and was replaced by the concept of *entitlements.*

The ethnicity of the language, itself, need be of no great importance. After all, to Phantericans the capacity for gossip was a natural endowment and was also extremely patriotic. Trivia of the thought and word carried a premium value. Babbble for whatever its intrisic worth was admirable and laudatory. An extraordiary system of commerce it was! I wondered if Dr. Kennison had had anything to do with helping to establish this unique system of weights amd measures, since he was an expert in diametric-system measurement of *thought ions,* the molecular potential of brain energy and neural transmission. There, it seemed to me, lay as to where we might find him at work.

Presently we came to an open meadow, glittering beneath the forest canopy of climax trees. *Pimento Squanus,* and red berries caulght my attenltion. The forest opening was filled with strange outcroppings of quartz of milk-white, scintillating schists and tortured strata of pink and red granite that sparkled in the tinctured light. One of the giants noted my bewilderment, he who carried the scales.

"My humble friend, when the chamber is full and a minister is weightlifting, so many of these golden winks are used to measure his words that, truly, our government cannot coin them fast enough. However, we could not live without them, for weightlifters give balast to our sysrtem. And the checks and balances I've heard about in your foreign system of government are made obsolete by the introduction of our highly-valued babble and gold waffer. We think we are among the universe's most advanced people.

"But why legislate at all?" I asked him. He was unable to reply to my blunt qustion, but only shrugged his massive shoulders.

"Oh, holy, benevolent practical government!"

"A variation," I noted but still I was puzzled. There was another curious observation I remark on. It embarrassed me to note the Sycophantic inclination to gaze at my boots, as wishing to own them. I shifted my backpack load on my shoulders, and even as we walked along the trail and my boots gathere dust on their tops. Sycophant removed it as soon as we stopped, as a consequence of which the boot tops remained highly polished and dust free. I was astounded to watch the Sycophant lick them as tribute to an icon of power that they apparently saw in their American instruders.

Strange, too, that I hadn't noticed until we were in the meadow light that each of the giants wore a felt hat that was divided phrenologically into the right brain and left brain, whose subdsivisions into attitudes, habits, talents and passions had been etched onto the hat. And I was again drawn to their heavily bearded gaces, their beards appearing to denote, wisdom, achievement, intelligence and strength. Truly, they were a unique race. Soon I and Dr. Barodin would meet the Grand Wizard, the Merlin of the Domain, the shaman of shamans, the knighted and noble Geru of the Chancel, the consummate ruler of knowledge, wisdom and Phanterican Affairs. He was, as we would put it, an Agent for all agencies. It was from him that we would gain access to forbidden parts of his domain in our search for Kennison. the desperate—trapof death.

At the crest of a small hill, where brambles partially blocked the way, we … I … saw the white flash of a foot or a dress of some sort and hard the needles crush. We encountered the female of the colony, a woman standing as if confronting us, fully seven feet tall, bearing in her hand a boglet filled with wi; ne, or so it appeared. She spoke not a word but tendered the goblet to each of us who in turn sipped. Wine of the flowers! I surmised. She apparsed harmless, although she carried on one hip a revolver, gotten from someplace, who knows. A rescued seaman, a pirate.,.? Babbling at first withthe others, she at last confessed that she was the wife of Kennison, and that the Government had assigned her to that role.

"I am Lejah. My husband is my mate by our Holy Govemement's decree. My husband is Doctor Kennision. He is head of the Department of Disinformation," We were absolutely astonished at this revelation, struck dumb is a tetter description of our reaction. We had found him!. Lejah offered to lead us to her contractual husband, a novel twist in our journey I had not expected. But if he really *were* Kennison….? what then?

Chapter 4

Into the labrynth

We entered, that is, I and Dr. Barodin, entered their world beneath the face of a cliff, streaked by rain corrosion, that rose up into the mists. Within minutes in the tomb-like blackness I felt my body rising, as if deprived suddenly of the anchoring of gravity. We were entering an electromagnetic field that cancelled out gravitational forces: that was obvious. We—I—ascended to the extent that I feared my heard might strike a rock ceiling. In this total absence of light the Phantericans emitted a pale yellow phosphorescent glow from their eight finger tips. Lejah seemed to be content to remain with us. I suspected an ulterior motirve, since she was the wife assigned to Kennison. What was her purpose for being here?

The hand gestures of the Greeter Sycophants resembled a sort of neon symbolic language. I had no other way of knowing where they were. The rising of my body abruptly stopped. One of them nudged me forward while still in my state of weightless, suspended gravity. I heard a voice. It sounded strangely monotonal.

"You have come to visit us, Doctor Galway. 1 am honored." came the voice as if disembowled. The phonemes were robotic; I was familiar with them in my laboratory work.

"I've come to look for Doctor Kennison. He is missing, as you well know.

"*How should* I know?"

"Don't these little officials consider you—omnipotent?"

"I fear his research suffers from his absence, not his loss to you personally, Doctor Galway. IN anyh event, you won 't get to him without a fight ... and we are prepared to claim him as ours."

""We are impatent and our mission is ... or should be honored."

"Fools, mad perversions of science to feed your pride and international status." Galways felt a blast of cold air upon his face, striking him like a hidden fist in the darkness.

"That is not our understanding. Sir, we are scientists, I and my friend—whom I can't see in this infernal dark."

"The dark is only a condition of your mind, doctor. I am the Wizard Most High, the great conjurer of history, the sorcerer of all magnitudes of human conception and plentitudes of earth's invention. The planets did not predict your arrival so soon. One of our telescopes is out of adjustment. It is prudent we hear only our voices at the start of our ... relationlship. I have send Lejah to keep you company and to respond to your needs. You are in our hands completely."

"I'd like a little light on—on you and—just where are we?"

"You will do well to follow my advice—do not tamper with our laws. The sharp edges of stones in the walls of the tunnel began to irradiate thin outlines of amber light. "Do not urge upon us the frantic time-space continuum of your own small world, Doctor Barodin. I read your thoughts. Our time, for example, is not your time, since we here in our glorious realm travel at a speed that is faster than light. That translates into your eternity. You are in the Modulation Zone."

"Gee, thanks, Colonel Wizard ... you are a wizard.... maybe you're not a Colonel ... but whatever ... you present yourself as a conjurer.... We are not simpletons. This ... this region is within our known world—in the Caribbean Sea."

"Why don't you tell the guy not to talk in riddles, Galway."

"You joke with the Wizard." Another blast of air struck Barodin like a fist. "It is possible that our world within yours can detach itself at will. Our technology is superior, our scientific wisdom is far more advanced."

"No doubt that accounts for Kennison's overstay of his leave."

"His leave?"

"He disappeared on his sabbatical."

"I'm glad that you understand." At this point, the Magnsificent One, the Wizard Omnipotent, Chief Priest and High Sycophant made his actual appearance. Lejah was at his side.

She She wrote in the air with her finger, as if with smoke: "Your silly notions of independence are cancelled. As the Wizard's Messenger, I declare you smitten with a terrible hunger and thirst. Comply with our wishes and you live; defy us, foolish beggars, and you die. I give you life."

"My messenger has spoken for me. Do you arrogant ones understand?"

"No."

The dark lightened like a deep shadow passing overhead, to display in his regal splendor the Wizard, in a coat of golden mail, in his hand a book of some sort, possibly his country's laws, his broad face and high cheekbones deepening the set of his lustrous eyes. One feature struck me as both amusing and distorted, as if a disfigurement. When he stood before us, he looked at our heads, agiganticus specimen of this world we had just entered. Yetr his people were mere pigmies beside him, where they surrounded a niche in the wall. He appeared as if a sculptor's creation, made from engraved marble, suggesting to anyone outside this land that Lejah and the Greeters were his angelic attendants. Real angels? I thought to myself. Absurd, and I'm sure Barodin agrees Within the space of three minutes we were transported to a room, octagonal in shape, trapazoidal shafts of light flooding the molten floor, and steaming fumeroles around the walls emitting a noxious sulphuric smoke. This atmosphere seemed pleasant to the Phantericans, ruler and subjects alike.

A table fabricated entirely of silver, legs fashioned like the heads of an eagle, a vulture, a raven and a Pterodactyl, grew bright under rising sunlight that pierced the cavern roomat a distance of some 50 meters above our heads, reminiscent of the Egyptian Temple at Karnak, and the Stoine henge onthe English plain, both Druidic tree worwship and Polytheism of many gods were thus far evident.

"I do not think you will e able to find your friend," said the Wizard. He prefers to remain hin his new state as an official Anchorite of the realm. He can do his best thinking, reflections, when alone."

"You mean … he's a prisoner, a captive."

"Don't think for a minute you can take him back with you. I know that's on your mind. But for your own lives, at this moment imperiled by my tamed Pterodactyl falcon, will be spared only if you do not force my hand."

"And the Great One has assigned me to him as his wife ... as you understand the arrangement. You will never take him with you!" she said in angry defiance. Her manner was obnoxious and possessive. It was almost Edenic.

Like the armada, if you will, that flew over our heads as we arrived, one of the hideous Pterodactyl vulture-like raptor creatures, whom they revered and worshipped, flew scorchingly close to our heads, as if we had disturbed its sprimitive nest. As it flapped by with slapping wings, it screeched and opened its scissor like beak as if ready to chop off my arm. It opened a gash in one of my shoulders. Lejah laughed with a low, insane sort of laughter, as if comprehending all yet understanding nothing. a manifestation of the true split personality. A word from the Wizard put the primieval beast to silence and rest, perched upon a rock ten metere distant and eyeing us with its red bloodthirsty eyes and snapping its long scissor beak.

"And you were saying ... you wish to find your friend. But, gentlemen, you cannot invade my land like pirates and expect no bloodshed?"

"O, Great One, do not confuse our mission with your fears of visitors."

"We have our ways of getting rid of you, if we find it necessary. But Lejah will lead you to her mate's retreat. There you will learn from your ... erstwhile ... friend that the conscince can be metamorphosed into will to *duty,* will to *power* and will to *death* ... the three choices we give to our captives." If *power,* you dare to thwart me. If *duty,* you must vow to become Sycophants. If *death,* you will be put to the test to quality ... by rebuking our sages with oncontrovertable arguments. So, prepare ye the choice, Foolish Ones.?" And who were the *Sages,* I wondered.

The Wizard disappeared as if a curtain had suddenly dropped in front of him. And Lejah was left laughing in her incomprehensible way, beckoning for us to follow her. She trailed behind her, as if the train remmant of a wedding gown, a fragment of ... laboratory smock such as Kennison has last been wearing when he disappeared. Her actions suggested the training of dogs to follow the scent of the quary, a harkening back to human instinct which these folk continued to display in their actions. After all they had threatened us with death by dehydration and famine, in a word, with extinction. The summons was a humiliation to both of us.

Chapter 5

Justice Delayed

My time in jail is hardly worth noting; it was neither a dungeon nor a country jail as is oftten depicted. I and my three fellow inmates were tethered by light chains around our necks, like dogs with collars, and were given a small yard of five by five feet, about the length of our tethers, to roam about in. We simply had to be careful of not to entangle ourselves. A robot "slave" delivered the food to our "cell" area, where we slept on bamboo beds, covered with rattan covers against night rats, and insulated with yak skins. We did not have to endure semi=tropical rains, which came in about May.

How we found ourselves in jail defies common sense. Lejah, whom we were led to believe would take us to Kennison, her government-appointed spouse, somehow took offense at my cavalaier manner and amistook it for disrespect. I would have to go through an ideological cleansing first before she would risk exposure to my infidel ideas of matrimonial union. And so I was interrogated by giant freezes of characters sfrom off the walls of Greek temples, bronzed—though how inthis darktunnel system I did not know. Their eyes flamed with yellow fire and they seemed to emit little runts of satisfaction when I had answered a question to their satisfaction. The dialogue went like this:

"You deranged dogs from another country assuyme that we are primitive. What is your faith."

"I had to say it was Christian, though that was rather a lie."

"You believe in god worship?"

I said that I did. They asked if it was one of their gods. I said, nay, it was Jehovah. The interrogator, with a withered hand and a beard like a bushel basket of goat hair grinned through his beard. His wite teeth were luminiscent, like a fast paint job on a cheap motor car. He was their master at interrogatfons.

"Get down on your knees," he told me, after a long pause, as if trying to select a punishment for my beliefa. As soon as I had taken the position, he flung onto my back and strapped it down what felt like a saddle but was, instead, a backpack—we had left ours when the Greeters showed up, "Now, now we go to see my mate." I realized that upon my back was some sort of crude recording equipment. I did not know that it contained a lethal skin-contact reagent together with instructions for my disposal in the sea surrounding Phanterica, to be bourne there by a selected Pterodactyl, bird of death. Barodin went through the same interrogation and process for prisoner punishment. It was obvious that wee were being prepared for some strange event, but what my ;mind could not conceive. I thought several hours had passed; instead, my watch told me that three days had transpired, as if in a slow-motion dream.

What was most unique about these Phantericans was their sense of time; thus Tashca, who had made himself almost invisible during these proceedings, continually referred to the continuum of time from which I and Barodin had come. We were being held not because we endangered the realm in any way, or were potential troublemakers, but we were held so that doctors could study our behavior, there being a wide range of deviant behaviors strange to the Phanterican mindset and their society. There and now for personal insult, was the real reason for our captivity. For example, distrust of the government is not allowed and is highly suspect Conversation, except for the most intimate, must be conducted in the presence of another person, a witness to the correctness of speech word choice and compulsory ideology. Of course, Dr. Barodin and myself were not at all accustomed to such flagrant evesdropping, a state of mind that discloses an irradicable paranoia—called *sharing* in this society. That innocuous word carries the stench of an inquisitorial government, represented by our captors.

As in the Medieval times, physical fetes of endurance determined guilt or innocence of a prisoner—his capacity to endure water dunking, flame to his hand, stretching on the rack, torture by fire,—as were

41

Shadrach, Meshak land Abednego in the holy word, and exzcruciating assaults on human flesh as by the Spanish Inquisitors The Phanterican method involved weightlifting. Weightlifting! Can you believe that! The plaintiff and Defendant in any case at bar were put through a simple, crude test of lifting weights, a literal feet. They were compelled to hold an immense stone weighing sixty to eigfhty pounds sover their heads until they dropped it.

With proud scientific foresight, Martyrs of conscience, with psychological motives, bearers whether of guilt or innocence, had long ago been eliminated through evolutionary improvements upon the human soul and psychethrough what we knew as genetic engineering. By the system of Central control of wedlock and conception, the Phanterican *State,* if you want to call it that, had inbred so adroitly as to weed outundesireables. Thus it was that these old-fashioned religious human behavior areas—such as marriage and the paternalistic family— became merely tokenized, peripheral to survival functions of social justice. It was my opinion that the Phanterican tests for justice represented a reversion to past methods of proof. Justice, to my mind, is cognative, not physical. Hanging, electrocution, medicinal poisoning and beatings ere all of them *prima facie* evidence of guilt where, in certain cases, guilt is proed by circumstantial evidence. This forensic route gave mind primacy over matter, a situation consistent with governmental breeding programs to produce the perfect speimens. Nobody, it seemed, wanted to bve bothered by looking at cripples, treating disease or accommodating deformity of any sort, for all those adjustments were destructive of the happiness of perfection.

Indeed, in past times it had been the number of *yeas* or *nays* either side could marshall as witnesses that determined the lightness or its worthslessness of a case at bar. Ten guilty nays were superior to one or two innocent yeas, backed up with tangible evidence. Therefore the defendant was often summarily hanged. That left no room for a rebellious pleading, new evidence, a retrial or appeal, with the *corpus delecti* speechless in a wooden box.

We found something of a reminder of those techniques in Phantericaa, much refined. Our enemy in this new land were the forces of scientific sperfectionism: scientific mutation, genetic enginneering, modular grafting, molecular transformation by ionic sequencing, and most hideous to me, the time-compressive disappearance of future time into present duration. Time was simply not coextensive with human activsity but merely edited out those events, mannerisms, dreams, expections in a Sycophant's life that would threaten the existence of the State. Simple logic told me that such a State demanded a dictator. The Great One was he, I was to presume.

Justice, as we knew it, was a travesty. The sheer system of numbers was so reined that anyone who was impaneled in the cardboard, facade jury could cast a ballot *en absentia*. The jury of a democracy being a microcosm of popular unananimity—they voted with a special ballot of rocks. The Greeks practiced balloting with stones The ancient Hebrews their instant-verdict justice—a form of vengeance—by stoning the accused. There was justice in the rocks.

In Phanterica, the system of rocking, or rock tossing, became popular, as in ancient Israel, long perished. Its legal custom of stoning was, however, justice delivered. Men with corrupt minds turned askew by ideological isolation, discovered that they could make large gains from the gullibility of the people. They simply practical on the natives. We were unexpectedly stoned as we followed Lejah; she did not look back. I took a hard blow on my back with a rock and Barodin was bleeding copiously from a head wound. We ran. I saw nothing of the ambush possess, which it appeared to be. Possibly they were just renegades with a hatred of strangers, aliens, Lejah scarcely looked back. I picked up one of the stones; it was pumice. I threw it back at my invisible attacker.

When I complained to Tashca of this treatmentto, he replied, quite appropriately, "Keep in mind that the system of justice in Phanterica has shaped itself from cryptic, molecular thought.   O n l y the stakes cn be measured but not the intent or the ambition."

"Yes, and what if we're killed?"

"Ne grateful for the change," he anwered blythely, s if reciting a change of address.

"Have you no compassion? I asked.

"I cannot help you," he replied.

Within twenty-four hours, I saw the jubilation on his face, a key in one hand. I released myself and Barodin from our chains. But our trip with Lejah, the rock ambush in the tunnel[11] Where did dream and reality join. I felt confused. Tashca only said that the Great Wizard, hearing of our unfortunate circumstances., had commanded that we be released. Our chains had dropped away. And so it was. Tashca informed us that he, too, was no better informed than we and that we ought to seek our friend in the most lieely places, in the Hall of Deliberations, in the University classroom, perhaps in the places of carrousal and most certainty in one of Phanteriea's mamy Laboratories of Mitigation, so called because almost all science was designed to mitigate Sychopnant pain, discomfort and disease. Intergalactic space travel was a genuine cathartic for the Phanterican soul Lejah led us to the Hall of Deliberations … I assumed.

We followed the lovely mutant Lejah to the Deliberations Chamber of the Great Hall where, after kissing the carved stone hand of the Procurator, or governor of the chamber, at the entrance doors, we observed a subaltern receive a silver urn from an aide. Sulphurous smoke issued from the urn. the Subaltern breathed in deeply of this smoke for about a minute.

"This little ceremony precedes vote upon a new law, gentlemen," Lejah explained. "Observe, please, the deMcacy of the operation, the attention given to details of the ritlual and the reverence bestowed upon the ceremony."

Then it was that I was shocked, for there in a bloack robve witha gited golden sea burd upon his crown stood our friend I glanced away at a cmmotion, and most unexpectedly Kennisonwas no longer there but instead a proctor with a sword in one hand. Swinging it swiftly over his head and cutting the air witha swish, he appeared to attack us, myself and Barodin, with his Claymore sword. We took cover. Lejah laughed a shrill girlish laughter, calmly seized the sword from the Proctor and striking it thrice ona rock proclaimed that the some thirgty members in the chamber, attired in leather hides, should stand sourround us threateningly, attempting to dsiscover the temper of our wills and our prside. But Lesjah curbved their appetites for death.

"Where is our friend, Kennison … he was here just a cmomdent ago."

"He cxonsults with the Wiard to decide what we should do to you. You are disgusting aliens in our land and threaten our ways of life."

"What! Just the two of us!"

"We see you as an army ready to set aflame our city with your junk science."

"We are well credentialed."

"A tremendous weeping broke out among the Chamber members, for I believed that they wept not at our claim to scientific knowledge, but for their country of Phanterica.

Why do you come here?" Kennison asked.

"To take you back with us."

"Never. I am content here."

"You are cleansed … brainwashed … by the State of Phantrerica.

"I am well satisfied that I have done right. Go, the both of you before you lose your lives." At these words he vanished as in a vapor, leaving behind the golden crown of a seabirdupon rthe ground.

These remarkable folk had discovered the secret of transpositional molecular separation and reconstitution.

Then, up the aisle of the Chamber, the subaltern gave each in turn a deep drought of the poetent rose and sulphur emanation. The fumigation intoxicated these ir imaginations and caused them to accept the words *consider the proposition* as if the words themlselves were a magic potion. The invitation to thought appeared very seductive, as lawyers often enjoy thinking for effect without any significant content. I was told by Tashca that Greengrocers, stage drivers, preachers and bridge engineers had long ago been stricken from the the Great One's list of Deliberators.

After this sharing of the sulphurous smoke, each Delbiberator took from his gray chasule—each one wore a chasule over his piestly black cassock—a piece of paper and a stub of charcoal. One by one they inscribed their talismanic symbol image on the paper. The silver urn made its second round and the Deliberators of this enclave, dropped their talismanic scribbling into the flame. The urn returned to the Subaltern, the Commander, lin effect, who sat quite still, watching the proceedings, his head propped up by two bamboo poles between which lay suspended a cardilnal cushion. Upon this clushion he rested his chin whitest deep in thought.

The light in the chamber changed from a twilight glow to a brilliant orange. A large tell clanged, like one of those attached to a steam locomotive, and the Commander mumbled in a spiritual language that sounded much like that of an lauctioneer … or a teacher in tongues of my day. He recited the names of as he pulled them wilth his bare hand from the burning sulphur smoke rising above urn. When all the names, purified by the sulphur, were counted and transcribed on the aall behind the Commander, the enclave got up and changed their seats so that they might view the propositions from the viewpoints of the other members of the body. I had always to remind myself that molecular transposition of deliberative thought had its value.

"You have just seen the pasasage of a new law that will require all Sychophants to swear allegance to the the law book of our great leader. At this moment an amazing thing happened: From the bowels of the ground m where the well used to be, there rose up a great bubble of molten glass, all aflame, that contained by some mysterious nuclear electrical force within its spherical shape. Yet it was not hot to any touch of the flesh. The Commander pitched the papers, presumably law papers, withdrawn from the urn into the molten globe. Waving his arms as a solemn blessing, he watched the globe disappear back into the earth. I learned that this was sympathetic nature's acceptance of the magical wishes of these noble Sycophants of Phanierica, who, having harnessed for generations past so many of nature's forces, had at last entrapped the very core center, or a piece thereof, of the earth's hot mass, and that this volatile entrappment acted as a natural curative furnace for spiritual thoughts. Rather like the fashioning of pottery I thought I suddenly came to realize the reigious significance of the Deliberators' thoughts, which deserved to be purified by fire.

A Sychophant seated beside me nodded but remained as solemn as a monk. A small clatterr of laughter erupted from the floor, but the Chairphant waved his tome of rales in their direction, and it abruptly ceased.

"We try to discourage laugter here in this chamber," said Tashea," and we do so by elevating pain to the status of state welfare, highly desireable, to be endured with pride."

In ancient days, I mused, the ability to laugh at the ridiculous had been somehow closely associated with intelligence., In this chamver pain was enobled and all manner of laws devised, I assumed, to mitigate it, the replacement by various elixirs and stratagems of, let us say, clean living. Truly, these were a remarkable people. Then, again, what were they to do with Dr. Kennison?

I remembered my mission and hastened to leave the chamber,hoping to meet up wit him in the cloak room, but Tashea's strong hand and will on my coat restrained me. "He will not recognize you." Lehagh had disappeared, having led us to her *summa bomum* mate,

"I doubt that our mission will find success here in this chamber."

"We have just begun," said Barodin.

"The man we search for was at least not a politician," I said.

"He had his own laboratory back in Jersey," Barodin replied.

"Take my words for it, Do nort show rebellion to my countrymen. Phantgerica is inhospitable toward rebvellious aliens."

There was sno rebuttan from the otter members?"

A scowl showed on Tashca's face, "We censors the one another here in Phanterica—in the interest of efficiency in government and purity in human relations."

"I see, I see," I replied softly. My first wonderment was slowly changing to fear.

"Just remember, Curious One, that we Phantericans are an advanced race."

"True," said Barodin. "But do not forget that we Americans are among the most perceptive of peoples. Comes from our survival past. Your children are pauperized in mind and soul, condemned to future passivity, because they're forced to bow before your government and become slaves."

Without any announcement, as the bailiff before of the judge, the the town crier the village news or the ... the President before the Congress, the Mighty Wizard appeared without any prelude. He stood brilght under the mirrored sunlight that pierced the cavern stones from 50 metres He stood upon his council table, his bare toes of his holy feet grasping, clawlike, the wingfeathers of a giant condor etched thereon. My eyes burned from the brilliance of his dress, the arms and hands akimbo and almost human, and much like the appearance of his own people. He had sheathed himself in reptialian scales of glistening sequins of black, purple and green, his head Hashing fire through eyes that seemed not unlike the rubies found along the trail. A fine moustache adorned his upper lip and a broad beard, groomed like a opera singer's, graced his chin. With one gloved hand, he slowly spun the electromagnetic force I stood trapped within, a motion that swung me labout so that he could scurtinize me, much as he might have a specimen in a jar. He moved with sinewy steps to one side of the council table.

The music of harp and flute came from space, his speech was not unkind, deep, from his chest, as he gestured like a ballet dancer with elegant hands to emphasize his words.

"Do not take me for a fool, Doctor Galway. You have already formed a judgement of my people, We're far beyond the world you come from and so—hold your tongue. We are not interested …"

"I have only looked, O, Wizard. I have not judged, Imperial Omniscient One of Phanterica."

While he paused a flute and harp melody of exotic notes, some refrains quite beautliful, ethereal, came to my ears. At the same time while the music played, the table of wlith the engrved raptor appeared to float so as to keep the shaft of sunloight entirely upon it while the Wizard spoke.

"You will not understand why …"

"Stop. Your speech offends me. I comprehend. It is you who do not. Yes, I know that you have come here to find and take back to America Doctor Kennison." He smiled through his great beard. "But he will not go with you."

"We already know where he is"

"Do you now! Another of your foolish enquiries. Naturally, however, we still have need of him."

"You have just admitrted that he is here in Phanterica."

"We never denied it to you." He removed a gold box from his cloak and inhaled deeply of its contents, which I took for a drug. "I will personally see to it that he eludes you. That is all I can say. He is, of course, alive. The Imperial Wisdom of evolutionary ethics mandates conformity to our laws to the ultimate. We toleratre no rebellious spirits here. We move in another time dimension—a distended time which has miniaturied our lives and distorted space but which shapes our bodies, compressing our lives and thus enabling our science to compact its discoveries. Join us and you will learn many of our secrets."

"Do I understand you to say....?"

"Enough of your politicizing, your sticky and insolent protocol of language! The historicity of progress precludes man's volition for change. Science dictates all matter!"

"Test me, Great One, and see if I don't understand."

"Very Well, arrogant intruder! Do you know about ... do you even understand 'subliminal adaptation ... progressive lineal growth ... or retrogressive evil habituation or, again, autotonic projection ... combined with all the cabals of doctrinal reasoning you can deivise? Utter simplicity, that is what we stress."

"Yes, I daresay," said Barodin."

"I carn learn much from your people," I said, trying to turn away his wrath. We do share an audiometric commonalty—our language."

"You swagger where there is intellectual emptiness. Your traditions and your men of history you treat with light contempt as figures from some almost forgotten fairy tale."

"And what does your civiliation offer—robotics, inbreeding and the manipulation of molecular matter to recreate life. Your children are mere breeders."

"How blind you are! By my authority they love and admire."

"Hate, is my guess."

"They are shrewd microspecimens of adult macrospecimens. Nothing that you know about remains for them to find root in. They have passed through forty thousand years of evolutionary change. They play and are neither in panic or agony over things they do not think are losses. Things in surfeit no longer matter to them. This accounts for their great contentment."

He had finished with his lecture on state doctrine, I assumed. He had one admonition for us both: "If you try to leave Phanterica, and especially this city, without knowing the way, you will surely get lost. Almost one thousand miles of tunnels in Phanerica remainun unlighted and only crudely charted., As quickly as he had come, he departed from Ms council table with the engraved raptor. So, too, did the sun that shone on it go out.

"It appears as if we have barely begun, Barodin," I said with a heavy sigh. "We don't know what project, if any, Kennison s engaged in-some form of experiment in government, or the particle physics of human behavior. Who knows? He looked enraptured...."

Henceforth I would operate on the "uncertainty principle"—which would mean exclusion of all data not productive of at least one, maybe more, certainties, We would have to increase our momentum in the search, that is to say—force multiplied by time ... and our energy, or force multiplied by distance-keeping in mind that if we stay on his trail, our combined energies will transect those of Kennison.

"I'm certain—as you must be, doctor Barodin—that our neutron force will collide at some point in time with Kennison's mass, as it were..,multiplied by his acceleration in whatever projects he is performing for the Phanterican State."

"And when that happens, we won't delay, Galway, my friend."

Of course, both Barodin and myself believed that *free will* was an illusion, and so, mathmatically and fatalistically, we believed that we would once more meet up with Kennison. We could then figure out how to get him back to America. Particle physics would determine the results of our search.

Outside the chamber of Deliberations we heard a loud ruckus, which unidentifiable noise put us both on instant alert.

Chapter 6

Tower of Learning

Certainly the peculiar ways of these Fhantericans had their genesis in education, I thought, when, at that moment, I was roughly handled by Syehophants wearing fiery armbands and dangling from their hips some sort of weapon desgined to demoleeularize an enemy of the State. It had become apparent to me that the people feared to be contaminated by the mindless application of principles of evolutionary pragmatism—which to them represented a synthesis of progress. They did posess a small grasp on freedom of thought, but feared to express it lest they be seized and *collaborated*—made to pay the State penalty for free thought which consisted in synthetic evacuation of their minds by moleclular freezing with a chemical caled Hydronmcularcortozine, The *freezing,* so called, was chemical rather than thermal.

Were I and my friend Dr. Barodin to be used for psychological geldings in the train of evohrtionay thinking by these folk? I had to meet an actual Phanterican scientist before I could reach an answer.

As we raced along through their tunnel system astride our pinkeyed albino horses, creatures that knew every twist and turn of the complex cystem, to some other venue, a drip of water hit my face from time to time, as cool drafts from pockets of forced air refreshed us from time to time. I smelled the clean smell of machinery oil and heard the hum like bees in a wall of hidden machinery. Scree had broken from the walls in certain places and fell into the murky, opalescent light of pearl like brillilance on the water-slickened stones. I heard the singing like wires singing in a wind upon a ceiling where a vast army of cave bats

51

glinted like blown leaves in the faint light, bloodshot eyes catching mine occasionally, their wings fluttering as they clung to places in the rocks.

"Barmouse bats—keep the insects down, the air clean," Tashca remarked, seeing my crouch over the white mane of my galloping horse. Presently we turned into a vast rocky area that lay above ground and in a natural drawthat was lined with exotic ferns, labvrynthian vines and tropical flowers. "This is our modst modem, up-to-date training academy ... which may interest you learned gentlemen." Without saying a word, I entered a room reminiscent of armories of ancient times that contained armor, swords, spears, shields and replicas of every fighting weapon known to uncivilized men, including daggars, mortars, canons, and hand arms of an infinite varilety, "We cherish the history of death, my friends, death caused by these infernal machines of human invention. And gunpowder. You will observe the extent of man's ingenuity for snuffing out life." I stirred uneasily and dismounted. "But don't be impatient. I will show you how we *begin* life. Our lifesbond factories are models of efficiency, cleanliness and production. We can produce zygotes of any human characteristic you could wish for." He sounded like a man out of his mind—or a chicken farmer whom chance had put in charge of our mission. I would not tolerate this cursive, intimidative handling for very much longer and whispered my intent to Doctor Barodin. He nodded.

Scattered around a great out of door clearing were children of thirteeen or fourteen years of age performing acts that would outrage civilized *mm* of long ago. With lifesized dolls, fabricated of plastic and fabric in official Phanterican reformatories, the children were by proxy techniques of surrogacy performing the most immoral acts. An instructor, formerfy in my century called a *teacher,* was showing these Innocents the most obscene anatomical acts and telling each how every sexual aberration should be accomplished. They listened in open-mouthed wonder, only half comprehending what they were hearing.

"The ultimate triparte goal is knowledge ...information ... understanding," Tashca whispered. "We have centuries ago dispensed with what you once called *wisdom,* that understanding that came from the crude and barbaric crucible of knowledge and experience combined. But here, where we control all of these little Sychophants-for their happiness, let me add. There is no reason to discuss experience ... or even to champion it We tailor experience to the State's demands, wisdom eventually atrophies and drops out of the equation like an unused limb and these children are left only with knowledge ... inculcated knowledge. Knowledge comquers fear and moral taboos and all the prohibitive *mores* that thwarted man's search for happiness in your world."

Monstrous!" thought

But how could children grow up and never experience the feel of a baby frog in the palm of the hand, the smell of a dog's wet coat in the rain, the sounds of the waves breaking on the shore, and the babbling of a brook over stones, the taste of ice cream and the feel of wet sand under the feet? and in a word corrupt the freshnes of simple natural experiences. There were so many things to feel touch, taste and hear. It baffled me how these folk could so isolate their progeny, *exile* them from life's experiences. I shook my head.

"Information is like heat-absorbed by the child," he said. "No distractive connection is tolerated here-"
"Like a parent instruding ... " I suggested. "Exactly—more like a religious prohibition," He smiled.

At the close of each segment of the childrens performance, loud and sensual music, a cacophony of drums and harsh harmonies flooded the outdxoor classroom amphitheatre, which, by the way, was lined of a kind of metal that amplified childish laughter and whimpering cries and made the rocks appear to shudder with their echoes of galeic mad laughter. There was that dynamic in the children, a roving, I call it, toward futile understanding and mawkish laughter that was neither human nor adult. I shuddered when I heard it.

But here was absolute safety, I surmised. The pitch of the decibels was so loud my ears hurt and the drums so explosive that the ground literally trembled. I had to hold my hands over my ears, yet the children did not do so, since they were by this time in their lives almost deaf from the booming, crashing, screeching sounds of Phanterican music—a continuation, I surmised of the deafening *cataract guitar* I had heard earlier but could not identify.

Psychedelic lights of the sun's intensity played their kalaidescopic fragments over the walls of the outdoor chamber, even while these imps, their faces controted by the horror of the fearsome sounds, formerly known as *rock music,* worked to try to throw off the ill effect. But—that was the impossible. So that they simply watched, bemusedas if numbed by it all, both sitting and squatting on the floor like madhouse inmates, traumatized by the music. A few of them lost bladder control in their terror, contorted in the agony of their learning sessioa Then, just as suddenly as it had begun, it stopped, and upon their faces there appeared expressions of immense relief and relaxation. First the pain and then the relief, habituating them to pain but resigning them to relief induced by Phanterican wizardry, the remedy for which coming from the government, would be paliatives of money, *entitlements,* pablum-like condolences and powerful sedatives. The out of doors setting masked the insanity of the show. All of this juvenile transition was called *sensitivity training.* How do I know this?—one of the smarter children told me,

"This is how by degrees the children learn to thank their deliverers from pain."

"Why start with pain in the first place?" I asked in a simplemmded way, somewhat intimidated by this cruel extravagance of the demonstration.

Tashca looked at me, stunned. "It is the pain which animates them to great deeds—not treacle ideals, freedom and the likes of that snobbery from yourt world. Pure pah-it conditions as well as instructs. And mind you, that pain is world-wide. We here in Phanterica try our utmost to import the pain overflow from the outside world to add to our common pain-habituation stock."

"My God, what are you saying?"

"Simply this: that one can never know true happiness unless one has endured excruciating pain. Therefore we elevate pain to the role of a priceless, let us say, aphrodesiac of suffering in order for the people to experiencre their greateast happiness. Also, selectove pain is good for the Government's drug industry."

What sort of masochistic madness was this, I wondered, but I remained silent, hoping to stumble onto a clue as to the whereabouts of Dr. Kennison, or at least not to impede any important revelation that would assist us. Any probing enquiries into Phanterican misconception of pain might suddenly alert the auhorities to the purpose of my visit which was not simply to find Dr. Kennison but to abduct him back to the States—nbeyond the reach of Sychopnantic fixation on pain. And of course, with pain as a state-sponsored indullgence mind-altering psychedelic drugs and Middle Eastern escapist opiates were rife.

"We are conditioning them, our people—an ongoing process," our guide explained in response to the expressions on our faces. Tashca had the curious *habit* of kneeling, taking our hands as if pleading for mercy, begging for tolerance

"I am familiar with the Pavlovian experiment with the dog, yes. But these are … not dogs. They have souls."

"Unmitigated rubbish! They do not have souls. There you are, my friend," he said in a way that settled any argument "The State of Phanterica is a great conditioner."

"I'm not surprised," Barodin said.

Undeterred, Tashca went on. "We are able to mutate the sensation threshhold by introducing contiguous stimuli. As other stimuli substituting for the one conditional stumulus come into play, a reward by our Wizarrd for hunger, first stimualted by the gong you see hanging over the sun spot, created the need for satisfaction."

"Clever."

"Very … and your Dr. Kinnison has innovated many versisons of this kind of official learning."

"Only the one is a false hunger, the otter a real desire to be met"

"How pereeeptive you you, Dr. Galway! But the proocedure isw totally ethical! False deprivation, thus fabricated allows us to turn the children over to the Great One, totally, He then has the option of supplying the satisfaction to his proteges."

"Show me what you mean," I said, altogether skeptical of his words. Tashca clapped his hands and the Phanterican teacher herded the children into a group and with an instrument much like the cattle prod of old, yet with very low voltage—more like a trickle of a feather, he urged them to form a square. Tashca spoke in a high Phanterican dialect which I had not yet learned, with a sort of falsetto voice.

The teacher selected one of the little girls to climb upon a high swivel bench, turning her about like a manikin doll figurine show piece for all to observe. She appared to enjoy the attention. He spoke into her ear, and she clambered along the length of the turning table, then slid to the floor.

"What was that all about?"

"Little girl fantasies coming into play early in life, the desire to show off natural beauty, the desire to imitate boys by climbing trees, the urge, later in life, to confront deadly enemies and share glory with the boys." This next remark was perhap the most astounding of the entire afternoon. "The teacher can implant any fanstasy he wants into their purile minds. Now wartch closely."

One of the boys, at a signal from their teacher, walked over to a heavy wooden beam and began to climb toward the ceiling, much as natives do in the islands for cocoanuts and bananas. When he reached the heavy trusswork, like a fly he hung onto the beam, gripping it with fingers and wrapped feet, completely without fear. And then, leaping to another beam by the awkward use of his small feet, he descends to the floor.

"The secret of what you've just witnessed? A monkey—he has been infomed so many times that he has ancesetral *monkey* in him that he feels he ought to act like one."

"Great Scott-that was millenia ago! And the kid puts up no resistance?

"None—you see, they are under my hyponosis," the teacher explained. "Oh holy, benevolent, sacrificial government!"

As to their textbooks," Barodin thought to enquire.

Tashca spoke briefly to the teacher who then, upon a signal, spoke into a large copper horn from the open end of which there issued, instead of words, pictures much like a movie screen, The machine translated vocal voice patterns into images—a not altogether new technology. The teacher explained, "You will notice that each child on his and her simple slate, received the same message without comprehending it. The *tabula raza* effect, said the teacher, "in which the child needs only memory without interpretation to recall when he needs to. After all," he said," Phanterica has survived not by interpretation, which is obstructive, but by pure information, which is constructive. Morallism so often ruins reason, makes it a bigabear in Phanterican minds."

"No room for thought," I said in my quaint, simplistic way.

"Thought! About what-all is settled, provided and beyond contradiction." said Tashca."Nothing can be learned in the presence of understanding, for that inhibits the free flow of information by virtue of obstructive experience and angry contradiction."

"Even experiment in my laboratory is just an ... an experience and no more."

"You think yourself wise to mock our ways, Doctor Galway. We understand, even if you do not., Facts are all that are required for life to go on."

"No morality?" asked Barodin with an unusual show of uncharacteristic meekness. Tashca looked at him as if he regarded the Doctor of Cultural Anthropogy as a complete and unredeemable idiot.

I stepped in. "What my friend means is—no morality, no interpretation, no conscience. I, myself, am beginning to see."

"I think you both had best stay here tonight and have a long talk with the teacher, whom he called *the professor,* a thin, angular, bony fellow, slightly hunched over, who never smiled. He brushed back his long, yellow hair, plaided in the back; but it was the moustache that seemed to smile, piercing blue eyes remaining cold. He was dresseed in a gown that was open at the back; it resembled a surgeon' or patient's gown. His restless fingers flagillated like short tentacles. He appeared to send his emanations of thought through the minds of his class of about twenty children, who were dressed alike in green togas and skull caps of slate color.

A most extraordinary thing then happened. The teacher, with the help of spirit aides that seemed mere winged blue dragonflies, mounted up into a podium that stood beneath a great chunk of unshaped granite rock. It moved gently, pendulum fashion by the force of the earth's rotation, moving restlessly above his head as he spoke.

"All ancient value sounds are programmed into the Rock-Demon, sluch as HO-N-OR." The monolith, probably of some 30 tons weight was held in place by a single strand of high tensile wire. I marveled at the metallurgical wisdom invested in that single strand. He smiled. "If I so much as dare to interject my personal values, whatever they be, if I had any," he smiled again, "that rock would fall and I would be crushed. Know then that it is a vallue-empty yet cogently brilliant science that holds that rock up. What good are acursed values in the face of imminent disaster? Tell me that ... learned men!"

"No!" said Barodin in disbelief.

"Let me answer the wonderment on your faces," the school Master interposed. "That immense rock weighs almost thirty tons. In the mass-energy equation, e=mC2, as on all planets, foreign and domestic," he smiled, "that stone weighs almost twelve million megatons when you consider the co-extended ratio of weight to size compounded by interstellar gravity. Time-movement changes the outcome; the equation stays the same. Being scientists, you understand. The wire that holds it suspended above is made of Taxibalnium, an exotic metal formed eons of time ago incombination with Titanium. In those times, when atomic bombs were detonated—and it took only four or five—in sufficient numbers, their explosive force rearranged the molecular structlure of certain metals within the upper crust of the earth, in the vecinity of heir detonations. And so we have this ... wire, if you will, drawn from that material. As a metalurgist, when I am not teaching, I tell you. You must want to go up and take a closer look at it."

When the Master pushed against the stone it *moved* ever so slightly. He was without fear; I could not stand long beneath it, nor could Barodin.

The—wire will hold that tonnage of weight permanantly in suspension ...?"

"So long as I abide by the rules of the State in all I say and do." We here in this Elysium of learning have complete and total control over the curriculum."

"Who knows when you deviate from the curriculum of the State?"

"The blue dragonflies do," he said, pointingto the gauzy-lwinged insects with long blue scaley bodies that flitted about the stone, as if searching not for human lies but for moisture. "They will be the carriers of my words, I'm afraid. If they can carry disease with their bite, they can also carry doctrine deviations. That is implicit in their very existence. We have conditioned—programmed is the correct word—even the insects to obey. In your movi3es, do not the very birds obey commands?"

""My friend," I addressed Barodin bluntly, do these people strike you as intellegent masters of seience ... or jiust what?"

"He speaks foolishness, Galway. Take my word for it. His is pure delusion ... madness ... fentasies of the imagination."

"We will at least have to pretend, won't we, Galway. We want to get out of here alive."

"You have already witnessed the efficacy of our pain-restitution activity. Most enlightening, isnt it?" Tashca asked.

Yes, I thought, in another way that makes them our enemy. A law of physics informs us that for every action there is a reaction. Should a stone, an inert thing with internalized energy, be fearsome to us? Should these insects that are said to be hearers of perilous news on their fragile wings deserve our avoidance?. Great Scott! I should hope so. The characteristics attributed to these objects amazed me-a form of animism, special mystical spirits in things of the lower orders of nature. And these folk believe that … illusion of reality. We should take great pains to watch out for our own safety, Galway."

"I am of the same opinion."

"Look out, Barodin" I cried as a snake of monstrous proportions slithered across the cupola of the academy room, slashing here and there with its great salivating fangs. Even Tashca ducked down.

"In what are the children being instructed?"

I foreknew his answer? "In life processes—daily performance. We have actually been able to eliminate much of the ancient and metaphorical sort of schooling you two scientists are familiar with. Our machines work out mathematical problems. Our scientists apply the useful functions of our laboratory discoveries. Yet we are still discovering many new things. You smile. Literature, the arts, philosophy, yes, even religion were discarded centuries ago—by your time continuum—because they interferred with those who now hold the reins of power. Permit Ime to use that ancient metaphor.

"Life processes are common to all life, are they not, Tashca?"

"True, true. Eating, sleeping, navigating, procreating, dabbling in colors and shapes now and then so that the children do not become mere drones. Come over here and observe more carefully."

I watched. I saw that the children played with great abandonment in their plastic dust, making water from their small bodies to shape Phanterican horses and bats. They appeared to enjoy chaos, squabbles and fighting, in ecstatic lostness with their confusion and, to my eyes, their general mess."

"But they are—*creative*" I tried to explicate.

"Oh, yes. We have a solid curriculum that allows a little wiggle-room for what we have not yet been lable to remove—that part of man's nature that reaches outward and is most—I curse the confining word— *exreative.*"

"That's the God in him," said my friend.

"Syllogistic nonsense—the pride of your rationalizations! Don't ever mention that name again, Doctor Barodin. God *is* dead. He has been dead for centures and centuries."

"An ancient slip of the tongue," Barodin apologized.

"Just remembver, gentlemen, that we, that Phanterica has reached the highest state of civiliation not with the help of any mythical god but with his own unaided efforts."

"I quite understand your position," I said, beginning to fear for our own fate, therefore sounding conciliatory.

"Is there more to this-learning regimen, that you've shown us?

"Oh, yes. Come along into the antechamber, the adjacent cavern, and observe for yourself."

I followed him up toward the light and into a into the ravine complex, flighted mostingenuously by an inner waterfall that carried light down from the surface, much like our own core-light conduits in our hospitals. There, scattered across the sloping terrain other children sat, mingled and like adults, in imitation they embraced one another in connubial imitation, in sexual positions, squirming activities and actual performance. Others not so engaged were busy breaking up rocks with mallets to construct pathways, thus learning early the value of work. I thought of a similar work scene I had witnessed in a German prison camp. These activities were forms sof adult cruelty foisted on their young to prove the ffieacy of reason over morality, I suppose.

"You wonder at such maturity," said Tashca. Such comprehension, such passive adaptation and acceptance of our ways."

"A little strange, 111 admit," I said.? But tell me, when are they taught … lhen do Ithey learn?"

They are learning by watching and imitating. Science has approved this tim honored strategy to link the young to the old."

Dr. Barodin dared to comment. "In this incadescent air, these Phsantericans are alive, vigorous, immenselsy vital and technically brilliant childre."

"They appear to be barbaric and ignorant," I suggested.

"You are in the twilight of skepticism. With our faith in ourselves and not the State, we have difficulty in distinguishing the enemy from a friend. While you in your civilization were worked to extreme in your fright over dying."

"We had to survive, often dying in the attempt."

"You were—and are—obsessed with age. To us that is inconsequential."

The dancing children feature themselves as a "Symphonie of beauty and color," said Tashca.

I observed their gross deterioration in vocal ability, conversation being almost non-existent among them There appeared to be, instead, a comity, a common likeness of understanding that eliminated the main purpose for conversing.. Yet with a macabre sort of fascination I watched their emaciated, bony, shrunken bodies twitch and girate. They twirled to the discordant music of a flutist, the strands of their silken hair swirling in the air. They mingled, bent, lept up flinging their legs wide apart, then pirouetted, dipped, held one another in vulgar embraces, suggesting sexual actions, multi-copulation. The light threw this bizarre scene into relief when they converted to silhouettes, when in fact the backdrop was struck with a bkzde of burning magenta light. The children seemed not to mind that they had an audlience, for they were totally enwrapped in their dancing, mere moving shapes against the light.

"They are everlasting," said Tashca. "They do not stop dancing. Since we control all energy sources, time and the life of space within Phanterica, we have converted them into our tireless escapade, our unending enjoyment of the raptures of the flesh."

"They are ... old," I said with sudden insight.
"You are forgetting your time perspeertive. Foolish fetish! No, Doctyor Galway, they are young by our time measurement Doyouhear>?"
"Quite plainly, sir."
"Mount up, then!" Tashco ordered, borrowing a phrase from Western movies.

I thought it betrayed a subtle Phanterican sense of humor. And so off we rode, back down into the labrynth of tunnels, leaving the experimental school behind. I called his attention to the mounds that had surrounded the school of schist. As we rode, on our albino horses, our guide explained.

"Their purpose, you ask?" He laughed. "My Curious One, we Phantericans have long ago surrendered purpose to the Government and now we live within the protection of its spirit. *O, holy, benevolent, kindly government."* He patted the top of his head.

"But they were built, they exist."

"If you must know, those mounds contain the contaminants of our city, the molcular sloughing off of aberrant ideals. We keep all political factions under control. We simply bury them in those above-ground containers—deals that might poison foture generations. I'm certain you don't understand, since you and your Mend are idealists."

"We try our best," Barodin answered.

"Never forget that we are a molecular society. Some of the crude excrescences of your day we have captured. When a ship went down, when an airplane was lost in a storm, when men were about to drown without cause or reason or a single trace, it was we who made use of their knowledge for our civiliation, my good doctor."

"Drowning seamen, crashed airplane pilots...."

"Since you must know—we have a most ingenuous device for salvaging derelict survivors of your way of life. We encapsulate them in an air bubble that instantaneously derives its inflation air from molecules of sea water that surround the crash site."

"As you hearing what I am hearing. Dr. Barodin?"

"I'm afraid so. Is that possible ...?"

"Our government operations room tracks all ships, airplanes, pleasure boats—yes, even swimmers—who find themselves trapped within our electromagnetic ring of energy. Essentially, they then belong to us. TEven eventually hey love living in captivity." Barodin and I looked at each other with expressions of incredulity on our faces. The little guide Tashca seemed not angered but bewildered that we did not comprehend his revelations.

"Come then, I will show you to the Opprobrium Room, or the equivalent of what you once called a *museum*. Death will not harm you or insult you there."

We wheeled hard left and through a small underseas canyon in which water thrashed around us and a torrential waterfall beset us on one side. I was almost certain we would drown. Our albino horses plunged on, however. At a distance of less than half a mile, we entered a great enclosure over which, hanging down from the ceiling, there prowled great monster cat-like animals mewing and hissing, and showing tiger heads, dinosaur tails, scales and gaping toothed jaws. How they roared and raged! They ravaged the entire cupola of the immense room with their throaty growls and incessant roars, like trapped beasts, as indeed they were.

"Do not fear these overseers to our museum, gentlemen. They have only one duty and that is to protect the history of we Phantericans have assembled in this room against exploitation, molestation, vandalism or theft. They are very efficient beasts."

"They appear to ... to walk on air," Barodin commented.

"Good observation. They in fact, do walk on air, since they pace back and forth, caged animals, on an invisible maze of aerolofted platforms comprised of solidified molecules, much as ... well, as ice, is in your world of knowledge.

"But their catwalks, or whatever you chose to call them, are not really solid constructions. Rather, they *seem* to be so, since they are invisible. "An optical illusion ...?" I surmised." "Precisely—one of our chief principles of molecular manipulation. By reversing the polarities between electrons and protons in the typical air molecule we produce not neutrons but rhaptons, whose billions of miniscule charges act to support mass, or in other words, the weight of the animals you see."

"What exactly do you call this place," Barodin asked, breaking his reverie of incredulity.

"This is our Time Suspension Assembkterium."

Now I saw it!—how bewitched the Phantericans were of their exhibits, their modes of existence. They held their relics of Phanterican society and culture for analysis, and ongoing appreciation of their ancient beauty and for the skepticism and curiosity of visitors. But what visitors—if not survivors of wrecks on the seas above? In one niche stood a table suspended by molecular legs without visible substance. Upon it was set the typical meal of ground fish, brought in by the Pterodactyl fisher birds we had seen. Included was a ladle into a tureen that contained dessicated snail shells and a cornucopia, I assumed, of exotic plant life. Slaves to other cultures, I learned, captives of Phanterican astronomy went through the actions of serving four Sycophants who had no discernable physical differences. And did not appear to be hungry.

"They all look alike!" I blurted out.

"That's as it should be. Here in Phanterica there is no competition to discern differences, either learned or gifted. Therefore, there is no anguish of competition, no feelings of inferiority, no nipped pride or self-satisfaction. *Equality* to the utmost is our creed, as you can observe from the display."

"Boring, don't you think, Doctor Barodin?"

"At least … not very enobling."

I watched a group of mechanical, robotic orchestra musicians playing a piece of chamber music by, God help us, ancient Mozart. Or *was* it Mozart? Each of the musicians was clothed in rags, the cello, flute, viola and pianoforte were absurd elongations of the real instruments, much like the distorted reflections one might see in a bent mirror. Their bows were warped like long bows, sawing with ridiulous regularity—but Mozart music it was not! The fingers of the musicians matched the strings like thumbs fumbling for latch strings. The faces of these Sychophant musicians looked macabre, as if life had gone out of them, eyes vacant, chests hollowed and the flesh drawn like parched skin stretched over the bones. Likewise, their hands showed this unearthly aspect. They were producing, despite these seeming drawbacks, the etherial music of a classic imitation, a sound, except for the viola's notes, as if played on clothesline wire and tin dishes.

Through all this strange show of Phanterican learning, we remained astride our albino horses. Of a sudden like a clap of thunder a loud voice boomed out, rumbling through the stone tunnels and caverns about us:

"You two Aliens are now our prisoners! Consider yourselves kidnapped!"

"Kidnapped!" I shouted. Barodin turned pale.

Chapter 7

Kidnapped

"We've been shanghaied," I exclaimed to Dr. Barodin, who merely shrugged his shoulders.

"What else can happen to us?"

"I'm afraid even to think about the possibilities."

As surely as the rain fells from the clouds, an immense ringing that burst our ear drums came from nowhere, a raging horde of Phantericans all armed with vicious pronged—fly swatters and they began to fan the air before us as if, we being insects, deserved to be to deprived of oxygen and mashed lifeless. They were, in their way, on the attack against foreigners into their midst One of these swatters, oblong discs of a translucent glassy substance struck Barodin on his elbow, opening a gash. One grazed my head. I picked up a rock—we were defenseless—and began to flail out against our attackers. I knocked down several, amazing myself with my trength, for these folk were big and bulky by any standard, clumsy afoot. They spoke in a gibbrerish I failed to recognize. Their leader came forward.

He was gigantic, a head shaped like the hourglass we had seen previously, in his hand he grippped what appeared to be an enormous fly swatter with horns that could kill or cripple its victim.

" Why do you trouble our people"

"We ... trouble ... the people," I repeated with surprise and incredulity. We are ... scientists on a vlisit. Did you ever see a scientist who travels without a purpose?"

"He growled something indistinct in meaning, and then seizing both myself and Barodin he juggled us in his massive arms like beach balls, back land forth, thrown about, pitched up into the air, mauled and, bleeding still! from the first assault. He then set us once again on the ground, all done as if to intimidate us, certainly not to demonstrate a genial welcoming.

"Our leader detests your presence here in Phanterica. We wanted to barbeqcue you until Hrothgar spoke his wisdom."

"My God, cannibals," was all I could say to Igmar.

"We are your superiors in science. We chose to dress like this because it keeps lus close to nature and to Hlrothgar's earth," Well, as soon as he had said earth a violent trembling of the ground transpired and a raving about ten meters across yawned within a scant metre of myself and Barodin, with the expectation, I suppose, on the fanged warrior's part, that we might fell into it, though as for why I could not fathom.

"Extreme environmentalists in a State, I thought. Barodin winced when one of these warriors twisted off the watch on his wrist and, rendering it in half, attempted to lie it on with fir strands for earrings. Pitiless ... and totally absurd.

""Guess he likes the sound of its ticking," Barodin responded.

Just as suddenly as they had appeared, they depargted, like animals that answer their master's inaudible whistle but not without leavmg behind vapors of sweat and urine that literallyl turned the surrounding stones into cold moleen substance, like a boggy tafly-just as some insectsand flowers trap their prey with a sticky substance.

As swiftly as the hawk dives down to seize its quary, we were lifted by electromagnetic forces yet beyond our comprehension or control, and were sped conveyor-like thorough a labrynth of tunnels, with only the luminous hands of Tashca to indicate where we were, as if we could know. This experience I have to give in greater detail Thugs, we called them at home, shrouded us with bands of copper more like throwing barrel hoops over us, and fixing our bodies in a kind of perpetual rigor mortis, even while we lived, we were, I should express it, magnetized toward a destination, which came into view with a blinding brilliance. I smelled the odors at once of a laboratory, the pungeanee of formaldyhyde, hot glass and solutions of one sort sor another.. No prison for us? Were we—valued captives, valued for our knowledge as Dr. Kennison must have been valued for his.

We were set down in amid numerous glass retorts and other paraphanalia of a working laboratory, there to confront the visage of a beareded monk-like captor who greeted us with a smile, touched each of us in turn so that our copper bonds fell away, nay, vanished and our body motions were instantaneously restored. He toughed; blut he appeared to have no mouth bvehind the snowy beard, only those huge eyes and fen ears.

"I am pleased to see that you have arrived without harm," came this deep, gutteral voice from behind the mask of villainy, if ever I had read a face.
"Sonow—nojail?"
"We do not believe in prisons here in Phanterica, They are a waste of human lives. Much knowledge and many skills are time tested under—good behavior/" He let out with a great sigh, and beckoning to an aide he had two chairs brought up to his desk, situated as it was within the laboratory proper, almost hidden by beakers, vials, retorts and a maze of glass tubing. But our familioar surroundings were only temporary. We could not forget that we were enemies of the State of Phanterica and therefore had to be closely watched … and tested for our reliability.

"Although this is a laboratory, you are still prisoners."
"I surmised as much," I said with deliberate acid in my voice.
"You must realize that you will be bound? Not in chains—crude hysteria of a gone world—but bound by a ring of electonic magnets extending from your head that will prevent you from … flying away … from wandering, accidentally, into an illusory freedom."
Two chairs were placed down and we seated ourselves. "I am Professor Martok, the Ingenuous. Do not doubt what I say or the power of my actions. Again, I am who I am-Martok. When I say to you, do not lift your right arm, you will not lift your right arm. Try me."
"You first, Galway," Barodin pronqrted. I tried to lift toy right hand but found it utterly impossible.
"And you, Doctor Barodin—do not turn your head, and do not speak for one full minute."

"He's-this is somel kind of a trick," I said to Barodin, but he remained silent, his red and eyes fastened on our Captor Martok as if in a hypnotic trance.

"You will follow me, you will want to but you will not be able to, as if you are paralyzed We are working on that aspect of medical, clinical neural paralysis. We hope to rearrange the neural impulses electronically so that they bypass any point of injury." He paused to see our reactions but we sat as mute as mummies. "That is another story for a later-chat? Hmmm?"

I did not wish to know Martok any better than I already did, although Ms theory of a transitory paralytic injury sounded fascinating.

"Come with me." We started to rise but found neither of us could. "Arise, I say and come with me," whereupon, with these words we could move about quite freely. We followed him and it seemed that with each step our amazement grew. I searched every face for some tell-tate familiarity resident in the features of my Mend, Dr. Barodin. And—I still searched about the laboratory for a glimpse of Dr. Kennison, but was unable to spot his familiar face.

My first impression that this was a foil-scale working laboratory was wrong. For, layed out on the floor in squares of obsidion and agate was a sort of chess board for matches between the intellectual giants of our world. They stood ranked around the edges. I thought I recognied, Kierkgard, Sartre, Heddegger, Hegel and there, there aloof and to one side as if existing in effigy, I saw Bewethoven and another not far-distant likeneses of Aristotle and Plato. What sort of charade was this! Was this another American version of Mme/Toussaaud's wax museum? I was baffled, confused. Was I living among the dead? Had I died and did not know it? I began to look more thoroughly about me. The room was immense; Corinthian columns rose to shadowy rafters, the tarentine walls glistened while creeping about behind the columns were figures attired as cupbearers shrouded in black and wearing golden sashes and cowls that hid their faces., a coterie of altarboys, as it were, in a hostlery of Western civilization's Greats. Within the squares—the floor resembled as an immense chessboard, these greats gambled in a way that suggested chess playing. Great intellects—gambling? Why, most certainly, it occurred to me, since they all, to a person, believved in the integrity of chance against which they threw the assaults of their gifted imaginations.

"There is Dr. Kant," Tashca pointed to a man with a small sharpnosed face, gottee beard and eyebrow moustache, who was dressed in a pointed cockade hat and sat with fierce and burning eyes, poised over a sheet of paper. I am therefore I know that I am. But there was no pen in his hand. He, in mime, pointed at all of the "chess" pieces, instrrumemts,even the brass retorts galvanometers, centrifuges miniaturized, bunsen burners for rooks, adopting the analogy, I asumed. In a minute or two he and issued directions and one of the cupbearers stepped into the arena to do the Doctor's bidding.

"There, too, is Maestro Schopenhauer" said Matok, who was the host for our tour of welcome. I saw a rather portly man, hardly a pale and hungry Zarathrusta, dressed in business garb, sporting a large black beard beneath furrowed brows, the complexion white in palor as if he sufiereed an inner gastrointestinal malady and loss of blood. I noticed the great philosopher's polished pump shoes, his small hands, almost those of a girl. He smirked placidly, sweeping his arms about him and drawing up his chest. He would flagillate in triumph as he pointed to other of the scattered laboratory pieces that were being maneuvered about on the floor. What a weird scene this was, that these great men should behave like imebeciles of a madhouse, using common laboratory instruments as pawns for their chessplay! I had to presume that Discoverers' Chess was their game as they contested against each otter. Bafflement, irritation, acute vexation and envy were written all over their faces.

"You will observe the markings on the floor, Captive Galway." the gutteral voice of Martok directed.

Several of the engravings on the squarea bore the words DOVE OF LOVE. Casting my attention around the room, as best I could ascertain other squares bore the words TRUTH and others JUSTICE, GOODS, REVENGE and one engraved square with a stake through the figure of a martyr of science, who was burned at the stake as a heretic, were the words EVIL and DEATH. These squares were occupied by the previously-mentioned game playing pieces.

The clothing of the other prisoners, as I assumed they were, intrigued me. Berkeley—be had revealed his convict-keeper's name to us. was a smallish fellow, cleanshaven in a pointed hat and tweeds, smoking a pipe; Kierkgard pinkcheeked, blue eyed in a voluminous boots, the Frenchman Sartre wearinghorse blinders, stood out as a diminuitive fellow with a large Gaulic nose and bad teeth. Heddegger appeared tall, slender and urbane, wearing a monicle and chain and smoking a Spanish cigar. Crouched as if to attack religion, there played Hegel, the indefatigable German so short he looked like he had been turned lengthwise to stand, gold chain tying time to his anatomy, sharpbearded style he had borrowed from the Dutch. All this panoply of philosopher genius were pushing icons of IDEALISM, IMPOTENCE, RELATIVE UTILITARIANISM, INVOLUTARIANISM, NATURALISM, EXISTENTIANALISM about on the floor, colliding with one another in an effortr to cast he oppossition off the floor, and out of the game. They Manipulated DEATH and LIFE, GOODNESS, TRUTH, LOVE AND JUSTICE with much like the bunker-car gang I knew as a boy, slamiming their favorite philosophic pieces into one another that stood in the way as they sought a position. Yet they refused, with apologies and courtliness, setting off across the floor only to repeat the collisions,

"Now you wonder why you never found Trath," Tashca said to me, after I had watched this melee for some minutes. "Only in Phanterica do we we possess Truth."

"Oh, and what is that?" I asked, naturally skeptical and voicing that cynicism of most American scientists, hoping for a casual answer.

He exclaimed in a feverish voice, "Science—that is Truth, man originated, man directed, man oriented and man affirmed: Science!"

"Man's senses."

"Usually though not always. The fragrance of a rose can be identified and analyzed chemically, but as to why it produces the pleasant sensation in our olfactory sense—the arrangement and composition of the molecules within the flower's juices does not explain the phenomenon of fragrance entirely."

"Then there are questions unanswered by science."

"For the time being. At least we have long, long ago—fifty thousand years ago—given up dependency on any supernatural answers."

"All phenomena, all masses moving with energy through a time-space continuum can be reduced to molecular analysis?" I asked.

"Yes."

"Then I am here by fete.?

"You might say so. Not by ray deconstruction, you understand, but actually in a different form. We are livng light, you could say ... Even Scripture, your bible says, ye are the light of the world.

"Is that relevant?"

Tasshca did not answer. But then with great enthusiasm he said, "Much of the molecular composition of our flesh represents captive energy as mass—and even sound is energy, given unique form in notes and vibration waves. Our flesh by negated voltage can be translated into and received as the energy of light. We can travel by strikes of light to a transponder that reverses the process by which, as I say, light energy translates into recognizable human form."

"Did you get all of what he was saying, Galway?"

"Hardly understood a word of it. I'd have to see his calculus first."

"Our friend, Doctor Kennison—is he now shaped into a bolt or flame or … photons of light … with due respect to Planck's quantum theory of light"

"No."

"That's all you can say—no?"

"We kidnapped him, as we did you. He is no longer safe in the time-frame of your world."

"I … we value … our world of science values his training, his knowledge."

"We value his contributions to the physics of light, naturally: transpositional molecular physics of energy exchange in transubstantiation analysis." Here Tashca broke off, and I cast a parting glance at the philosopher players scrambling around on their arena of idealisms within the Time-Suspension Temple.

"Ah … er…. Tashca, I have just one question," I said as Martok led us, like blind men, away from the playing arena, "Do you plan on keeping us—frozen thus, petrified, paralytic here in your electromagnetic enclosure? He remained silent, perhaps embarrassed at our perspicacity. I followed up with—"Sinee the players can do no good, why not mummify them for all generations in perpetuity?"

Martok roared with anger and in his wrath reached over, picking up a bunsen blurner, and threw it at the wall. "They are fixed where they are. They know how to spring the trap of time fixation and therefore are able to appear perpetually. But they love our world of Phanterica. It is inexplicable how they can … attach themselves to a retort that boils base and acid into a gasses. Tranfixation is the only word for it." He pulled a small black book from his pocket and made an entry. "And in time you, too, will not want to leave and then we will release you … after which liberation you will want to remain here, forever.

Another Sycophant joined Tashca and us, excited by our presence, loped ahead of Martok, who was obviously leading us to—

somewhere. As if he had overheard our thoughts, he said,"I take you to the work station where you will work on a experiment in molecular transmogrification of spirit into a basic molecular equation. It is a very difficult transition. You, Doctor Galway, will be very helpful to us, since you as a cultural anthropologist appear to have some sense. Barodin can help us to identify the kinds of sign waves pecularar to certain molecular substances." Truly he lived up to his name of Martok, the Ingenuous

"I'm—my specialty is physical anthropology," said Barodin.

"All the better. We have fragments of bone, pottery and, yes, even dessicated flesh, taken from specimens alive millions of years ago. We should like for you to render a judgement as to what we can best do with this knowledge."

"Why, I should be delighted," said Barodin. I was a stunned. Such cooperation, unless feigned, would end our mission here in this otherworld.

"You're a damned liar," I whispered.

"We must pretend … we must play the part of the foolish gullibility."

"Yeah, we'll we've done pretty good so far," I whispered.

Bartok was speaking. "We have manged to combine all the enchantments of nature with utility, Guest Aliens. We Eve the life of the happy savage, even while enjoying all the benefits of our marvelous science."

"I've enough clues to believe Kennison is here, Barodin … in Phanterica. If we can only discover what experiment he was at work on … if we create suspicion our quest might suddenly end without hope of success.

"Play the part of a wise and old clown," said Barodin, still speaking to me under Ms breath.

"And you friend, imitate a credulous dunce. We can still do any-work, Martok hands us."

From a table Martok handed each of a set of dissecting tools and an instruction sheet telling us to begin, and where—better sooner than later. The dissecting instructions were in Phaaterican polyglot. At this point an honest-to-goodness mummy, such as I had seen in Egypt, was wheeled in. The Sycophant who had slipped into our midst, alongside Tashca said, "You will both do well." Martok smiled affabfy and touched my arm and Barodin's shoulder with his finger magic in those godlike, mystic finger ends. They burned brandmarks into our

our flesh, the stench of my own flesh I shall never forget. Despite the pain, I remained calm.

At least in our position, I thought, we would be able the better to track down Kennison and find out what they had really done with him. He had left certain clues behind as he became increasingly inoived in Phanterican life-until in the end he became of them, naturalement, disavowing all that he had learned that was of secular interest . I knew that when we searched we would also have to explain the clues as he went and exploit them. Each clue, I had realized, represented a dimension of Dr. Kennison"s capabilities, left behind, I am certain, with the intention of using that character quality later.

Here's one of the three figures who had greeted us to the domain cave entrance, the rod-bearer, said, "Doctor Galway, you can not ever have met the equal of another from your part of the world." His words were an enigma to me.

Now that we were prisoners in the Phanterican laboratory, I flinched when I thought of how they could use us to inflict pain on our "colleagues," But more importantly, it came to me one night as I slept under the moon on a mattress, I was told, filled with paper money, that they could still taring us before a judge and try us for unnamed crimes-It was becoming pellucidly clear that the moral nature of unhindered conscionable right and wrong had no place here in Phanteriea. Each of took his dissecting tools and pretended to begin a studious sudy of the dessicated mummy, wondering what would come of this sudden plunge into learned biotechnical anatomy. Then, a most extraordinaryl thing happened. Just at I put the tip of my scalpel blade to the mummy, it moved!

Chapter 8

Prisoners of Phantoms

Since the excruciating night when I had undergone laser surgery on my time-space continuum, within the phrenological area of my brain that interjected autonomous impulses into my biosehedule, the elementary lower brain areas, I was ready to observe thorough the eyes of my host, Martok ... and to avail myself of every chance to find the missing Doctor Kennison. That rationale belonged to the more cerebral, an incurrable left-sidedness, though I was far from prepared to undergo the corrugation efforts that most Phanterieans' head shape suggested—a pragmatic bifurcation into right and left lobes that was visible on the surface. I considered myself too old for such shaping up.

"Where the devil is the wheelhouse?" I asked Martok, thinking to suggesting mariner terminology since this whole island resembled a great vessel of stone held together by incalculable plasmic forces, its invisibility resting on the principle that an object will appear to bend in the light when placed in water. By a complex cordon of mirrors,concealed from the air, the Island is made to disappear to be, in effect, *bent out of sight* from aerial observation. That was the explanation I had received—from Tashca.

"I believe you want the Multilinear Room—what some of us call the Room The Secret Compass."

"Well, whatever in blazes it is—which way do we turn?"

Martok drew us into an ironclad doorway and beyond, a stone bairier of morticed rocks that swung inward. On the other side of that door lay a bronze wheel on a flat rose colored tone that resembled the compass rose on mariner maps. The hidden terrors within the soul of

Phantericans became evident at once because of these reinforced security measures. But what did they fear-was it perhaps Kennison whose modern science acted as a terror goad to their inner insecurity? Or were the lost squadrons of airplanes, the floundering ships, the pleasure craft the nemesis of their precautions and scientifically endangered living"

The interior of the room vaguely resembled the bridge of a steamship, except that I saw no pilot wheel or marliners binacle.

"Do not ask us about the steering wheel. I see the quizical looks on your faces. Our govrnment keeps it locked up in the Master Wizard's chambers for fear it might be used to misguide our nation. It is the *Wheel of Freedom.*"

Barodin spoke oiut: ""Freedom will … mislead you?!"

"Preposerous!" I said.

"No, rude Alien Galway, it is you who will … or could … misuse it to destroy our people. And since they have lost their yen for freedom, it is best we guard it under lock and key. We—that is, myself, our liege leaders and the Great Wizard—do not want the common people to know it is hidden since it is inevitable they will thy to they will steal it They'll surely misuse it"

"I'm not a man to trifle with, Martok. I am a doctor, a a surgeon of the past, an anthropologist. Freedom is a great boon to science."

"It leads men to pray for peace, and prayer is strictly forbidden here on our … island."

"But not free enquiry? Come now, Martok. I don't not need to repeat my reason for coming here in the first place."

"Permit me, sir, to doubt your words … since few scientists think on the same level of magnitude at the same time"

"I … we will find him."

"Don't trouble yourselves."

"I tell you, he is either a prisoner or … or is transmorgrified … or … he is dead."

"Clever assumption. No, he is not dead: that's all I can say."

"He is useful to *us*" I said.

"And so to us. He is our … you might say, one of our major resources."

"He knows much about Einstein's theory of relativsity—its applications, the nuances of its construction, the consequences of its application."

"So ...?"

"He proved again and again that Relativty is not a theory. It is a fact." I asserted.

"I see you view us with skepticism."

"Our eyes are clear, Doctor Martok. The Doppler application *has* enlightened us? Theory becomes facts which merge with Infinity."

"Yes, and so you see life, fantasy, fact, movement just as we do in our wonderful land of scientific *Man Control.*"

I stepped over to an immense flat-like rock, The Wheel, through whose veined and scored transluscence a light shone and within which there was water that dampened the action of the needle, pointed to NW—as a mountain climber's compass, with which I have had some experience,

"I would say, right off hand ... that we are Captives of ... Phanterican ideologies?"

"Our guest is exactly right," said Martok and smiled. He pulled at my elbow, drawing me over to inspect the compass. "This is our three-point compass: *time ... space.... motion?*

"Martok, this place is an Island ... a rock-steay island anchored in the ocean floor!"

"Phanterica is a *vessel,* we prefer to think. It shifts three centimters every one thousand years. Small ... but it moves. It moves at twenty-four thousand mliles per hour through space, interdicting time only where the earth transects our course and the apogee of the moon. Spurred by the moon's weak gravity, we—our island-continues on at the same rate through umimpeded space. Yet at the rate of motion of three centimeters every one thousand years."

"That's time's duality?"

"Its bifurcation ... which makes time ubiquitous and ... user oriented, shall we say?"

"Does the Island conform to the curvature of space?"

"So you know about spacial curvature, eh? Immense, incalculable, electrodynamic forces circumscribe an arc path, trillions of arc paths intersecting ... with occasional collisions ... like an inisible net through the endless void"

Barodin's thoughts were similar to mine. "But then the curvature of space implies fixed limits—apogeotropism and epicenter, eliptical, parabolical, perfectly circular...."

'Wo *movement* is perfectly circular. That is what your ... Doctor Kennison demonstrated to us, since energy tends to undergo changes in an apparently erratic manner—like arcing electricity-therefore, throwing off any precise curvature to the body's arc of movement."

"I see," was all I could express in astonishment at the doctor's perceptions. Tashca, who wsas our silent shadow through all this dialogue, looked at us through squinted eyes.

I asked: "But Doctor Martok. If energy simply transfers from one object to another, from one motion to another, from one cataclysmic phenomenon to another and is never lost, ought not that energy to *contain* ... rather than to ... *disperse* and to expand the boundaries of space?"

"Contain ... contain what?" he replied. I have long held, my Captive Apostle"—he smiled directly at me—"that the sun's energy is not the only source but that identifiable masses, rings, peripheries, globules—whatever you with to call *them,* are ... free energy and they draw spacial objects outward into other dimensions of time and so tend to disrupt the perfect curvature of space."

There you go again with that word *perfect,*" I responded.
"Limits ..."
"Space has no proveable limits," Barodin interjected.
"And so no discernable impediments to the continuation, forever, of this—*floatilng energy,*" said Martok with a smug grin.
'Doctor Martok, I perceive you share some of his ... Kennisons?.... thinking on the subject."

"Let *me* take the theory one step further, " Tashca said. "Although the curvature of space limits are real—and we know that energy changes expression, transforms, animates inanimate and animate nature before our telescopic eyes, and influences our paradyms of analysis, there might well be another spatial phenomenon on a collision course with ours, like two beacballs thrown toward each other."

"We can only assume that our constellation travels in the arc of a limitless curvature," said Martok, "and therefore energy fully dissipated—not extinguished, you understand—will create more and more dead stars as electromagnetic forces within each body coalesce and snuff out the energy of light ... light, of course, being the fundamental energy."

"Your choice of words is not precise—but it is knowledgeable, Dr. Galway. Recall what would happen if all the neutron masses in tknown and observable atomic nuclei were packed in together without any space or distance betweens them. At the size of a pea, they would weigh ten quadrillion-million tons. In the absence of molecular energy, you have inert weight, dead weight."

"The universe is a clever opponent, is it not,?" said Barodin.

"Sly, devious and fascinatisng, like a seductive mistress," said Martok with a smile.

"Why, then, do you breing us *here* … *to* this compass table?" I asked.

"This is our … your phrase … out conversation piece. Our government guides its direction and motion by this very instrument."

""Imposslible-the ethical governance of geology and …"

"And choice of direction? No? We truly know where we are headed. And you … you simple ones in your land—do you know where you are going? You have lost many fine aviators who relied on your defective compass, whose electomagnetie signals were dispersed and and therefore misleading.

"Toward ideals, if nothing more."

"Exactly-nothing more, the emptiness of a nino-direetion

I and Barodin stood in shocked silence, amazement clearly written on our faces, while Tashca and the Master Host Martok regarded us with benign smiles of contempt. What could we do but stand and inwardly resist all temptation to flee. Yet to where?

In the days of old our government at home kept locked up in an air-conditioned safe the measure for an ounce, a pound, a pint, quart. It maintained the perfect clock to establish Greenwich time, it established the measures for a yard, inch, a foot and a mile. Here, by this compass we are told that there exist only the true measures along the space-time continuum. I was puzzled. The barbaric Greeters with the scales and the mystical rod returned to my imagination. If direction is only linear, how can it then be a selective and fuctional part of choice? How can measurements be accorded values for use in comparisons and in telelogical constructs? I asked Martok about these things,

"A yard changes its one-dimensionallity when compared against the speed of light—the ultimate measurement, fester than which nothing moves and therefore everything can be comnpared. A light year is verifiable according to that speed of 5,280 miles per second. What if the speed is slower, is not the yard within the mile changed, the inch altered; the concept of weight in the E equals MC 2 equation changed, or mutated

… I prefer to say? I think so. Since weight, let's say a pound's measure, moving at a slower sub-light speed, becomes less than a pound—we have then the diminished moon's gravity, which moves through space at less than the speed of the earth. Take another measurement—an ounce of liquid impacted by gravity assumes a freer molecular state when that gravity is lessened and therefore it no longer weighs the same; nor is the volume-ounce one ounce but perhaps more than an ounce, the pressure upon the ounce having lessened along the space-arc continuum. Water is denser at the colder depths of the seaAnd for that very reason, my alien pupils the bodies of the lost have never floated to the surface. The decay gases do not collect in cold water."

"I think you come to close to what I call Phenemoninal Transmogrification," I said, "or thought changes induced by molecular infusions—like bone marrow,"

"Our body systems are closed systems. You know that Doctor Galway."

"But.jnutatable."

"Now you are beginning to talk like a Phanterican, Much of what you see in our land is the result of beneficial mutations—encouraged by our government. *Oh, Holy, Kindly, Benevolent Government.*"

"Back to the compass," Barodin reminded us,

"Look!" I cried out, "We are in movement. I saw a tiny deflection of the needle—almost, Hike an unsteadiness rather than a course deflection."

"You are right You saw that deflection—toward Dishonor!"

"Dishonor!" Barodin exclaimed.

"Right!-marking a heading of two points north of the nebulae of Obedience."

"But you can't equate physical nature with moral laws, sir," I said, complaint in my voice.

"We have. We have!" said Tashca excitedly. "We Phantericans cultivate Purpose, as a seed germ, in a test tube, fathered together into our Doppler Changer—like nuclear fusion, almost—to summon up for us some knowledge, some figment of outer space. You can see that we inseminate the kernel of Purpose with complete and total Pacifity. That is our collective regenerate nature. Direction only, gentlemen Aliens. Our people are not competitive, avaracious, destructive as yours are."

"You have your elite members."

"Only as resource material/They assuredly are not pragmatic polity engineers," Martok said. "By fixing our minds on the concept of Obedience, we discourage original thought—which adulterates our purity. We, of course, must use measures to correct that adulteration. We also discourage random invention beyond what our staff invents, for such inventions are likely to distract our inhabitants from daily routines of lovemaking, euphoric pursuits and venues of masculine strength-testing."

"I see," I said. "But wouldn't these attributes have positive consequences?"

"You fail to understand that without a conscience, former men which these Phantericans represent could make true progress. We believe that we have successfully purged the rebellion from the hearts ... pardon me ... the psyche of modern man."

"I'm beginning to understand. These people know only what the Wizard's commands."

"Not only know his commands but execute them. And since we cannot fully purge instinctive attributes—man's incessant and bothersome trendency to name things he does not comprehend, like Adam—why, we sacramentalize the objects of nature: the nebulae, the stars, with morality names—of Obedience, Honor and the like, although ours is a totally a-moral community. We are proud of that ethical cleanliness."

"Total assent."

"I prefer to say-no risks, no riots. " Martok placed his hand on my shoulder. "If you will hold still for a moments you'll feel the floor beneath you move. We have scientifically accelerated the motion of the earth's tectonic plates and are sliding along the giant stone mass that transects the Northern Pacific Ocean."

"How....?"

"We cannot tell you but to convey and refresh in their minds for communal enjoyment the idea, the illusion of self-improvement, always an extrasensory illusion, we give movement to their feet.

"Again-direction?"

"Exactly."

"Like soldiers," I added.

"Do not mock us, sir! Here in our country you will come to know and observe the concept of what it means to be obedient to sterility of purpose. There can be no conflict of movement."

"I saw no signs of communication ... whatsoever ... to infer or command obedience."

"How obsolete is your thinking!" said Tashca. "The will of the Master communicates to every man, woman and, yes, even to children through extrasensory perception.?

"He has got to be your Master."

"We would have it no other way." Again, the reversionism in Phanterica. Martok raised his hands mid as if in supplication and like medals of honor attached gold wafers to our tunics. Phantericans earn them by babble, for the purpose of useful goods, the opiates, sex stimulants, alcohol and albino horses. Yes, those albino horses. Every Phanterican is privileged to own one in his lifetime. That is his vehicle of freedom if ever he is tempted to think he lives in bondage."

"Very thoughtful of the government," I commented.

"Yes, I'm so glad you understand," our guide said, acid n his voice.

"But lets go and see the Temple of Idols. There is where many interesting folk converge." said Martok,

"And perhaps-Doctor Kennison?"

"I wouldnt be surprised," Tashca said. "After all, he was and still is a scientist activist."

Chapter 9

Under the Gavel

When Martok condemned deviants from and protestors of the regime to the soEtary confinement of state ideology, his change did not speak well for his personal mutations. They did not add appreciably to his perception that I and Doctor Barodin-and the missing Kennison-would some day emerge to condemn Phanterica as a State constructed on fraudulent science, the science of death.

As if by chance, we found ourselves lhustled into another chamber similar to the Room of The Secret Compass. Tashca told us that this as where laws were fabricated Laws? Laws? What a conundrum! a myth of The Mnd, the illusion of cataclysmic presumptions.

"Where are the legislators?" I asked, a perfectly logical and sensible question.

"They are gathering wool." His exact words! mark me! I jest not.

We ascended stone steps into a room heated by emanations from the nearest nebulae.

"Have you in Phanterica no light bulbs, no globes, no incadescent lighting.?

He looked at me rather strangely, "We borrow what heat and light we need from nebulae, since it is great and readily availalble to our flame catcher." Flame catcher! He saw my bewilderment. "Yes, we have developed an instrument that draws flame-heat from the exploding nebulae into the orbit of our life planet by the simple expedient of carrying these elemental heat waves on the back of radio waves. I'm sure you are familiar with radio waves"

"Not a new science to me, to us. But carriers of heat …?!

"Very simple," said Tashca. The light and heat are molecular spinoff waves that synchronize themselves with invisible radio waves and catch a ride, as it were, into the orbit of our world."

"How amazing!" was all I said.

We found a place among the pumice stones, as in ancient Greek amphitheatre, only this magnificant theatre was entirely enclosed by shields of sound proof light the molecular ambivalence of the light forming an impenetrable wall of sapient molecules that blocked speech vibrations.

Down on the floor I could see the assembling of the members, who had finished with their task of gathering wool, meaning supporters. Sycophants seated next to me leaned over and talked to friends on the floor. Below, one of the legislators removed his transfiguration lens from his pocket and focused it on the scene about to take place.

I must describe this lens, pink in lits optical elements, about 14 inches in diameter, like a small telescope. Inside its prismatic optical changes, the Sycophants were about to filter out all obnoxious thoughts that issued from the minds and lips of the speakers, and so to arrive at a state of observed purity that even the holy Government could not condemn, indeed, could not discern one iota of questionable material. Theirs was a perfect forum, a cacaphonic gathering of words lacking all humanization so that the words, without human excrescences, could onvey the purest of thoughts only. This was the remedy for virulent propagands, for relilgious zealotry, for human desecration of the best in Kantanian and Berkeleyian reasoning. Pity was reserlved to gods and poets only.

This form of self-deception commended fraud as virtuous. I considered the methodology to be rather daring. Tascha informed us that we might procure one of these transfiguration lenses to share, as spectators might have rented opera glasses at one of our operas. By far the better quality of these transfiguration lenses were manufactured by a special division of the Department of Psychological Neutralization of the Phanterican Govrnment They were distributed among the citizens for spe3cial occasions, and for the business of the so called legislature, particularly those calling for criticxal thought. The other Sycophants in the galleries employed their lenses to observe the shearing scene among the Mediators. With the help of the Phanterican Government, the Sycophants avoided all forms of seltf-indicltment.

"The man in the great ovestuffed chair is a sage," Tashca announced, I could see his chair swinging slightly above the stage as he reclined therein in preparation to bring the Mediators to order. The speaker rocked, rather swung, gently in his suspended chair, there being no link frolm his cushions to the firm stoney ground of the podium. It was intended that this arrangement should lend an air of loftiness to his words. I could not help but laugh to myself over the literalness of the scene.

"Did you hear what was his message to the Mediators?" I asked Tashca.

"He asked them to grant fifty billion molecules of gold to float his plan that would increase the size of our island."

"And did they?"

"Watch!"

As it they so voted into effect the proposal, in this manner, that all the Mediators simply blew in the direction of the suspended speaker and he turned to the lee. That apparently was the right response, for he smiled. I discerned that this method of voting on a proposal involved less noise and frustration, that that it appeared to cast over the Mediators a cheerful wind, not at all unpleasant on that hot summer day, that created a pleasant aroma in the nosrils of all Government mendicants.

"What was the issue?" I asked Tashca again, trying to get a more definitive answer.

"Money—and since the words *repay, deficit and debt* have been stricken from the language—Oh, holy, benevolent, kindly Governrpent—money has a mere loadstone value. You in your ancient world once called it accumulation, coansumption and stewardship. We here all delight in weightlifting, an erotic stimulant as well. It has brought many mistresses to your ancient capital. Your mores are quite different. Our joys areasexual. Hark! He speaks, he who occupies the swing vote in the chair."

My eyes popped out of my head. Barodin was fiabbergaisted. Kennison with a bill!" It was he! the man we sought to rescue. He spoke.

"When SRA issues quasi sub-manufacturing notes on the Fill issues, and the BeEP leven congtinues to curve, it was found by collective transfusions of the RNG that GBY lacked sufficient gold for the *tregromianages* experiments."

A great cheer greeted his speech. I couldn't believe that our friend had undergone whas seemed like a brain transplant, from brilliant physicist to Sycophantic disorder of the mind.

"Have the Mediators greet by vote to trade with our foreign Sycophants?" Barodin dared to ask.

"Foreign!" Tashca exploded. "Yes, naturallly our superior people inhabit other parts of the decadent world."

"You mean they actually come and go from this … this lost world?"

"Our wise Wizard negotiates for the purchase, singlehandedly, of our albino horses. His great brain was designed to confuse other networks of commerce. His inpenetrable mind has even designed the web of our underground passages. He is a genius engineer."

"Will, that's some rlelief," I said. "For a mlinute there I thought he might be a madman, mouthing all that gobbledegook."

I looked around at the Operations Chamber. The Taschca smiled benignly upon me, who must hav appeared as an innocent child. The phosphorescence of the rocks illuminated the ceiling and added to the nebulae light, as I have described. Atop each stalgmite, as soon as my eyes could adjust to dimmer corners, I made out hollowed out seats where the members of the assembly perched, quirte thrfllingly amongv these immense limestone formations. Our guide pointed out ten monkeys sitting on a ledge and the flury of large bats that swarmed in and around the speake's swing chair.

"You recall the emblem?" Tashca enquired of us.

"About evil—see, hear, speak no evil?"

"Exactly, only those represent in our vernacular the alternative to the trio familiar to you. Sylcophants of Phanterica have a fair and politically correct a choice. It used to be called situation ethics. Now is is simply the right of radical choice. When you seethe schoolroom, you will learn that toe mention of any moral value there in Phanterica has deadly coinsequences. Morality is eprehensible … except where gold wafers are involved. Morality, the old self-righteousness sort, brought on disease and unmitgated hardship because it meant self-deprivation and worship of a non-existent God Thank god it is now purged from our consciousness!" Tashca was qusite blown out of shape by his own exasperation.

"We say … see and try … hear and disgorge, and speak and confuse. We Phanteicans find solace in chaos, deeming the rational to be so pernicous and destrucrtive during the age when you lived. To put it simply, chaos is ur natural element."

"And they, all ten, emblematic of Phantericans' deepest desires?"

"What on earth are those Mediators and Deliberators doing?—they hold a flame to the rock as if it contained a mystic message carved thereon."

"You arre exactly right Perceptive. They translate the message of the native rocks … the grains in the stone … the fracture lines, and striations if there are any. Each mark bears a significance as to future events, snd … barbarians will invade, escuse me … no offense … striations, the wicked will emerge from then-graves and … fracture lines, many sadly going into exile. A sorts of mystic prophesy in the rocks."

"The discoloration …?"

"*Rust*—pontification wins arguments…. green mineralization … the lost will commuunicate with the living, and the silvery mica—purity will sustain all Phanterican life."

"The rocks are … message bearers, are they not?"

"And so we meet here to read the stories of the rocks and vote on the dreams of the Proterean body of our domain. Nature is our liberator, our mediator, our deliverer, our god."

"I'm beginning to see that," I said, understanding even less than when I first entered this phantasy world.

"Precisely. You see. The notion of purpose no longer exists in our thinking or our vocabulary. We find that eradication of teleological ends expedient as well as life giving," said our guide.

"Then how did sclience ever advance to the sublime state?"I asked.

"Speculation, not purpose. The latter is a fiction to explain the former methodology of locating a phhenomenon like the tail of a comet."

"Then you do not plan, scheme or contrive ..."

"Never, never use those words. They are forbidden by our holy, beneficient government, who has full control and privilege alone to use them."

"I see" I said lmeeky.

Do you feel that you understand out system of government?" our guide asked.

"Oh, beyond a doubt it is magnificent!" Barodin replied.

We had all but forgsotten our discovery of the *great man* amid the debris of these empty conundrums of Phanterican philosophy. He has made his proposal before the Mediators in their Operations Chamber and then he had disappeared from the scene as suddenly as he had arrived, a shadow of a figure. Tashca blandly and with ingenuous innocencer eplied to my query:

"Your frilend now sproudly wears the label of

Transfixed Autonomy, one of our highest awards for diligent service. You will, find "Doctor Kennision hard at work as an alchemist, learning the secrets of our molecular transmutation of the elements. But— he remains invisible while working with ... sensitive Phanterican data.

"You surely don't take him for a ... spy," I said/

Tashca said nothing in response for a long moment, and then he said, "Not Doctor Kennison but ... you, our alien ... refugees. We distrust your mission and therefore ... we believe that you have come here to Phanterica, not by accident as so many others have done, but to learn of our foturistic ... ways."

I and Dr. Barodin could not have been more astounded by this suspicion. There appeared to have been much cordiality shown toward us, and now this ... Then, it reoccurred to me that we had always been under surveillance. What had we a right to expect in this dark venture?

Chapter 10

Before the Committee on Dklinformation

Why I, we, are surprised that these seientMcaMy-advaneed folk should use steam to generate electrical power baffled me—until I realied that a most ingenuous engine called the *Extrapolator IX* converts steam into an inhalent productive of euphoric hallucinations. It was to amuse my guards that they had outfitted their cell block with such an instrument Barodk was frightened by the very novelty of the engine. With scarcely an effort, it was possible that we could break out into spasms of uncontrollable laughter, like mad men, victims of Hebephrenia. But we found a way to turn off the engine by voicing its code from our cells, a voice recognition mechanism that Barodin was experinced in. This skill comploetely mystified our jailors and gave us a chance to scoff at their *science.*

I lay down on a bed of sea kelp; the effect of the iodine in the kelp was to restore my sense of calm overnight and reduce my anxiety I had thought that we were prisoners in the laboratory; but such was not the case. There was, also, the outside possbility that Doctor Kennison might also be a prisoner there I identified him once for certain, when he spoke so eloquently in his alphabetic lingo. But then, our jailor, in one of his euphoric moods blurted out that Martok had successfully rendered Kennison impotent before terror—at least the evil if not the life-threatening component thereof—by removing from him his *conscience.*

How in blazes could that be done except by the ancient methods of bramwashing-terror, deprivation, incarceration, utter dependency, and, most fearsome, self-abasement akin to moral suicide. The civilized conscience was, after all, a product of centuries of cultivation and refinement We were yet to experience the full realization of what psyehologifeal imprisonment meant here in Phanterica: it meant simply the loss of one's identity. In the place of a conscience, voeafeed in our outlook on life's important issues, we were given an identity number tattooed with a floral pigment and a shark's tooth on one wrist. Not a few of the elder members of Phanterica took special pride on their body tatoos, performed by the same method by a tatoo specialist often *referred* to as *Doctor.* lie had no need to solicit clients, since the wrist tattoo was almost invisible and did not embrace all the quirky ideologies of the Phanterican people. It assumed the natives' dignity and recognition of reigious faith and social convivction. It was the equivalent in importance to social correctness, a sensitivity by which a man verbally identified himself. The Phanterican authority, comprised almost totally of fanatical liberals, seeks to increase by any means possible this utter dependency and thereby reduce personal pride in achievement and strength that issues from having defeated hard circumstances. This program gives novitiates the power they seek.

Our deepest fears were to be realised in the interrogation soon to befall us. I would almost rather fell into the gravity well of a starry black hole than endure what followed I knew they were planning to use us. Tashca was summoned elsewhere on his albino horse for other duties. We were under the control, much as the general population of Sycophants, of the Wizard's Elite corps for our bread, our clothes *and our amorous petitions* par boudoir, including the very act of procreation, These purifications, they were called, by enforced silence and robbery alarmed me when I learned of them from our euphoric jailor. Neither religion nor common decency nor moral codes could insure sexual purilty; that was the virtue and province of the Phanterican Government, a notion that appals me even to write it down.

Soon were at the mercy of the Ethicists Board, otherwise known as *The Executioners,* as they called themselves. Martok informed us of these things. They, nine in all, who weighed our thoughts like gold wafers, stressed our nerves like calcineous waves of lignum vitae under pressure. The elite Ethicists altered nature's parabola of spectrum gasses to conceal their true colors when they spoke, just as they asserted widely that man can control rings of gravity and therefore stellar orbits and that the ozone layer of the earth can be affected by human intervention, like a massive holding of the breath by Sycophants in the Colony at a specific hour and minute of each day. The temorary removal from the atmosphere of their exhaled carbon dioxide would, they believed, significantly improve the ozone layer. It was a part of the Phanterican delusion that nature had to be concealed, changed, controlled for man's comfort and safety, and that he need only to will the remedy and it was done. God was nowhere to be seen.

Our jailor, whose name was Garrunide, led us into a cavern of the sort I was not accustomed to being in, its high rock ceiling dripping with strata ooze from the Pleistocene and containing rich carbonates, lime and sulphur. The stalactites virtually gleamed irridescent hues of orange, yellow, white and rust in the nuclear, slow-burning torchlight. The cavern was below the sea but not far distant, for I could hear the pounding of the surf through the shock patterns of the metamorphic and sandstone overlay above. The sea, once lower had honeycombed through the walls long ago, gouging out this subterranean cavern where we stood But these ingenuous people had shut out the sea and sealed off all waterways, passages for currents letting continue the slow, steady dissolving action of mineralized seepage water. A cataclysmic movement of tectonic proportions had made further precautions unnecessary. For the sealed cavern now lay below tidal levels. The sound of a stormy, pounding surf was often upon the rocks situated over our heads. Only the translucent beaiuty of the walls showed through the plastic sealant of strong, tensile, durable micro-silicone plasma. I record these details for future use should we ever escape.

Torchbearers moved among the ghostly forms of prisoners, in and out of the shadows from all directions. I sat perched upon a outcropping above the level of their bobbing heads. Their milling about, reflected from the smoking flares into their palid faces, eyes shadowed into hollows giving a bizzare aspect of semi-death to the scene, like a waiting room in hell. Their master was about to begin. He was not Garrunide hit was apparently the Warden for this loose assembly of his charges. Hie Scorpion, so called because of his massive jaw and claw-teeth, was the chief Justice of the Elitists. He would control the events about to transpire. Had I, Doctor Barodin or any otter prisoner desired to escape, where would they escape to?

Tashca, returned from his mission of disposing of unwanted babies in sea coffins of shaped coral. He sat us down on a cushion of mesmer leaves, found on the hypnotic tree Mesmerieus, which we were told grows widely in that country. By chewing its leaves, or coming close to the tree in bodily contact, the illusions of the brain change, the phantasms of mind alter, the states of consciousness shift. Here, here is where Sycophants make the laws of their domain even as, while doing so, they conveniently adjudicate any existing relevant breeches of Phaiiterican *codes of disinformation. Convenience* is an all-powerful motivation in Phanterica slince the ethic of *work,* as we know it, was abolished by decree long ago.

I pulled a small volume from my rucksack. "Here is a copy of our, of my Country's, Constitution," I announced with no small pride. Tashca thumbed through the pages, well worn by my own perusing. His small, barkflaked nose wrinkled up, his saphire eyes ignited, turning cyan with anger that spread upon his ashen face. For virtually no sunlight comes into Phanterica. He scowled "We do not tolerate such rubbish here," he said with immense disdain. "We condemn it … though you obviously do not."

"It is not rubbish where we come front It is the law of the land." "We here give great credence to the impact of personality … what you called *charisma.* He who possesses the greatest charisma controls the greatest number of people. I should think you would understand that since personality trumps law in your land."

I showed him a photograph of my girlfriend and me on a fishing trip one summer off the Florida coast. He tore it up before my eyes. He waved the thin fingers of one hand, webbed like struts in a bat wing, and from the darkness came a savage looking head covered with beard, bushy eyebrows to mask his face and provide a form of camouflage.

"Here is our prototype of charisma. In feet, that is his name, *Charismatis,* meaning charmer." The beast growled. "He can be summoned to charm millions and that is why he is omnipresent." I reckoned him to be an unkempt tramp, a fakir. Tashca clapped his small hands and the image vanished. "He is like our instant judge and mediator. With him around, we need neither court, judge, jury nor interrogators, the ancient artifacts of your obsolete system of justice and avaracious government

But, here … chewonamesmerleafand observe. You will learn from what you see."

A ridiculous-lookling gathering of the nine tall Sychophants, the Elitists known as *Executioners,* looking swathed in bandages, their probing eyes shadowed by black cowls, took up their places behind a stone revetment.

"What is this all about?" I asked Garrunide, our jailor

"You gentlemen of *The Committee of Disinformation,* our noble executioners, *Ethicists* all, we are ready for the proceedings on … censorship."

"Censorship!" I exclaimed. "Who are they censoring … and for what?"

"You are a fool to ask such a question, Galway?" said Garrunide. He shook the dust from his wig raid reattached it to his head. His and his colleagues' white faceless shadows created the semlance of a death ritual, their movements causing a strange rush as of a great wind through the cavern.

The nine *Executioners* in pristine gauze raiment,the letter "P" embroidered on their chests, bore in seven immense baskets, slung between great wheeled sleds of timbers, all encrusted with shells from the tidepools outside Phanterica and drawn by a team of more pink-eyed, blind albino horses. This I could surmise, while I busied my troubled thoughts with idenentifying the shells, cockle, conche shells, rose tulips, blue agatha, pink and acquamarine reef branches … A thought occurred to me that chilled my blood. These Sychophants were the cannibals of the future, who feasted on the achievements of civilisations past. I was to learn that the contents of the baskets were books, mainly, and documents, letters and such produced by civilized minds down through human history. Now I began to comprehend why I and Barodin were brought to trial: we were well-read literate men who had an understanding of civilizations past. Those simple facts made us dangerous to Phanterica … as perhaps they had of Doctor Kennison.

From the center of a ring formed by these nine Executioners there lept up an immense towering flagon of flame, a geyser whose white-hot heat I felt, and rising above it a synthetic cloud of stone, fuel and evanescent vapors as from a well of gas. It appeared to be a crucible flame into which, one at a time, logistically and with a sense of destiny, perspective, horror and anger, each *Executioner* threw whole copies and remnants of books that these government *Executioners* had censored from the translated languages of the world. Just as I might have suspected, like the barbarian Visgoths and Vandals that invaded ancient Europe's beginnings of eivilization—these Elitist *Executioners* operated on the ultimate premise that when you control the minds of men you control their actions, their society, their civilization. And when you control their passions and natural inclinations, you direct their destiny. They achieve that degree of control by gradually *disinforming society of its hisltory.*

"Pernicious vice—such destructive information is not tolerated here!," said Garrunide.

"What ... what else!" I shouted into the roar of the flames, the mute and unspoken panegyrics of book burning, the ancient vicious pagentry of milling disinterested witnesses, the rite and ceremony of the death-deed for civilizaation. greeted by savage shouts of approval from witnesses. Yet the paradox challenged: how could these folk sustain a status of *enlightened* when they destroy the sources of that enlightenment; books? Were they god-possessed? I came to realize more and more that *speculation* was truth in action for these people, a searching to be resolved or expunged. Surely these ceremonies must in time deplete their stocks of learning, I thought. All of those unfaithful to Phanterica must be considered as culpable when brought to trial before this cracilble of flame. Fire to reality was the act of these people's judgement. It symbolized their intellectual suicide.

The Chief Priest Executioner Scorpion fixed his dead eyes upon the flame, his voice monotonal as he chanted, his as immobile as a mask while he worked. I was watching some kind of primitive exorcism-which had nothing to do with me or Barodin, since we were mere prisoners. Was this cereemony for my benefit, to intimidate my conscience and curb my learning? The only resolution to this inescapable phenomenon of burning a seemingly bottomless supply of book and diary fuel, paper, speeches, letters was that the Phantericans reproduced them in order to destroy them. They whetted their appetites for censorship through these purges of original rebellious, disobedient, conscience-stricken thoughts of other men. Their access to the planet's knowledge derived from ship captains, sailors, airplane pilots, passengers who had been captured and saved by the electromagnetic ring that encircled Phanterica and for which modern civilization had no explanation. Their destruction of great thoughts and observations from these sources, integiments of disaster, was cyclical and without conscience. I was beginning to assemble the pieces of the mystery of Doctor Kennison's abduction, which it surely was.

Suddenly the Chief Executioner, stepping out from the other eight Elitists, started over in my direction to where I sat, his eyerows arched, his chalky white teeth gleaming in the phosphoresence unique to the cavern. On his forehead were the letters *FIE.* the "P" emblazoned on his chest shone in the murk. The book burning had seemingly acted like an opiate on him.

"Do not fear," he said. "I am not so different, merely changed. I once captained a great ship that sank ... and these savior Sycophants rescued me from drowning. I am eternally grateful to them. I have fiirnished them with nautical lore and books from my shipboard library. Evolution has neither added a rib nor removed the tail vestige from my person." He came close and appeared to smile. "What first attracted me to you was your personhood," The High Elitist of the Executioners said. "Here in Phanterica personhood ranks higher than intelligence, since the one is akin to godliness and the other is distasteful because in centuries past is proved so ... inconvenient."

That mere intellgence in an advanced civilization should have reached so low an estate may cause some historians to wonder; yet I had come quickly to realize that the creative intelligence was dangerous to possess in Phanterica. Morality, I learned, was the bastard child of intelligence, "for centuries a greater hinderance to ultimate and total success of evolutionary perfection," intruded Warden Garrunide

"That is how you killed Dr. Kennison ... removed his intelligence by *disinformation,* reduced his identity to nothing, obliterated his conscience for your purposes. Did it ever occur to you that you are deadly to civilized men, sir?"

"It is you who do not comprehend." said Martok, who all the while had been observing the scene from the shadows.

"Your Mend, Doctor Kennison, is free to come and go as he pleases, Banile One."

"A prisoner like me, is that it, Martok?"

"He is a resource," the High Ethicist replied.

"Who corrupts your society? Barodin asked.

"There in your own words is more of your old corruption," the Priest Scorpion exclaimed. The flanks silhouetted his dark figure, looking awsome and threatening to me from where I sat, and bigger than life.

"Hear me. Listen to my deliberation," I cautioned the priest with a sudden burst of courage. "You fear the flames will die out when you've got no more books to burn?"

"Ask them, those write books as purveyors of foolishness, to fabricate new laws in the guise of interpretating old traditions. We can wait."

Barodin gave in to a sudden anger. "They will never die; not ever …!"

"Those, Despicable Ones, are the flames of everlasting truth."

"A purgatory for knowledge is … is truth?" I asked.

"The burning of knowledge commits murder of the intelligence," Barodin offered, who had listened quietly, deep in thought. "Tell me then, what do the tetters *FIE* mean on your forehead?"

"Mine is a worship cicatrix of dedication. Found only in the devout … for an Eternity."

"And what does that mean—what only is found in eternity?" I waited for a deluge of philosophical thought, a plethora of Phanterican wisdom. The Chief Ethieist, who was indeed a Priest, reached out fingers with claws on their ends and raked at the cuffs of my prison coat. I saw that he wore no shoes and that his feet were also clawed.

"They failed to evolve-the retrograde claws-the wretched destroyers of those volumes." The flames had shot higher with added fuel of books and papers. From between the Chief Ethitist's' lips there spun a luxuriant gossamer which he sought to stick to the stones where I sat, but, failing this, he affixed the fine thread, a spider-like extrusion, to an adjacent rock. Vibrating slightlhy in the unsteady air currents, the sheen of its saffron color in the torchlight cast a hypnotic spell upon me and Barodin; yet being men of considerable courage, I at least sought immediate redress.

"Why are we kept in here … incarcerated, Priest?"

"Disobedience. Leap from that rock and my gossimer of *illogic* will ensnare you."

"Soo … that's what happened to our lost friend Kennison, is it?"

"Your colleague is free to come and go as he choses, Banile One We wanted you to see our methods of enlightenment."

"Then where is he? Come now, Priest Scorpion, you don't fool us. We are not idiots. With your system your purgatory fire will burn out without books to burn.:

"Reason, reason is our defense. Evolutionary science has weeded out spurious constructs of reason and fallacy in science. They are the playthings of ambitious men in politics. You are aware of that, Doctor Galway?"

"Yes, yes, of course."

"I have it now," the Scorpion cried out. *"Your* singular objective is to advance Mankind's enoblement, to see him as perfect. Well, let me tell you, sir, perfection after centuries of arduous labor, is now *ours* to claim. The Sycophants of this domain are *Perfect.* Call that Utopian if you chose."

"We have no scheme," Doctor Barodin said. "We are scientists only. Politically, we are always correct. Do the waves of the sea beat down upon the rocks with the purpose to wear and break them down. No, no. We only observe that they do so. We eschew purpose."

"Just so ... as we disregard reason." He stopped spinning his gossamer-"Your logic is dreary, good doctor," he said and lay back restfuliy on his own webbing. Remember that inanimate nature entails design with purposeful rules. There is no reason they do so, and the politicians cannot concoct one."

"Exept maybe ... the ... *ruling* principle of longevity, resistance to chaos and death. Hmm?" Barodin queried, I was stunned by his penetrating question.

"Like good living habits." I added felicitously.

"The laws of these Executioners are flexible. Bending with the winds of circumstances, they survive. That is reality, Galway," The other gauzy white robed Executioners with black cowles continued to feed books, papers and documents into the roaring singular flame. They worked with dead-pan expressions on their faces and with a certain slyness that made them secretive.

At last when I could withstand the apprehension no longer, I told the Chief Executioner that I and Barodin would now depart this inferrno of righteous ignorance.

"Since you are brought before us because of acts of disobedience, I caution you against trying to escape."

"We have never condemned your colony."

"Nor will you do so this tme. Your actions attest to your corrosive suspicion and disbelief."

"We are entitled to our opinion,"

"There's some more of that slavery of indulgent faith, in your God, in your founders, in your great men. But to what avail? To the end that all they have created will self-destruct in our fire, our fire here in Phanterica. Do you doubt my words?"

I said I did and even allowed myself a slight smile. "He turned to Garrunide and said to the chief Jailor; "Take these madmen *Operations Room* where we will dissect their brains to discover their transgressions against us. Take them away, Garrunide."

And so, while a new load of books and documents were hauled in and the process begun all over, to the accompaniment of immense cheers from the spectators, our jailor led us to the *Operations Room* in which, as I partially expected, giant Sycophants, like those we had first seen at the entrance, would try to stiflle our speech by placing our heads in a gag cage, a literal wirebasket within which a tongue screw captured our tongues and held them there for long periods of excruiating pain, thirst, hunger and torture. Thus the system of jusltice in Phanterica would amend our speech by cutting it off altogether with these *chastity cages*—all speech pure, undefiled, empty of meanings except scientific and correct to the nth degfree in its dogma of the perfect state. Barodin and I looked despairingly at each other as each of us resisted not the encasement of our heads in wire cages. Garrunide's henchmen left us alone to contemplate our fete.

Chapter 11

Captives In Effigy

"Look over there in the corner of our Deliberations Chamber. A doorway to the Operations Room."

I had never seen him. I can only guess. I had not entered the chamber through the main portal. This man was the Gatekeeper, the doorman to the Operations Chamber. He was seated on the edge of a small subterranean pool, formed by the closure of a spring to the sea table. He did not move, but simply mumbled. "Is he a … prisoner?"

I regarded Tashca for an answer.

"Humbled. His conscience has been carefulluy removed by an overwhelming superabundance of rational meteorological ideas, rocks, to be sure, placed upon his chest—the location of the conscience—during his trial But felling to liberate him, he is partly restored by rthe Wizard to perform duties of discrimination as doorman for this chamber."

A group of other Sycophants in the chamber were visible—our guide explained the others were at their usual spas for the day. They too passed the Dorman but averted their eyes in an indifferent manner.

"He will not move. Catatonasis—I believe you once called the condition-induced by chronic and extreme fear that the slightest movement can invite injury or death."

"He will not move?"

To do so requires a conscience, a motivating energy that has already been removed from him."

"*Will* cannot drive him unless he has a conscience," I surmised This native Sycophant with the face of a boxer dog, large limpid eyes, dressed in a goat-Mr shirt and red livery trousers, was a curious relic of old. His feet looked shriveled, due to his immobility. He had, our guide said, uttered dangerous tilings to the people around him. And they, in their ignorance of what he was saying and without sight or imagination, they had condemned him; for they too were dependent upon non-conscience and had delivered him up into the hands of the Specal Committee of Ethical Ineptitude.

"The Ethicists!" I exclaimed, having already encountered them, the Executioners in the Deliberations Chamber.

"They are the Thought Removal Committee, done through shocks of intense humiliation followed by grieving communally, over his demise while he lives."

"But why?" I asked again, now completely dumbfounded.

"It was a technique developed in classrooms for young children in … in your day, if my paleontological memory serves me right."

"He must've done something wrong."

"He sold Opinion pills to the populace at large."

"Sold … what! *opinionpills?*"

"Yes, they are purgatives in the form of polls. How you loved polls to replace thought and action!. Well, our Opinion polls are intended to get one to vote for his own thoughts even if they aren't altogether his convictions."

And so this poor fellow … " Our guide shook his head sadly.

"Forever?" Barodin asked.

"I'd like to talk to the fellow, if it's okay with you, Mister Tashca."

"Fine with me, but remember … he is … afflicted."

"Sir, I hear you cannot distinguish one right from another wrong."

"When I was sa boy the teachers thought they'd improve on my father's faith, and so they taught me how to clarify his values."

"Well, then it *has* worked."

"Oh, no sir. I find my job obnoxious and wish to steal every chance I get. I think the people are fanatics and the government is commanded by God to take care of us."

"Commanded by God!"

"Yes, sir, since my father was useless, a derelict in his duty and my mother, she is begging at the door of the Charity house."

"I see, well at least you do respect work."

"Don't ever, ever say that word: *respect.* Yes I work but only because if I do not the Committee of Disinformation has promised they would shoot me."

"You poor fellow. Well, they are vicious aren't they."

"I wish I could get rid of them, but I guess I will be under their control forever."

"That is sad." I left our conversation at that point. "Muskovich, he's the keeper of the Operations Chamber. He was an immigrant like you. He was accused of conspiring to overthrow the government, or so it was said of his intention. And the Wizard, with the concession of the Operations Personnel, have provided him with this rock-a symbol of their derision."

"How ingenuous!" I remarked.

"Now you understand. Ingnenuity without purpose and operative within the blessings framework of our holy government. Oh, kindly, benevolent govenment—that is the *modus operandi* of so much of our life and activity in Phanterica."

What was the source of those pills again?" I was dumbfounded.

Smuggled in. And may I say two lotharios who wished to destroy the unananmity of Phanterica. He must think, eat, speak and little more. You doubtless have wondered why we say, *Oh, kindly, benevolent government.* That is our trademark here in Phanterica, since our government is of the most advanced sort. The answer is very simple. The apparatus that controls all Sycophants in Phanterica is the stable warp of our own time-space continuum. We are, in fact, magnificent, giant creature men who appear dessicated in the flesh and diminished dimensionally because of your faillible measurement-perception stamps us so in your brain.

"I don't lunderstand what you are saying," I said.

"Of course you don't. We have sped past you eons of time ago and therefore to yoiu we appear retarded. Our science is measured in quanta of light years of exploration and ..."

"Wait, now my savvy giant of a friend. Where are your discoveries, how have you escaped this island domain, what achievements can youl show me.?

"A misconception. These rocks mark only the outer physical fringes of our time frame. I could take you out among the stars in a microsecond. We have harnessed their energy, we comprehend the quadrarational boundaries of extra-nuclear physics and discrepancies in time measurement in radically different moving bodies. At this very monlent we have placed almost eighty of our most kinesthetically adapted citizens into orbits beyond your comprehension. They are not exiles. They are our heroes. We have mined the globular minerals from the earth's core and readied our domain to cast off from your world at any time. The extra-orbital gradients of all the stellar bodies are within our knowledge. We use them for comprehending medicinal cures you still struggle to find, cancer being one. Molecular transsitional physics has opened the gate to that microbiological hell of disease. We have measured the universe back to Ithe beginnings of infinity, a secret we share with your God. But we profane Him not; He has juried our explorations. In transition now is our study of exotic plant foods from space and the threats to your survival you call plagues. Our modes of sexuality are without question; some would even call us a-sexuai, but we do procreate more often than not clinically ratter than biologically. But we are happy. You still search for happiness and contentment …"

I shut him off. "I come not to steal or usurp your great knowledge. We search for our friend. When we find him, we shall quit your domain."

"You have already seen him—in the Chamber of Deliberations. That is all you will obtain of his presence."

"You are telling us that our mission is doomed to failure?"

"Only that it is doomed to disappointment Failure is not a word in our vocabulary."

"I see." I said.

I felt the eyes of the invisible *Wizard* following me. Of course I was helpless against his scrutiny, since he heard my ID frequency resonate with his receiver. My skin crept, my flesh tingled, I perspired freely, although the room was freshened by currents from the sea waves. In a lake of blue that occupied half the room, a miniature of realistic icons met my sight. Ringed by the profuse lichen green of the great chamber, there floated a small flotilla of dimuitive, scaled miniature replicas of sea vessels, merchant and naval lships, aircraft of pre-WW II vintage, fishing smacks, a schooner or two and an array of air force bombers

"Harmoniously they are set lin various possitions, as the Master encountered them, their quadrants variable according to the tlime, circumstances and navigation position when they came within our electromagnetic orbit of power."

Tashca smiled patronizingly.

"I thought you lived on purity, not on warfare." I said.

"You have such a quaint way of putting things, Galway. No, they are the baubbles of the past, they move by means of emanations from our great masters powerful brain, which we lesser Phantericans will never understand." He stood erect, a comical barbaric figure in his white robe, rigid and staring off into the rocks.

As I approached the Captive table, I was taken aback by what I saw. The replicas once home to missing sailors and airmen, as they appeared from a distance, were none other than models that moved about like so many chess pieces. "How ingenuous ... savage and primitive!" I thought."

"Welcome to our concept of war—deaths in battle, former human beings reduced to things and but for remnants, all in our possession ... quite appropriate, don"t you think so?" Tashca asked, looking up into my face for signs of the answer he expected from me. I kept my composure. "Sink, amass, divide ... the icons respond to thoe words," he informed us. They are his playthings. He also is chief of the land icons and the fallen passengers and military troops, captives here in Phanterica but put to good use, I can assure you."

"These icons, they ... they are strictly utilitarian then"

"They represent those transport ships which have fallen into the ring of time's continuum, and and therefore they are captives in our domain."

"The ships lost ..."

"The airplanes, squadron and single airplanes, that have suddenly disappeared ... *mysteriously* your press describes them."

"And ships, one naval vessel ..."

"Never literally sunk but, instead, enveloped by our ring of negative energy and, permit me to use the word, *captured,* seduced into our domain."

"But the lives...."

"All but a small handful, a few ... saved by our dynamics of molecular reenergizing of the subterranean waters in a way that provided both air and conveyance."

"Like an air ring, an all functhing float."

"Right, sir, you are perceptive! ... a giant flotation device you might call it. But these things I have already told you about, and yet you doubt Step over here, closer to the table." With a laser pointer he circled the ring of Translation—into which there steamed *The Beachcomber,* a maritime vessel, among the first to go under and ... over therte ... four airplanes of a squadron of eight led by *Pretty Lady* that suddenly vanished? Lost their way ... turned and headed out over the

South Atlatilc toward Africa, the press reluctantly said. Why? I could only wonder. By reverssing the deflection of the compass to read its opposslite cooridinates? Perhaps.

I was suddenly smitten by the appearance of faces peering down at the table, as if from the earthern darkness that hovered over the involved topographical area of the Caribbean Sea. Like ghosts, they seemed to crowd against each other, looking down as from a theatre gallery of an operating room. There were ships' passangers, the captains of vessels, the military pilots and airmen, the whole assembly shifting and moving about like roiledckiuds, all of them making up the assembly of the lost, those who had suddenly disappeared within the Triangle of Mystery. Yet they appeared as if alive *en absentia,* pushling and crowding over the table to watch, as if they too were just learning of what their fate had teen.

"The lost ones," Tashca said with great solemnity, "But not lost to eternity ... lost only to the denegrations, the shallow existence in your workt—I have to admit, the best parts we have ... appropriated for our use here in Phanterica ..."

These spectator figures that hovered above the table were draped in pale brown linens, their faces masked in personality smiles, their hands upraised as if to fend off some fete they were no longer subject to. They hovered there, amused, chattering voluably yet voiceless amongst themselves and promoting a certain kind of crowed atmosphere within the chill rocks of the theatre.

"They are diseussisng matters familiar to your world—how to remake the economy to their own dimension. All reflect a desire for ease from the weight of tasks we have given them. All respond to the Wizard's thoughts—all. Then I notices ... their eyes!

"Sightless, or virtually so." said Tashca. They live in the Master's past. They are like the fish in the underground caves of your own ancient Southwest They do not any longer need vision."
Intrigued I asked if they had ever seen any light here in Phanteriea.
"Only this phosphorescent sheen to their skin that bathes them like an elixir of chlorophil of lichens, which we have in abundance."

"Chlorophil … without any sun."

"Havent you noticed … rays of the sun deflect through the crystals of rock dykes scattered throughout our domain."

These phenomena all overwhelmed both myself and my friend Igmar Barodin, silenced by awe for long minutes. Elixir of chlorophil, pkythings, ring of negative energy, lost but not drowned…. What was it all about, I wondered. What strange creatures and their world had our rescue mission brought us to!

I was impatient. Last I miss some clue as to the location of Kennison, I gave atltention to the smallest detail of our surroundings. I had actually seen him in the Deliberations chamber. Of that I was certain. *He was* here, in Phanterica, that both I and Barodin confirmed to one another.

Unexpectedly, we heard … and felt … a gigantic cataclysmic rumbling of the earth, the slipping of a thrust fault, a geosysnclynal fault plane, with all its attendant tremors, rock collapse, strata dislocation, subterranean flooding, and seismic rock torture that, like the burying of miners, had hidden them forever from human contact because of their near signless eyes. They were the remains of *pioneers* of our advanced civilizartion. The word stuck on the end of my tongue.

"Actually, they more clearly resemblle us than you do," said Tashca, since their biological development was intermediate to you and to us," he explained. Was is possible I wondered to reverse the evolutionary biological strains of human morphology and reconstitute the primitive, Prehistoric man on an earliler and simpler plane of biological development yet gift him with the technology of our own contemporary America? How strange! I could not dismiss the idea.

I heard another deep-boweled rumbling in the depths of the earth. The phosphoresenee paled with the dust shaken from the root of rock and the stone walls. Screeches as from stalagmited creatures, like a million trapped bats, essentially prisoners like us of scientific advancement, now rose and fell through the Operations Chamber. I felt trapped, ambushed by rockfell, the spelunker's escapes closed up. Claustrophobia momentarily overcame me. I fought off panic.

"The Great One divined your thoughts, Alien. He has warned you with this rock jam. He has censured your independent spirit. He disapproves of your old immoralities. Yes, graciousfy, he removes you from our penal system of ... disposables? over beyond the chasm wall."

"Many thanks," I mumbled, "but why am I so important, both myself and my friend here, Doctor Barodin?"

"Your childish brain does not grasp nor fully realize that you seek the Genius of our scientific civilization, whom you hope to spirit away, back to your decadent surroundings."

"You sound like a political activist or a ... a socialist libertarian," Barodin intervened, scarcely reaking the truth of Ms words.

"You have already taken everything you need from him," said Tashea, refering to Dr. Kennison.

"Hardly. He does have a wife and son. Yet he had found a way to defeat death. His experiments are far from completed."

"In your world, he was in love with death, an oxymoron. Here he becomes death in order to discover—longivity, perhaps immortality."

"Look! Here is his photograph." I pulled a small locket from my pocket, which I carried to remind myself of what Kennison looked like.

"And what is *that*?"

"A photo of Doctor Kennison—a reminder to me."

"Foolish biped!" He rubbed his hands together and by neurological transference from the picture in his mind to the *generation* of molecular images from *mind energy*, his words, there stood across the sea table from us, the very life-like image of the doctor himself.

"Doctor Kennison!" I cried out.

"He does not hear you. I show you his spirit to demonstrate the quality of our reproductive science. We abolished your single-minded reflections of nature, your photography, millinnia ago. We now reproduce the spirit of the departed" He snapped his fingers, flinging his laser light beam into the shadows of the chamber and the figure of Kennison suddenly vanished. "You do not believe our science is superior to yours?

"I have little choice," Barodin responded and I nodded my head. That is ... unless, of course, we were delusional.

"Little do you realize what is in store for you, alien gentlemen. We ... the Magnificent One ... saved your doctor from de-molecularizatidn."

"What the devil is *that?*" Barodin blurted out.

"You are scientists.. You will find the Ice Room a clever demonstration of four states of matter where, in there, spectal changes will show our capacity to reduce human flesh to its electrical potential yet save the form and freeze the life for as long as we chose. We can also expel the flesh of a mortal like a time-fractional impulse that *places*—the better word of *shoots*—a person into the chocen dimension consistent with his life's interests here on earth. For we do admit that we are a part of your earthern world. Human life can be expressed in any one of those states, and yet ... yet ... translation either retrograde or progressive can now be controlled ... thanks to your ... missing friend. Remember, good doctors, that our time-speed continuum does not permit of choices, only observations and results ..."

"Like school children, I suppose."

"Exactly, precisely. Oh, you couldn't have uttered the truth more precisely, Doctor Barodin!"

I looked at my friend in wonder. We were far from done on our excursion, and it looked as if the Phantericans would try to match our expertise smewhere along the line. We could not be crertain. We suddenly heard the sleek, melodic music of Phantericans celebrating this, their revival week, as a time-honorsed pursuit. There was th flute and there was the mandolin.

Chapter 12

Is If Treason?

The Chief Magistrate occupied an unassailable position of wisdom, power, authority and invincibility. Lesser judges, barristers we might have called them, stood below a crenelated wall and shouted upwards to make their pleas heard The Judge, the most imposing, gargantuan of the Couriers, paced to and from on the wall, as he was wont to do in his chamber,as he considered our pleas, arguments, protestations and, ultimately, the sounds of rocks of justice dropped from the hairy hands of Gargantuan Judges in coarse black goat's-hair robes and sequinned powdered curly locks. The falling rocks represented the popular Elitist verdict. For the huge judgement and disinformning chamber was adjacent to the witness niche, spectator galleries and outer lobby, all carefully carved out of the native rocks and at this juncture crowded with milling Phanterifcan observers. There was about their presence a wierd and unearthly silence, as if they held their breath or stood mute and stunned by what they saw.

Tascha was back with us again. He explained that the gilded robe of the Premier Judge represented purity of thought, his long black sequinned wig unending wisdom given by the father of Phanterica, and his gestures signified that he appeased the unseen Powers of Contemplation by an amoral righteousness fixated on purity of thought and action. The conduct code of these people begged for an audience.

"This is where … justice is considered and meted out?" I queried Tascha. He seemed amused that I did not understand why a courtroom should cloister itself between g;ass walls bejomd wjocj tjere teemed acquarium life, lavender daylight plying inside the immense reservoirs of sea water, squid, giant tortoises, shark and porpose trios, millions of silvery, spotrted and striped specimens shifting and weaving in schools amid the enemone and planted sea grasses. Silvery twisted pillars confided the glass taniks, holding up a black timbered truss ceiling, the floor of schist, the judges' benches cast from the alloys and other benches fashioned out of bleached bones of prehistoric animals, this entire scene, visually and actively overlain by the deathly hum of monosylabic priest chants and monontonal music, as from an ancient monastery.

After my eyes had roamed this room, Tascha whose sense of thre bizzare never never faded, said to us, "You can say this is the dwelling place of wisdom, in the cleft of the rock, an imurrmountable wall flanked by seas teemning withs prehistoric fish."

"What exactly is the case before the court."

"Before yours—a woman, who is far too voluptuous for our simple contentment, is to get a hearing. Voluptuous in all aspects, wearing about her neck a pendant which emits a fragrant colored perfume."

She has survived., but what?" I asked.

"She has been accusled of a refusalt spy upon her neighbors, here in our beloved Phanterica, an almost certain fatal fault. She is also accused of trespassing on the Wizard's lands."

"She is … tannned!" I exclaimed, cognizant that all Phantericans were a bleached white skin color.

"Ethereal light, doctor."

The accused was placed on a huge wheel, more like a grist mill wheel than a spinning wheel. It revolved much like the potter's wheel of old, flat and of irresistable momentum.

"Prepare the ftask," said the judge from the height of the wall as he peer4ed down llupon Ithe accused like a sentry at the gate. The attendants strapped the girl to the wheel, tying her golden hair and with a great rumble set round rock into motion. The spinning disc with its victim bound thereon created a whistling noise, the breeze of felt on my face where I sat, on my stone ledge nearby. The wheel was given fifty turns, then caused to slow down and finally stop. The accused woman, helped to her feet, was told to walk up the stone steps to the parapet where the judge sat in a niche in the wall. The accused rose from off her torture wheel and, slowly, with great exertion, she mounted the steps to look the Premier Judge in the eye. The magistrate flung his black wig aside causing its oiled curls danced in the eerie torchlight coming from below. He pushed a stagger-counter into the face of the accused and entoned for the entire motley assembly to hear.

"This woman reels like a drunkard. She cannot stand up two minutes and then she is down again. This shows sensible men that she is guilty of the crime of spying on The Master."

A task-master seized the woman from her fallen position at the bottom of the steps. "Aren't there any words for the poor girl's defense?" I asked.

"Are you out of your mind? We have no defenders here. The State of Phantrerica is always right Its simply a matter of degree of guilt or its total absence that counts."

"No defense, no defense," I kept repealling to myself. "But what if she, or anyone, is falsely accused," I asked Tashca. "Gossip among the fair-minded is not unhard of in my country."

"Do you not know that we who have arrived scientifically are perfectly infallible? All we say, do and think rests on a scientific data base. We can err only in our calculations, not in our premises. And since the wheel of justice could have spun only forty-nine times, the magistrate would have thus reduced her sentence. But, as you can see, fifty it was, and the accused failed the only valid test.

"We are weeding out the misfits a few at a time … still. Hers was actually a very minor offense to the State of Phanterica. She appeared in the tunnels wearing an outer world tan. However, should anyone ne caught stealing he is thrown over to the other side of the wall, into the black chasm. Anyone caught having murdered another Sycophant is peeled, like you peel an apple, in la spiral manner until; finally only the core remains. This method affords our perfect democracy great cause for amusement. In fact, we take wagers on the length of the accused peelings, as it were." Our guide went into paroxysms of laughter.

"The state, who represents the State?" "That is the judge, as in Stalinist Russia … or///Caesar in Christ's time or … the master of his vlessel or … any dictator of past centuries. But then, enough of this.

What will they do to her now, since this is a minor offense?

"She will be condemned to live fore forty days in a burning wilderness of smoking pine needles and leaves to curee her of her fault?"

"How cruel!" I exclaimed.

"Well, we must maintain the purity of our Phanterica, you'll have to admit."

"I won't do any such thing!"

"Follow me if you want to see a real trial … for treason," Tashea summoned. We entered another smaller chamber.

The accused stood on a small dias that rotated like one of those gem displays in a New York jeweler's window. He stood against black velvet, beneath the crenelated wall where the jusge sat in an attitude of imperious majesty.

"How can anybody be accused of treason since the lack of a conscience rules out conflict of right and wrong and any discussion on loyalty. Loyalty I thought is a moral and ethical matter, a choice of ends and reasons."

"Simple," said Tashea brusquely. "Just as long as the ac-cused mimics the headmjaster of the Domain, as your priests did of old in imitating their Christ, he is pure. Purity we Phantericans test by light."

A brilliant blue-tinted light was at that moment cast over the poor fellow who appeared almost transparent in its intensity, a phenonomenon due not to detraction within the body of the acclused but to the x-ray character of the transmitted light. "The accused is currently in the plasmic state of matter, quite harmless. It is the gaseous state of spirituality that seduces and deceives, not the soliditty that harms."

"I see. So your scientists have made these states interchangeable by means of…."

"Quantum energy of light. Your Doctor Kennison showed us how to replicate cellular molecules in such a way that the very process can be stopped, like the shutter on a motion-picture projector, to arrest the transformation at a certain point." Tashea pointed to the translucent nature of the soul of the accused under the x-ray light. "In Phanterica we have advanced to the stage where man's inate goodness has finally surfaced and impateted all areas of Phanterican life."

"But I thought he was inherently wicked."

"Christian dogma. Not a whit of truth to it. No, in fext when a Phanterican sees another in trouble he sacrifices his very life. That is, he surrenders his very soul to amend failure of conscinece in another ... a conscience that does not belong in the human psyche or flesh. Show me that in your society."

"If he were dead, I mean the accused, carved in ionic, which is solid when not agitated ... crystalized by ketosis or negated by secondary fusion processes, I could understand. But to arrest a man's deterioration from solid to liquid ..."

"Death we have solved. He is in the intermediate stage and so is inert, completely harmless. Has he ingesrted some sort of poison? You have already been to our Ice Museum where specimens of this ionic arrest abound."

"Yes," we both chorused.

"Self-sacrifice is the way here in Phanterica. In matters of law, we have actually managed to reach that noble height where there is no longer any true litigation, in the old sense of the term, no adversarial contest, but only self-sacrifice. By suicide he confesses both to the crime of treason and to his benevolence which he shares with the government. Oh, kindly, benevolent Government!

"So this is your court of justice ... suicide right before my very eyes,"

"Surely you did not expect harranging, crippled logic, non-sequiturs, fallacies of the ego and the id and all sorts of perversion of the intellect."

"I do not know what I expected," I said. So this is the law in Phanterica!"

"Neat, wouldn't you say," Martok said. I had noticed his constant omnipresence as our Priest host. "The ancient law of the Chaldeans, Hebrews, Minoites, Egyptians and others were pretenses of justice. They left out self-sacrifice, which is enobling of the human spirit. The Japanese warrior code says the same."

"I cannot say anout that." I said.

"Doctor Kennison has taught us the art of conservation while he has been here. The great physicist has extended the old law of conservation of energy-no energy is ever lost-to control the environment. By the thermo dynamics of energy transfer, look. The rocks dissolve into spa like waters. See how the people splash about in them. The black skies whiten, turn cinnamon then blue, the sunlight activating man's natural appetites into needs, whcih the Governemnt is kind enough to satisfy. Observe the orgy of these people, happy at enjoying their little fiesta, voracous in their greedy hunger." This panagyric went on and on in praise of the Domain of Phanterica. As I sat there in the chamber I averted my eyes.

The jailor said, "You turn away. Well, then, the master has merely to cross his fingers ... see, he does it now ... and the rocks return to their hard, crystaline state once again. But the very vegetation becomes adornment for the Executioners. The Master Martok now speaks for the nine judges. "Umpaqua, lsusquanishs befetosh uuy ets vanmauguzell."

"They cringe."

"We express ourselves in ways curious to you," Tashca explained.

"You consider yourselves the master race, do you not?" Barodin enquired of the jailor.

"Do not mock us, Alien. We have achieved ultltimate simplicity, the throne of all laws, the foundation of all concord, the rule of brotherhood and benevolence. When we bless our Government, we bless ourselves.."

"Most amazingl!"

"Yes, lisnt it," he said.

"Well, I got that one right," I thought.

"In the opening—and closing of the case, I had witnessed a means by which the poison of treason was exposed, made totally accessible by way of transcendental light waves in the invisible ultra violet and visible blue segments sof the spectrum. So the man there exposed by the moral x-ray, on his velvet pedestal was guilty without his having spoken one word in his own defense. Our guide explained to us that treason can be chemically forumulated and when ingested appears under the blue ultra violet light. There, however was no cure for defection from Phanterican self-sacrfice. Serif-preservation was a thing of the past. Self-satisfection authenticated itself under the banner of State Wisdom. And so it was. So it was in this case.

His interrogator was feeding him safe questions. They are indeed safe for him, I asked with some temerity. "Of course, of course," Tashca replied.

Martok questioned the poor culprit. "Why did you join to be together with what is foreign"?" he asked.

"Oh, holy, benevolent, kindly government. So that I might convert non-Sycophants to our faith in ideological brain food that bears an official stamp-stuffs such as communlal moss, dry lichens and carob stew."

When the interrogation questions entered into the system of the accused, in the form of Centralized Crumbs, which we had formerly called handouts—the beautiful precept, and marvelous to wonder at-they did then pass from his mouth into his rudimentary belly and out again without their changing the man's behavior.

"Our Governments thoughts, by this timeless test, have proved healthiest to his and to our physiological systems. No ingestion, the purity of the accused stands unchallenged."

"Is there a verdiclt?"

"The verdict of the rocks,"

"Which is?" I asked.

"Self destruction by stoning."

I still could not be ceretain if Doctor Kennison was dead or alive, since under this systrem he had no chance to defend himself, and being a scientist he was not an expert in the law and so stood totally exposed to this form of necromancy.

The web that Martok had thrown between the rocks shone in the firelight. Its tensile strength, the gossamer fibres, almost invisible in the flamelight, showed me, at least, that I could not escape through sluch a powerful netting of gossamer. The sea beat powerfully on the rocks above like a pounding heart. Why indeed did I need to escape at this time, our, my mission being yet incomplete?

"A touch of poetry, eh, Doctor Barodin. Heartbeat, waves beatng superlative. I should confirm and conform you to the will of the Great One, our Supernal Wizard."

"His purposes ...?"

"His singular purpose, which I have just uttered to you—divulged is better—since he holds to it as a secret mantra"

"You say these things from the proud security of your spun web, Priest."

My accussation enflamed the Priest Martok. His face darkened in the torchlight shadows in the cowl he wore, his eyes flamed white with passionarte hatred, his lips scarcely moved within the bony structure of his thin face.

"O I have ample time," He said with great calm and assurance.

I could not refrain from dry commentary, to test his Majesty. "If there were not purpoe outside of Man in the universe, then Man could remake the heavens. If purpose even existed side by side with the angels, it could not alter the system of nature, inanimate and life-bleeding. The law of thermodynamics exhits direction and therefore purpose, since chaos is the state of non-purpose, and the conservation of energy in the third law of thermodyamics is one of downward direction and therefore of purpose. Does the blood course through the veins of a man, through the body of an animal to serve as function? I ask you, Priest Martok. Can function exist without purpose, and who establishes function?"

"We do—we here in Phanterica."

"Pride, abysmal pride. You Priests and ... godforbid Doctor Kennison, if he is not your slave and prisoner ... confirm the reality of function and therefore of design and so of purpose. They are all interlinked This is the geneology, going back to the beginning of creation, Priest."

Martok scowled with inner rage, "I thought as much—a cursed beliver in some sort of god! A curse upon you and your kind, Doctor Galway!" With these words the Priest attempted to throw strands of sticky webbing across the arms and face of the prisoner, capturing his animation, freezing lit but for quiverings of the web, his hands as tools of expression. But she foiled. As I lifted one hand to brush away the webbing, it dissolved with a puff like a powder fuse ignited by flame. The Priest stood gratified but in dismay. Quietly, as to a deadly foe, shaking in his wrath, he bid me continue.

"I comprehend chaos and anarchy as well as you do, Priest. I find in chaos the absence of design. The abyss of hell is chaos, its confines established by ... God, Anarchy, likewise, is rebellion against one or another design, but, as I have had no occasion to note in my long lifetime, I have never seen anarchy with a replacement design that worked."

"You have not searched diligently enough," Martok said. "We here in Phanterica, we scientists, can create chaos and anarchy among the stars. In the heavens, the nebulae are incipient chaos. When meteorites and comets spew into empty space, chaos reigns."

"Do they not follow prescribed paths of trajectory, or do they fly off directionless into the void," Barodin wanted to know.

"They do-the latter."

"Then why do they deflect from their parent bodies?" Barodin queriled.

"Why do the apples fall downward from trees—because they are ripe. Purpoe again, Priest," I said. "Or, at least a design of some sort."

"Utilitarianism-which we have carried to its fullest development," said the Priest.

"Your speech spins this tenacious web before our eyes. But ... so it was intended."

"My purpose, mine, Banile One, is valid because I sit at the feet of the Great Wizard."

Then we have reached an agreement. Purpose is real-but whose purpose?"

"I could call a slight shift in thinking on the subject.," he replied.

"No man desires to hide his innermost secrets. All Sycophants wish to confess their problems to the public by means of Omnivision, the transference of thought by close physical proximity."

"You have learned the value of interfacial thought, Doctor Galway. I would not have considered you advanced enough for that."

"By this means you assume that the wonders of nature are merely intuited out of chaos, but are not real You deny my own science of physics and anthropological study of Man, Priest. Intuition is valid if one accepts its premise of prescience, of some grain of foreknowledge. But then again, that is ... design, is it not?"

"Intuition has crowded out communication, which we are cautious to control here in Phanterica. And, shame, likewise, is a burned-out star, a black hole in the moral fabric of you ... you childish humans of ancient civilization. Shame was the product of conscience, which we have extinguished, abolished, exterminated as counter productive and useless."

"Then you admit the link," I said.

"Confess it heartily, but deny its existence-evolutionary science has expunged, exorcised shame from the humam psyche as a step in the evolutionary development of mankind."

"How neatly you encapsulate forty million years, Prtiest. The act of shame, the very appearance of it, once conveyed more than the words of exoneraton themselves. Behind you, the witnesses to your rite of destruction … see how they appear to be talking at once but when no sounds come out I might suppose that they are dumb."

"Mute but not unintelligent, Doctor Barodin. Do not mock me."

"They are only realists, must I suppose, for over evolutionary time they have come to distrust human confessions and have adopted the mummery 1 see before me," I replied. Indeed, only the guttering of the torches within the cavern, small squeeks, yowls and cryings of a pitiable sort, in addition to the scuflfle of feet and the rustle of clothing were the most obvious sounds within the cavern—apart from the increasingly heavy pounding ot the incoming tide upon the rocks above our heads.

"We cling to what we call the quality of life, Doctor Galway. You have never learned about this. In promitive civilizations such as you come from, duality of life was totally materialistic. Here, materialism serves us yet does not dominate out thinking or our ways. We are survivors of that fetish of posession and things."

"Are you, yes? Are you … survivors? You've destroyed by fiat all religion, except for your cult you call high-mindedness. Before me is the mummery of defeat of purpose, design, direction. Your laws of society are now, at last, the rudimentary laws of science and of nature. Instincts control your village, indifference its will, and chaos its people's lives. Thus you live in herds, being no longer capable of decisions, promises, originality, judgement or wisdom. Gravity to you is to fall to searth in an cxultic prayer, so-called. That exultation ushers in a popular zest for death through violence. That's all it means: a high-minded grasping for death amid its denial. Energy to you is responding to the Wizard's commands. Light to you barely touches your half-blinded eyes, eyes which appear as if diseased by cataracts but are instead, the evolutionary product of species adaptation. That is as far as I can go."

"Our togetherness is by choice," said the Priest, his voice weakening.

"All the worship, all the faith of antiquity is invested in the state of Phanterica," I charged.

"Which gives us here in Phanterica … purpose …"

"Without design."

"Direction, you have forgotten."

"Without wisdom."

"A curse upon your philosophy, Doctor Galway!"

"I have one last word to say before you return me to my … niche. Chance is the last barrier to your hypothesis, but it is frail, shallow, illegimate and unertain. Accept if you want that this rocky haven is the result of chance beating upon time and the sea upon these ancient stones. But chance itself is a principle that of itself must rule whatever it touches and is therefore foundational to chaos in the absence of design. Chance is random direction, but many directions nonetheless. Chance is a law given by a holy God to confound the Seers and the proud."

"Stop … you blackheart, you plagued thief, you renegade, you usurper."

The Priest spat out these words, the webbing continued to flow from his mouth as he spoke, moist in its wet newness in the torch light. I slid off the rock, it now being cold and clammy where I sat, and stepped to the floor, I walked through the new dense webbing, tearing and stretching it asunder to confront the Priest Martok, He expected a deed of violent vengeance. I raised my hand and placing my fingers over his lips, sealed them with a cod from the nearby pyre of flaming books. 1 closed his eyes by their lids while he stood as if mesmerized by my boldness.

"Now your senses are humbled," I said to hint "Your lips are closed, your speech is silent, your eyes are shut Night has descended. In this cavern you may chance upon a … a friend," I said to him, realizing that I had hypnotized him without making the slightest effort to do so, a new power that I had discovered within myself Realizing that we were free, I and Doctor Barodin promptly left the bedchamber to bump and claw and scrape into the fresh air above the cavern, not for distant from the outgoing surf. I stopped to listen from time to time to the beat of the breakers in order to discern my direction. One element whilch I had not anticipated in this absurd, mad doman of disinformation and non-cognition was-the animal, the beast of nature, I thought I had discovered it in man himself but how wrong I was! What most amazed me was that I was liberated not by jailor, judge or warden or Priest, but by my own efforts to contend with Phantercan philosophy!

Chapter 13

The Ice Cave Museum

I felt a heavy shroud suddenly flung over me, smelling of leather and bearing iron buttons with the Phanterican Domain seal on them.

"Where we are going you will need warmth," came Lejah's voice from the semi-darkness.

A cold and clammy hand caressed my face, a gesture I did not understand.

"Our keepers test the temperature of your skin so that they will know more accurately what temperature to induce into your shroud." Warmth from a distance, the remote control of surrounding temperature, was not new or fashionable but was certainly practical. We were surrounded presently by what appeared to be the interior of a glacier, blue ice enveloped iln its total silence of desolation. The cavern of ice provided interlocking platforms and roped catwalks up and down its sides. Within the middle area a sight astounded me." frozen forms of what appearted to be humans. Impossible! I muttered under my breath. Barodin was stupfied into silence. Mme Tousseaud's wax museum in London was no more life-like.

"What did you expect to find in our little ... iceberg?" the woman asked.

"Specimens...."

Like the backstage area of a marionette theatre we saw lifesize forms hanging by harnesses from the ice-rafters, their numbers beyond my guess. Others were folly encased in ice much as were the specimens of lost Norsemen and Northern Great tusked mammoths that had lain dead for millions of years.

"Here are your survivors of the Bermuda Triangle—I have mentioned it for the first time since Bermuda is a silent partner in our operations." There was no arrogance in Lejah's voice, only the grim pride of an idle and corrupt interrogator fixiated on death.

"It is I who decides on their … preservation. Lejah, who deposits their intelligences in these ice-tombs … I prefer to call them … displays.

"Whose purpose is …?

"To mine the world of its wealth in nowledge … knowledge only, not mores, values, laws or standards … just knowledge."

"But no Christian burial …?"

"Sir, you very well know that to chose to fly an airplane on a stormy day is a choice, and that if all the passengers are killed that choice to fly becomes a moral choice/"

"Only a circumstantial, not a moral choice. Any promise your government makes, any guarantee of safety by the ship's captain to his to the passengers is meaningless … when confronted by our,.. our electromagnetic ring of dispersion. Put very simply, we nullify the compass readings and from a great distance, shutdown the electrical grids of … invaders of our air space. Voila! There they are, those who survived!"

"In a word … you scramble the electrical impuses … " I did not finish. Barodin had turned a deathly white, under his fur shroud.

"There are your airplane pilots, and … over there … and alongside of them hang the surviving passengers from three ships, including one, possibly two, merchant ships that sank in the Triangle. The sea captain, two as a matter of fact..,.lifeless, by alll appearances, but potentially living in cold storage.

"They look dead to me. You could be exgtradited for … murder."

"Foolish Maurauder! You knew long abouy about suspended animation by freezing. But you did not pursue the wealth of bnefits it held promise of."

"We do not believe in freezing cadavers, sir."

"Suspending their life is the real twist to the logic. They are not dead. These figures … 1 chose to call them … quite unlike Mme. Toussaud's wax figures in her museum … are capable of returning to animation and life again, if we should chose to release them from their bondage of ice."

"I've heard of mastadons being trapped in ice and served up as steaks three thousand years later.

"Not really the same. All of my ... our creatures were alive when they were ... quick frozen-that is your term? One of the boys lost his arm in the sinking of the vessel he was a passenger on with his mother. There she is and ... there he is. He lost his arm caught in la lifeboat davit We quick froze both him and his salvaged arm and reattached it with a precision unheard of in common surgery. When quick-frozen we can remove any limb and transfer it to another, without blood loss and with the great craftsmanship that our method allows."

"Doctor Barodin," I said, "does this actually seem plausible to you? I mean ... do you think these ... cadavers are capable of ... life again?

"I hardly think so."

"Then watch closely." Lejah summoned an attendant and gave him an order to revive Captain Hennessey of the Beachcomber, an American merchant vessel that sank lin 1916. No sooner had the order been given than the figure came alive, and, beginning to squirm in his harness, was let down easily to the floor by invisible ropes. With a warmloth the freezer attendant removed te hoarfrost from his face, his eyes and lips." Greetings, Captain Hennessey."

"My ship, I've got to save my ship!"

"Sorry, Captain, said Lejah in the voice of sinister warning, "but your ship Beachcomber went down over three-quarters of a century ... years ago,"

"Impossible! Absurd! Why am I imprisoned ... here." He stiffly craned his neck around. "You're keeping me. You'e holding me a prisoner, I have to go up to the wheelhouse ... at once."

"Be calm, sir. There is no more that you can do,"

The figure of Capt. Hennessey, now completely thawed out, sank to the floor, despondent. "Nothing?"

"Nothing sir. You need not worry about your vessel. The maritime commission has assigned the name to its registry of mysterious sinkings ... no enemy torpedo, no deadly war sabotage, no weakness in the hull ..."

"My God, I can't believe it."

"I simply wanted to show these two scientists that we hold onto your information. We are peacelovers here, and when we discovered that your ship carried munitions to the enmy in England, we took action. How is still highly secret and very special to us. Yet … we give you peace of mind, meantime, with respect to your career as a merchant marine officer and responsible for your ship and its crew, you are not held culpable by the American Maritime Board in its sinking. We destroy, remove, all any lany ltraces of sabotage in our work to sustain world peace.?

The sea captain Hennessey stood, and as soon as he did so, the attendant upon a motion from Lejah, refroze the man. A nozzle sprayed foam over the captain, a foam that quick-froze into ice. While standing as a piece of stone on the floor, the attendant of the Ice Room Museum slipped the harness back over his shoulders and racked him up to the rafters again, on his face the smile of a kind of benign rapture. The whole scene had been so incredible!'

"So you see, we glean Information a little at a time, we save lives, we preserve posterity. Now you see the utility value of science, doctors … the magical dynamics of change. Indeed you have just received a lesson in the truth of evolutionary science for the miracle of suspended animation could never have come about without the intrinsic polarity of intermolecular attraction that makes luman engineering possible … and already in existence. You're a witness … quite feasible. Indeed, this is our time-space continuum museum, which has no beginning and no end but is maintained only by olur using temperature as an adjunct to medical surgery and a bequeathal to our world of your unexplored criteria of temperature negotiating."

"I'm tryling my damnedest to lunderstand this woman … but do you, Barodin?

"Partly. But I also know that when a body, whether it's human or otherwise, is subjected to extreme cold, and where atomic activsity lis reducxed to a near zero Fahrenheit, that body becomes brittle. If the sea captain had fallen, I daresay he would have shattered into a thousand pieces."

"Thank God, he didn't!"

"We have achieve absolute zero, I hasten to tremind you chaps," Said Lejah. "In your world the mercury can be lowered to about 490 degrees fehrenheit..but that is still not absolute zero.. We have achieved the limpossible.,.one of our secrets. We have created absolute zero—in here!"

I and Barodin both regarded each other in incredulous disbelief.

"Of course, as with any extreme technology, accidents happen. Just yestefrday one of our assistants dropped the frozen cadaver of an unknown John doe, a passenger liner survivor, and he … that lis, the passenger … shattered on the stone floor. It was impossible to reasemble the frozen pieces, and so we had to discard him as useless to us in our biological experiment."

"I see," I said, realizing the consequences of freezing a stiff to absolute zero and dropping him at that zero temperature. Barodin's mouth was still hung open at the announcement of the accidental shattering.

"I have a strange premonition that my friend Doctor Kennison may be hung up and frozen stiff in your cold storage. Mind if we look around?

"Not a chance but suit yourselves … he's to valuable to us in his viable state."

""I want to take a look."

"Do try." TLejah held up her hand. I wandered aimlesslyabmong the ice blocks and hanging cadavers, which they surely were, life-potential or not. But my search proved futile.

"You see>" she chirped smugly.

"What the devil are you doing?" She was on her telecell.

"Calling for Security.. The cold storage unit is like knowledge held in abeyance for as long as we chose. You might call it … a kind of frozen library. We dare not permit interlopers to access our museum. Yolur behavior is becoming suspicious, Doctor Galway."

"I think I'll just have a look around," said Barodin.

"I say you will not." Lejah this time withdrew a magnet ring from one pocket and flashing it thrice in the air, cast a spell of my friend, who just stood hypnotized … which in fact he really was … only by thermal means, not by psychological craft.

"Would you please release my friend," Barodin said in a commanding tone of voice.

"You must first swear that you'll not interfere in our frozen biotechnical experiment."

"I m sure he so swears … as do I. We personally believe that biotechnics will solve the problems of raising armies, eliminating disease, cloning the strong and the beautifull, and, in the end come to the aid of evolution's survival of the fittest?"

"Good, then we see eye to eye," said Lejah. Martok will commend you both. " As will the jusband that the State has assigned tos me—the man you search for ..."

"Doctor Kennison...."

"Precisely so."

"Have we been freed ... our sentence commuted?"

"You have been ... inducted."

"Inducted!. My God ... into what!" I shouted.

"And exonerated by the Deliberators ...

"Do you mind if we have a look around in this ... this strange domain? It's too quiet in here."

"Sound is excluded. Even our voices are nullified by dectrocharged air. We can take no chances in our ... museum of suspended knowledge. Do must steal or borrow knowledge without Martok's consent or you commit crimes."

"Don't forget that I and my friend here are prisoners of your ideology ... and that's a much more serious kind of crime, which denies habeas corpus to us ... you will admit."

"Foolishness! Your criminal justice system does snot apply here in Phanterica, The body of the victim for proof? We have frozen bodies we can use at any time to exoneragte a criminal from guilt. Have you forgotten ... we have destroyed, eliminated the conscience here in our little land." She paused to reflect. "In fact, we are running out of space and soon we may have to borrow a planet for future cold storage."

That night in our separate cubicles, silmilar to jail cells, I set about cracking the code for molecular stasis the scientific word for the freezing process and its gruesome death-like evidence which we had witnessed. When we should next spot Kennison, that would be time enough to set the formularized concept into motion and perhaps thereby save Mory Kennison for our world.

Lejah volunteered to say: "He conducts experiemts on social phenomena ... with rocks."

"But Doctor Kennison is a geophysicist, not a ... a petrologist or social engineer."

"We have found that specialization is a curse; it fetters the mind."

"I am inclined to believe that your people are—beastial, of a lower ordert than homo sapiens."

"Be careful of what you say, Curious Galway. I can withstand your insults but you must not offend our domain."

"But these ... hanging effigies ..."

"Potential living people..living once again ... if we ... if Martok and the Great One decide."

"They are ... people."

"Let me warn you, Galway,..and Doctor Barodin ... that if you try to interfere in any way with his work ... you know whom I refer to ... you could become one of those ... speeimens."

"You woudn't do that...."

"Science is more important that life to us here in Phanterica. We have, for your information, ongoing experiments on longivity, breeding for human perfection—a little assist to mother nature, of course. And, oh, yes, we've even got one in progress on mind control by cellular adaptation and cerebellum alteration."

"Impossible!" I shouted in the silence of our icy entombment.

"Oh, holy benevolent, kindly Government," Lejah countered. "There are many pleasant aspects to our scientific programs," she hastened to say. "For example, you hae a type of photograph known as laser three dimensional, do you not? We have one that is time dimensional, showing past and future in one revealing depiction. You have developed by means of a crude speaker systen a sound that is three dimensional. We have extended the melodic line from its past inception to its development and thence to its time recapture. Taste and smell have, I must confess, somewhat deteriorated here in Phanterica, though we can smell much better than your hounds of olden times. We can smell the dew on the grass. Sight and hearing, however, are vastly sharpened. We hardly need microscopes anyomore, our vision is so marvelous. The objects that you formerly could see only through the eyepieces of an electron microscope we can now see with virtually our naked eyes."

"Impossible!" I said.

"You keep saying that word. It was a barrier to progress in your time. The impossible is with us now the possible in Phanterica."

"Will we ever be able to speak personally to Doctor Keimison?" I asked.

"That remains to be seen," said Lejah with la cryptic, wry smile. "That remains to be seen. At this very moment, your lives are but trickle drippings from the mineral rocks. Doctor Kennison is this very moment activating the elromagnetic-molecular messages in the rocks, buried millions of years ago. In a word, he is decxrypting the voices in the rocks, molecular voice signatures, energy captured by the rock crystals. His work is of extreme importance to us. Thus, Rapturous Do Gooders, you face extinction by our jealous hordes who covet only our scientific knowledge."

Without another word, she simply ... vanished, as if she had been a delusion, a hallucination of our distraught minds. We were left by ourselves to find the way out of the Ice Cave Museum at which time, a screaming horde Sycophants on albino horses descended upon us. We luckily found a cleft in a rock face to hid in as the mounted brigade of horsemen warriors screamed past us. For the first time we actually trembled. We realized, also, that Lejah was an accomplice in what appeared now to be a subtle intrigue to get rid of us once and for all. We needed to find where a working petrologist might set up his laboratory. We had our first real clue from his ... government wife.

Chapter 14

Our Ingenuous Tortures

By now it was pellucidly clear that these giants of a strange land meant us harm, if not extinction, since the man whose existence we sought was of utmost scientific importance to them and to their own survival. In retrospect I should have seent that the congeniality of the guard Garrunide at the Ice Museum, even of our otherwise affable Tashca and the Nazi-like woman named Lejah were all in collusion to exploit our knowledge as scientists. Even the Chief Executioner, The Scorpion, the equivalent of a hangman, witheld certain cruelties of execution, tortures and the like, so that other interested parties, shall we say, could make the most of our presence in the domain.

I was aware that Kennison, by magical transfer subliminally of information, could reconstitute his very personality, as might a great actor, to become another person. That person was, indeed, Martok, the Minist4er of Dissinformation. I happened to mention to Lejah— Tashca was a witness to my words—that Captin Rollins of the American Destroyer *USS Rushmore,* was also a physicist who had taken to the sea by preference. I saw his frozen body hanging in the Ice Museum, as I had the living corpse Captaian Wethersby, a superb navigator of a made over sailing vessel, a British frigate that had disappeared some years ago in the Bermuda Triangle. As an experienced deep-sea diver, e was doubtless a source of much information about the Undersea world, its life, its geophysical nature, sea currents and the like. We both recognized old friends from the Ministry of Scientific Exploration and were appalled. My eyes caught sight of Rodger Tomilson, an astronomer of reknown and, another, Captain Holmes, a geophysicist of great reputation in the States and of eminentin Europe. The sight of these frozen figures shocked me to the bottom of my sensibilities. I was in a word, *horrified*. The corpse connection of both of us, Dr. Barodin and myself, had put the Phantericans on their guard lest we, somehow, steal information from their frozen repository. In short, they suspected us of being spies predators and possibly saboteurs.

Next, Lejah with motives I did not at first perceive, led us to an inner cavern that offered for our delectation a drop-off cliff which, when confronted with this trap, we might feel compelled to reveal the real purpose of our mission to her country. Lighted by freon torches and surrounded by a guard, we were captives on this little venturee. At the brink of our personal disaster she asked both myself and Barodin the basic physics of flight—the Sycophants possessed no knowledge except empirical as they watched the Perodactyls take flight to sea for the gathering of fish to feed the colonly. I explained the elementary aerodynamics of *lift,* the displacement of air currents from over to under the wing of an aircraft by the very foil of the wing, the displacement being induced by the power of engines that thrust the craft forward. They were fascinated. The big fellows, not underswtanding the import of our words, layed hands on us and for several terrorizaing minutes as a threatening gesture they held us dangling over the precipice. Had it not been for Lejah's intervention they would, these giants, most certalinly have disposed of us puny fellows like worthless trash.

The freon lights led us away from the perilous brink and into a labrynth of tunnels. Then once again the Martok appeared and spun his insidious spiders web about us, as if trying to frighten our psyches into catatonic activity. Or was the figure in the gloom really Martok? His voice sounded strangely familiar-rather like Kennison's!

Lejah-I supposed it was still she-took us to a great cavernous room with a faceted ceiling of glowing stactites where, to my utter astonishmentl, I recognized parts of saircraft instruments, a tail rudder, wheels ingenuously restructured as a wind gauges-air currents in the labrynthian tunnel complex could be very severe, upwards of 40to 60 mile per hour jet underground jet streams. Also in the room were pieces of luggage, a wristwatch with the words *US Army* on it, a ship's lantern, a binnacle, and a great assortment of gems mined from the sea floor. This was evidently an annex to their treasury, the final resting place for artifacts from another world that I and Barodin once inhabited. Lejah reached into a great kiln, unlit, and withdrew a dripping handful of gold coins. Stacked atop of and around this kiln were tons of goldbars, the likes of which one would have found at Fort Knox., These gold bars-and coins-were the salvage from vessels which had sunk within the Bermuda Triangle. Lejah hefted one of the bars and held it out to us. Tell us, she said, why your scientists investigate the atom. Tell us and we … we would like to share this gold with you.

I could not have been more astounded by her proposal. For we were not atomic scientists. I told her so, but she did not believe me, casting a wary, suspicious side glance at me and Barodin. Our expertise was only vaguely related, as was Kennison's, but then I had begun to discern that these Phanterican folk lived out their lives in a mazed trap of studied disinformation, possessors of which we were not.

Just as I turned to go, I heard a venemous hissing as of many snakes and spun around to discover that the gold ingots had turned into venemous vipers and, smelling our presence with their forked tongues, had turned their writhing movement toward us. Lejah laughed a most wretched, mad laugh and with a wave of her hand, like a female Moses, commanded the snakes back into gold ingots again. Her power was in her capacity to perform magic, this I plainly saw, Then, like a change in charcter, she vanished into the darkness.

What we had in store for us would have terrorised even the stoutest of invaders, which we were assumed to be by this time. Bearing a freon torch, Warden Garrunide ushered us into the presence of the Great Wizard, whom we found seated between two immense golden boulders on a cushion of thrashed straw—like a farmer in his barn, the image came to me. I did not underestimate either his cognative or his magical powers, but steeled myself for the worst of experiences..

"I am Asteremus, the Omnipotent," he said, his voice insinuating, filled with sounds of treachery. "I know why you are here. I applaud your courage—and your cunning. Yet I am still your host and so I bless you. Take off our sandals; it is holy ground that you stand on." At that exact moment my eyesight was stricken from me and I stood before the Master, blinded. "Damn-Galway, can you see?" He mumbled something about needing glasses, a foolish conjecture contrary to the reality that we were both stricken blind and now must beg for assistance. But that was not the only fracture of reality we had to endure. My legs suddenly seemed to be frozen, as if petrified by some alien agent, either a beam of sympathetions or a chemical linfused into our muscles and bones without our knowledge. But how-and what? This treachery could mean our deaths while we remained alive. Absurd to even mention such a phenomenon, since I felt nothing but the sudden tightening of my leg muscles, as though suddenly convertsed into brass.

Livilng tissue can be mineralized, but how-by the induction of a deliberate gangrenous interruption of blood flow, a spontaneous tournequet. Yet we were still standing. Blood molecules cannot ly transpose into mineral crystals to create a false "brass," a state of petrification. But we were untouched by any needle, hand or instrument. Instead, it occurred to me that by osmotic pressure a chemical of X unknown structure and campacity could perhaps ascend from the very stones we stood on in bare feet. This mad theory came to my mind. Then did our hands partake of this same frozen state. I say frozen yet there was no change in temperature in the coolness of the cavern where the Great Wizard still sat, watching us.

The thought of Egyptian mummies came to my imagination—they too had been mineralized to preserve their flesh from microbic putrifaction. But we still were possessed with blood that circulated, I had a pulse, Barodin could speak.

He then uttered words which I shall try to recall. They sounded like-*Alamadilish ven catorvbiliet'* But nothing else happened to us physically, except as I say, we could neither move nor gesture with our mineralized hands. Were we being prepared for something, an event, a painless sacrifice to the Great Wizardon his altar of gold?

While we stood there before the throne of golden boulders and straw, I heard Garrunde mimic a raptor bird, gutteral clucking; I heard the snarl of a leopard, the hiss of a viper close by, all of which sounds horrified me, especially since it was Warden Garrunde who seemed to be making these imtition sounds. I could not find any logical reason except to frighten us into further submission. Unable to move in our defense, a great Behemoth appeared from out of the cavernous darkness, thrashsing its tail and and emitting a snarling scream, its yellow leyes aglow in the torch light. As in a nightmare, the beast disappeared After putting on our sandals, we meekly let Garrunide lead us away, our frozen knees and immovbilized hands suddenly beginning to function again. The show for our benefit had been to demonstrate the Great Wizard's power, thereby to intimidate us further. He said to us while we remained mineralized: "I should like to inform you that your only path of escape is to adopt Phanterican beliefs." We knew, at the same time, that by imitating Sycophants, we might escape undetected. Until then, we were indeed in their power, that of a folk who had done away with civilized values and moral persuasisons of conscience. They had been emptied of civilization, one might have said.

We mounted up on albino horses for the ride of our lives, through the Phanterican maze of tunnels, how many miles I could only have guessed, perhaps only two or three. The entire scenario of events had so shocked my nervous system that I cannot even now recall the exact distance.

We turned into a wide cleft in the rocks and thence into a room brilliantly lighted with the same freon torches. I at once recognied the chamber as a kind of laboratory, filled with glassware common to a laboratory. Barodin and 1 looked at each other with a faint smile of relief. Perhaps we would find Kennison in here. With the help of Garrunde we wended amongst the work benches where Phanterican scientists were performing analyses and experiments. I expected to come upon Kennison at any moment. But that was not to happen An immense, inexplicable silence surrounded us when as if by earthquake or fiery implosion, or some other means sof devastation, the tubes, retorts, vials and other glassware began to move, twilstling and coiling and ev=nveloping us like an entangling force, surrounding me and Barodin with a sense of snakelike entrapment. *My God*, I thought, *what is this, the glassware coming alive!* I felt drafts of hot air touch my skin, yet selectively hot enough to soften the glassware as by bolts of random heat that possessed an encoded heat for one purpose only-to soften and melt glass while remaining ineffective on human flesh. Why, why was this happening to us, to encase us in glass, to further diminish our common sense, to blur our perspective, to silence our rebellion against captivity?

I called out to Barodin. His comment was, in retrospect, very funny, but it was not funny at the time. "Captives-weavils in a batch of soft spaghetti!" "Precisely," was my only rejoinder., equally as funny and inexact. Then a great discovery came to me, that Garrunide was, by change of character and appearance, actually Kennison. "Kennisonl, is that you?" I cried sout. "For God's sake, get us out of here.!" Garrunide said nothing, though his voice sounded like Kennisons, with whom I had worked for years and could recognize without a doubt. He had led us here, but for a purpose I could not establish. His little game …!

I try even now to solve the problem of selective temperature infusion, the objective this time: glass. Silicate glass crystals separate at a X temperature, softening, then eventually liquifying them. Perhaps that is how the Phanterican tunnels were bored, by softening the rock crystals with heat, a kind of directed volcanlic infusion of superheated heat. But from where, unless from the depths of the earth, through layers of mantle into the environment of Phanterica, all controlled as geyser-heated water can be ontrolled. I prefer to call this process selective carbonization.

We finally managed to disentangle ourselves, from the soft glassware, especially from the glass tubing, which presented a special problem, all without the help of any technician, who strangely continued to work at their benches unperturbved.even while the laboratory glassware snaked around them. Garrunide, our Warden guide, pleaded an attack of false pity., I remembered an old Gaelic myth which says that a man who is captive of evil can find his escape by singing a song to Gabriel in the language of Ancient Gaels. This Messenger of God will then bring obout their release. And so, taking courge I began as best I could to recite the petition to Gabriel.

> O, messenger of the favorite God
> Bend your ear to our lament,
> Cordon off the snakes of wrath
> And capture the birds of death,
>
> O, Gabriel, champion of faith,
> Messenger of God, hear our plea.
> Fix our enemies in stone and grief.
> Harbor the wizards in the deep pit,
>
> Make helpless the sins of Gael
> And tarry not for our release.

And we shall glorify your Master.
We shall triumph over Cain.

We shall burn Lucifer,
Amd we shall clip the horns of Rage.
Our lives are in Gabriel's bosom,
Our way is discerned by his torchl.

Our steps are secured to flee.
Now we kneel, hear our lament.
We are imprisoned, crushed yet
Not destroyed, thou canst save us.

The earth shook violently, as in a mining explosion and we heard distant screams, as if the entire island were imploding. Barodin and I made our way out of the laboratory, only to encounter Tashca, who had been waiting for us all the time. He was smiling that deceitful, limpish smile of his, It almost seemed that he wished to redeem himelf from his participation in any agony caused to us by our horrorific experience in the laboratory of living glass.

Do you two gentemen actually comprehed the meaning of-happiness?" he asked us. We were *gentlemen* now.

"When we get out of here we shall then be happy," Barodin replied. I could say nothing. We were intimidated, yet we had not found Doctor Kennison. *Happiness* was not on our list of discoveries.

Chapter 15

Their Happiness Syndrome

I heard, or rather overheard, in the Chamber of Deliberations, amongst the Inquisitors, that work was taboo in Phanterica. How the pristine alabaster dome-minarette-pueblo-like structures on the surface, the myriad of tunnels and the ornate interiors of the various chambers could have ben conceived and executed without work baffled me. Prison or slave labor, perhaps. But … no, the nature of the sophisticated robotic machinery I had already seen supplied the answer.

Yet the happiness of the Sycophants surely was not an outgrowth of their robotic society. How wrong I was! By comparison with theirs, our robotic machinery, as on auto assembly lines or in watch-making plants, was still in the primitive stages. I will furnish other examples later. Was there some kind of extra-sensory display of inertia, of human apathy that mechanization inthe extreme satisfied? Why were not competition, struggle, failure and victory more apparent? Why do I call their yen for happiness a syndrome? Simply because it has neither ethic, impulse, creed nor verifiable cause.. It just is. The were happy because they were happy. A silogistic conclusion that was patently visible the happiness that attended them whether they walked alone or grouped in an official assembly. They were happy because that was the natural state of their carefully-fashioned society of indolence, involving as it did a state of mind, a condition of lassuetude, a vision of convenience and molecular inertia much sought after by these folk.

Tashca explained their syndrome this way: We spend our time at useful pursuits. Leisure, your people call it. The old and elderly are the privileged, since the government that once sorely needed their support, can now disregard their existence. We call that Elitism. The word to us has the ring of supernal purity and innocence of motive, that was godliness to your in your religionistic society.

"It is surprising," our guide told us, "what a bowl of reconstituted grain once purchased in privileges. So well did this stratagem of barter work that no one thought to question it Work thus among the indolent was taboo, as it tended to harden the heart and thicken the palms and thus impact love-making. True, the Ethiefets might easily have supported the indolent. A taboo, however, against work among the impoverished-seeming gentry folks, was widespread. To them indolence meant thay were obliged to put on appearances of poverty by sleeping like dogs under old boards and and beneath bridges and walkways. No conning, 1 mused, escaped the indolent in the pursusit of non-work.

We had not gone but another hundred paces when I heard wierd music thrilling through our underground tunnel. It was a style of music which seemed with its first audible notes to to drone and then to roar within the near and distant caverns.

"Here. Sit right here." When I did so the rock, as f plastic, a kind of molecular adaptation, conformed comfortably to my form. "You can better appreciate the happiness of the music if you'll first taste this ravenous disk" He told me that the common people subsist almost entirely on liquids and lichens from the moist rocks … and on fish brought in by the Pterodayctyl bird squadrons we had first observed outside the walls. Tashca expeeted myself and Barodin to down a hideous drink, a sebacious sustance which tasted like bitters and looked like coal slurry.

"Drink heartily. That drink contlains all the nutrients you'll need down here." He followed this up … our meal at a sidewalk cafe, Phanterican style—with a pitch of ugly-looking ooze from mould on roots that protruded through rock ceilings here and there, root gardens he called them, culltivated just as if they were hoed and watered above ground. I have never tasted such brackish betterness … and hope that I never shall again,

"Doctor Kennision … eats this stuff?" Barodin asked.

"Loves it, literally! Consumes it with relish! You see, it's brain food. Almost all of Phanterican activity is cerebral. We do not require huge chunks of hideous dead beef to survive down here,"

"Well, I'm certain glad to hear that," I remarked. "Without potatoes and gravy beef would suffer,"

Meantime the fat uristric music we kept hearing went into a cresdendo which the Phantericans thought best when played loudly, a blaring to match the vibes of their drums. As an amateur musician, I noticed that the music had neither a key nor a melodic line but, instead, was a chaos of sound with only a few consecutive notes that suggested a tune standing out from the mixture. Its reason for existence was completely pragmatic, like clanking water pipes or the thunder of a piledriver. To their ears music that replicated random noise was more gratifying than melody, since melody was to them counterfeit but noise sounded like reality. They would have found musical contentment in a boiler factory, I was certain.

This music is very popular. Its words, when they could be discerned—Phantericans were in the habit of mouthing their words—are laden with happiness sentiments. The music presented itself as the valentine of public domain.

"Yes, I can hear that it is," Barodin shouted over the din.

Some of the giant natives, made so by consensual choice and governmental favoritism the purpose of gargantuan physical size alone, held blaring wind instruments. Others of them pounded with their giant fists on hollowed out tree trunks. Still a third groups, with thick, blunt fingers, thrummed the strings that resembled shimmering wire.

"Tuned to a nicety," Tashca commented, as if a master musician, when, in fact, he was probably tone deaf. "Note the strings—made from spider gossamer, believe it or not, a thousand strands make up one string."

"Amazing," I replied, scarcely knowing why. The fact that I was here was amazing.

The musicians play on strings that are toughened and strengthened by the breath of dying men to give them elasticity. They are then strung by a master crafrtsman who secures the fore and aft ends into the bow of a truncated harp. They are a big folk, you'll remember. He tunes the gossamer to a fineness of pitch inaudible to our humanoid ears, and he then coats them with beeswaz as protection against the elements.

These musicians did truly like to play on their strange harps out of doors, so to speak, for we were almost always under-ground. They did so while other natives frolicked about and made wicked and obscene chirpings with their dimintdtive mouths. It was always desireable that a young man should at least aspire to play their cataract guitar—as I have heard it vulgarly called. The name did not, in feet, suggest its real sound. Having accomplished this sort of music, the young musician should have of necessity become deaf by the age of twenty or so, and like the Chinese condubines who bound their feet, be inacapble of escape from their style of music either from a lack of hearing or an endearment to the musical style-both ends being the ultimate pleasure of its devotees.

If the young man failed to make the category of The Deaf he was deficient and was given lessons by sitting in a sound chamber for 10 to 14 hours a day with only this wierd sort of music filling the small room.

Then there was always a question of course, as to his sanity; to obviate all explanations he would customarily take to opium or hashish or one or more of the stringent psychedelic narcotics. In consquence of these odd habits, our guide explained to us that this unique world was peopled by guitar strumming idiots and lofty thinking visionaries of different descriptions, often adorned with long, unwashed hair … or no hair at all … whitest sporting grungy clothes and affecrting a manner of humilty that repulsed the more sensitive men born in the conmmunity. These were neither the beatnicks nor the flower children of the 1960's but their spirits were kindred, and I saild to to Doctor Barodin, to whilch comment he remarked: "Purely a cutural design."

"You will find these notions about our happiness art curious," said our guide. "In your country your advertising is your vulgar functional art. If it can't be useful … like plumbing or a man and a woman on a mattress … it can never be art. Happiness is the only legitimate feeling we tolerate here in Phanterica, call it Utopian if you like."

"I think Doctor Kennison made some modest pretense to playing the violen in his leisure time."

"We do not have violins, only harps strung either with spider gossamer or, shall I say it?—with criminal entrails to replace cat guts. But we do have any forms of art

"To relieve boredom and ... assuage the savage; breast."

"Beast," Tashea corrected. We do have savage animals down here, but our knowledge of animal lore has enabled us to put most beasts into a trance before they attrack ... great horned bats, two headed snakes, sightless amphibian monsters whose venom is lethal to the touch ... and other native specimens."

"They where is your happiness? Do your folk ... draw them like pictographic art of the ancient men? Art is to please the senses," I commented., feeling rather foolish after having done so.,

"The creative intuition is what we stress. Literally ages ago we abandoned all formal rules for art. Rules are a curse to art."

"Then your ... paintings? ... are artistic anarchy."

"You might call it so. We call it total freedom in art and the only one worth considering. The causes of revolution and war and social upheaval render any pretense to art negligible, thus the past becomes false to the present. Art is forever contemporary since it never looks backward."

"Just like the ... cataract guitar?"

"Precisely. The sweet nothings of yesteryear are vapid, indolent, worthless and without meaning. For this reason we never regard our arts as fripperies.... The work of Picasso, Gauguin, Daumier in posters are the cutting edge of socal unrest and so they constitute ... art. Most classic are was revolutionary in one way or another," he finished.

"And necessarily social," I said, warming up to the subject.

"Now you see the truth. Art must be social, must be revolutionary, or it is stagnent." Our host's small mouth puckered into a smile that revealed teeth like splinters of obsidion. He went on. "The result of social negligence is the condemnation of the arts as fripperies, worthless preoccupations and meaningless ... doodling.. A faith in the worthiness of the creative process, with sound critical reasons to reinforce the creed to believe in their worth, is supplanrted by society's ... your society's ... efforts to return into new balance the injuries to perception and execution abitilities caused by war and crisis. Survival, class conflict, merhantile preoccupation are the sigpans of growth and change, but always uneasily in the direction of ascendance of power, survival and escape. Moderation, reason, balance, fine discrimination, which give depth to social perceptions, are neglected while society attempts to resolve its alterations of the old status quo.

"My, that was some disquisition," I said slyly. As a Cultural Anthropologist I was astounded by his insights and knowledge of our ways. I couldn't let him go. But would you simplify for me."

"Of course, You are our Alien guest With social upheaval come changes in the arts, with stability come acceptance and rules. With vulgar individualism comes anarchy and artistic oblivion by a culture."

"So that ... here....?"

"We strive to maintain a lack of social balance in Phanterica. We promote the arts by this means."

"I don't suppose I'll ever understand," I said. feigning dimness of vision.

"Not unless you are willing, like your scientist friend Kennison, to discard all learning, inventions, science and pleasures to begiln agaln, as sit were, indulging yourself in the happiness that only we know but that is irrelevant to the present-day outer world.."

I could say no more. I was not entirely happy with my exploration of the elemernt of happiness among the Phantericans, for whom I was starting to have some small admiration. They appeared to possess the courage of the ancient explorers.

I am still a prisoner with Doctor Barodin in your domain," I began, for the idea had been on my mind all night.

"Although you are aliens, we cut our guests some slack. You cannot know what happiness means until you attend a wedding here in this underworld of Phanterica."

"It is ... relevant?"

"Couples are known as spasmodic couples. They love withsout clutteing cities with offspring., yet they are under constant surveillance by trained psyciatrists who use Doctor Kennison's invention of the throboscope to assess their condition as a couple. I know, I know—the good doctor was in the process of perfecting its measurements when he—disappeared from your view, Aliens. Moral law does not exist in this domain, and so guilt for sexual lifestyles bear no onerous of painful self-conscious guilt, but, instead, we're purged officially by the Govennennt ... oh, holy, benificient government ... of any ... consequences. Marriage here is therapy. What you call the Sexual Revolution is but a compound of gnorance, about sex, psychologically, biologically and spiritually."

""Just what is the course of your information?" Barodin enquired.

"You've been to ice museum. They are our singular source."

I remembered the frozen cadavers who had disappeared in the Bermuda Triangle decades before, representing to these folk living-non-living books. There can be *no* morality either in suspended animation or in death, I mused. Every tendency toard morality was discouraged, if not severely punished, depending on the context, whether classroom, church, business, playing field. But then, these familiar institutions did not exist here. In this the Ethieists were our enemy. The free mingling of husbands and wives was permitted and even encouraged, urged, so that each Phanterian should not see his mate but once during the whole year. When after this time, the couple do return to each other, physicians than appliy the above named instrument to determine by a mathematical formula whether harmony or friendship differs from those of others around them. I tried to remember certain animals that had the same habit: leopards, the big cats ... penguins ...?

And as to the formula 2/16 5/6988.5 (over_ 188 + 16 it was and still ;is used widely to unite old cronies and discover new mates with a celebratory accuracy. By its consistent use, erotic scientific phenomena had already been established—that marriage is merely a pragmatic solution to unexpected events, and that love as we know it is an inconsequential and purely chance element in all spasmodic marriages. Our guide informed us that Civilization does thereby advance. But now a real marriage I was invited to witness. which, as I look backward, seemed to have been played like a sporting event. We must remember that Doctor Barodin and myself were the enemy and that we were under constant surveillance—by interloppers who were paid in gold wafers for their pains.

Chapter 16

Contract or Covenant

He weighed in as a heavy, in boxing parlance, the unforgetable little Greeter at our intrance into Phanteriea who carried the scales about with him intended to weigh alien thoughts and attach a value to their character. I find out now his name is *Mathus.* No last name since Sycophants bear no last names, their forehead identification chips being all that is necessary for contracts, associations and just getting along in this strange land. I forgot to explain. At infancy an electronic tracking chip is implanted in the infant's forehead and it remains there for its lifetimds, identifying him, locating him, tracking his movements and overseeing his social ... airangements. The Great Wizard has only to access the directory of his inhabvitants, and a chip number for his quary, and he can then access the Sycophant's life details.

Phantericans had navigated from all corners of their floating rock ship, by the tunnel system, by scallops that resembled bubbles and were, indeed, aerodynamic, and by trek over the mountains. They had come to watch the wedding of the bearded giant known as Mathus, the Greeter and Assessor. Unlike many important events here, this ceremony oceured under the open sky. The natives had arrived in their very best suits of skyfoil, aluminized fabric of rare design. Some stood about the central islandette in the midst of a lake, the altar site place for the contract to be formed. They agitated their large hands like swimmers treading water, while they waited for the early evening event to begin.

There intruded abruptly into the throng the fresh news that a well-known one of their number had crashed on the way to the banquet. But since Pbantericans held no fear of death, having conquered its outrageous terror by delusory sublimation, they regarded their soul visitor as being unharmed; his injuries were illusory. In feet, all injuries, the Phantericans believed, were to them a form of self-admiration which they were loathe to let anyone mend or paliate. Several of the commuter baloons almost collided but fortunately did not. The Government indeed allowed these folk to observe their sacred festival days but, I learned, seldom if ever do they keep the time of day, for their lives consist of passive obsession toward Rothgar, their Wizard and, very much like school-ground children, they engage in active play-making amongst themselves. All during these pre-celebration festivities I, of course, kept my eyes peeled for the ever elusive Doctor Kennison.

Gone, I presumed were the romantic courtship overtures of the traditional couple toward each other, as was culturally condoned and blessed in America. Here a marriage ceremony was performed in full dress, like a sporting event of the first magnitude. Its honors, its courtesies, its bloodletting—the last one being totally anathema to the ideas of *union* that I had always treasured, a notion that apparently contradicted the honor of their society, which, being valueless, could lay no claim to honor, a moral value.

Tliek … traditional … marriage would occur not between Principles but between their effigies, their surrogates or stand-ins, just as in motherhood of surrogate women provided the gestation service to the sterile spouse. Under circumstances of wanted surrogacy, consensual acceptance, which is to say, the bondages and liberties of mere love-making, some marriages often did occured in which the constestants were truly happy. It was the word in its broadest sense-*happily* joined together.

On this particular day the … contestants … had already arrived, the surrogates to the marriage. The crowd was assembling in their colorful baloons, paddling here and there in the warm air, squeezing in, balloon beside balloon to get a glimpse of the marriage ceremony. They grew increasingly restive, then the musicians anived—who rested upon hallowed rocks, tottering and swaying with their limber horns, and blasting away in all directions. The stringed instruments of twined spider gossimer across hollowed tree boles, I have already described; the drummers hamnered away with stones on nearby rocks to warm up. When the larger body of musicians had arrived, some 250 in all the bamboo horns clashed in all keys with the concheshell horns. To fabricate horn reeds, bones of fortuitous enemy invaders were sliced thin, whitest I saw some unfamiliar harp-like instruments that were (I was told) laced with fhe guts of Kayss birds, an advanced specimen of the ancient eagle and of the immense *Gypnotic Prowler Triped.*

The male groom, a selectee of the Government, here to be married had let his hair grow down to below his ankles where he kept stepping on it. Thus almost tripping himself, he was forced to knot it and cradle it over one arm. Most of the service was conducted in silence, escept for the music, the Phantericans having created the sort of bottled jug noise, shrieking on bamboo flutes, hammering base notes on the skeleton drum and rattling their conche shells, all rather primitive instruments but they had been created anew—or from words spoken to them by survivors who presently hung in the ice cave museum.

Rocks of black and red pumice were strewn about the ceremonial venue,which was, I supposed, the natives' notion of flower petals. Existing *in* virtual isolation, the Phantericans knew nothing of guild crafted horns, stringed lutes, gambolas, violas and the like. The harp or lyre was their sole invention. Their music pierced the ears, but they enjoyed it, being as I correctly deemed, partially deaf. There were no jazz throes of innovation but, as I have said elsewhere, the rendition followed the sound waves of virtual chaos. The musicians were totalfy naked, thus no manner of custom or dress detracted from their music while, *au natural,* they played like children, with an abandonment that 1 would describe as highly innovative chaos and sophisticated noise.

With passive indifference I watched the events unfold before my amazed eyes. One naked section of the overall "orchestra" consisting of six or seven musicians, you may call them so, found places atop rock outcroppings where, like ancient bagpipers they might sound their several instruments individually, all the while sitting cross-legged above the contending marriage partners. Like a vanguard of lookouts amid a cadre of soldiers, they watched, tootled solemn notes, and honked on their colorful conche shells. Under the setting sun, their parchment white skin, so deprived of sunlight, literally glowed in the translucent golden light, their deep and moody eyes roving about the assemblage in the stony field.

Since Phanterieans, and particularly their omnipresent Rothgar the Wizard, had disposed of the nuclear family through attrition, and had dispersed mutations of conception into embrionic laboratory dishes for experimentation, the ancient custom of inlaw intrusion was not at all observed. It was lost in history's timeless logic of annonymity and then— oblivion. What was not upheld, observed, and practiced was allowed to die by negligence, a tactic used by outer societies to rid themselves of unwanted babies. In the name of government efficiency, Phanterica bad adopted the pracrtice with vigor. Alienation—if not by neglect, then by violence. Even as I watched from between two immense boulders, I felt the effects of this sinister alienation upon my own soul. Phanterieans, despite their common heritage, their community in pitch dark cavern-sharing or perhaps because of it ... were essentially strangers to one another. And I shared that feeling, that intuition of having been cast into the reincarnated vagabondage of primitive animals m the primal forests. I had not forgotten the guardian beasts ot the outer walls, the behemoths, the pterodactyls and vicious coiling snakes.

All the while I feared for my life, for by this time I and Barodin were marked as *dangerous aliens* for being out of sympathy with the Phanterieal culture and way of life. And I knew nothing, except by deduction, of their ethic of respect, if not reverence, for life, I presumed they had none and therefore it was *we* who were imperiled.

The evening came alive with neutron torches fed by electrons flensed from pure rock flakes, their blue and amber brilliance casting myriad roving, elongated shadows across the nuptial field. Their white chalky skins reflcting this strange light, the band sat like enigmatic rock burls adorned by the light, emitting not a whimper from horn or shell, or tipping the drum from time to time. They appeared like pyretic accent-marks perched atop the pumace rocks.

The first event, in what was beginning to resemble an Irish wake, was to be a wrestling match as nearly as I could make out. A frocked prelate in a long cassock his head wrapped in cannonic leaves, raised the hem of his garment. His albino face, long eyebrows, pointed beard and delicate hands roved over the corpulent flesh of the antagonist. These actions ritualized the marriage ceremonies symbolically, the wrestling mimicry ... presumed—suggesting the inner tides of the combative contract about to be formed.

The other combattant was huge, having fed mainly on clams-allowed to mating couples—and on sea kelp. He struck first, wrestling with the cassock of the garbed figure in the prelate hat. He broke one aim **of him I called *The Divine*** by a sharp twist behind the back. He then flung him against a rock, his body dropping limp like sackcloth to the ground. Blood flowed freely from the mouth of the recumbant cassock figure, as if he had received a mortal blow. A cluster of Sycophants retrieved the body from the foot of the great red stone and secreted it out of sight in the woods. The nuptial band struck up a few raucous sounds of music, pausing for blasphemous and arrogant statements from the victor as to the purity of his victory in his attack. The encounter was over. The torches and weird music filled the black night sky. What did all of this prove? Why? I kept saying to myself. What did this scene have to do with a contract or a covenant of marriage? The victor giant with a superhuman strength, seized one of the torches from the hand of its bearer and pitched it fifty meters into the night sky to signal his victory.

One must remember that these players in the prenuptual scene were mere players, symbolic representations of the couple to be joined, and their little play was simply an inactment of common marital traumas. So it was here in Phanterica. Such a scene had a *purgative effect as clinical results showed,* said Trovar, our mentor for the exhibition, he who had Greeted us with his scales at the entrance to the Domain.

The crowd of a thousand or more grew riotous with the excitement and the show of victory distemper. A group of Phantericaas armed with molybidnium visors ran the celebrants through then bore them off the nuptial field. I struggled to withhold judgement; the scientist in me at first would not permit me to become a participant but rather a diffident observer. Momentary I accepted that status. Barodin had turned pale, allowing for himself a slight margin of humanity.

There appeared to be no concept of mercy in the folk of Phanterica, much less any medical expertise or its applications because of their latent religiosity. Of course, I had not seen all of Phanterica. Without fear of death, why survive? I thought. Or was struggle to live the essence of living to die? These folk lacked elemetary compassion, in my view, and therefore justice was alien to them, as were fundamental concepts of love in its many guises. Science, it appeared had leeched out basic emotions of the human race and in their place had installed cruel reason, barbaric retribution, the madness of destruction for its own sake, and any ultimate act that resembled mercy. I was in a philosophical quandry. These creatures of advanced civilization would simply fling aside the wounded and dying and, with a great show of pretended brotherly love, lift the rod-wielding combattant victor upon their shoulders and bore him from the nuptial arena. I now owned the secret of why our early Greeter carried an ordinary iron rod: for retribution and for magic.

An official of some rank smeared the big fellow with the blood of his victim to signify victory to the wedding couple. This was called a *rite of extrapolation, the* display of animus, force, the omnipresence of the capacity to harm, or to permanently maim the female—or the male—spouse was resident in the actions of the surrogate partner and specified in pre-nuptial agreements, In our county such mahem was made to appear civilized by court procedure, One's legal victory would sit upon the shoulder of one's former partner for the rest of his or her bondaged life.

The wedding ceremony, the actual one and not the mocking one, had hardly begun. The balloonist guests were mere jostling figures of flaky light and shadows. The torches seeming to ignite their flesh from a distance where the torch bearers stood on the perimeter of the arena The musicians had not yet stirred from their rock pedestals, swaying only when the noise wailed and shrieked and rumbled beneath the flickering starlight. Their ashen white bodies looked like snowcaps fixed upon the blackening night rocks.

An orator emrged from the edge of the spectators and entoned, like a Greek tragedic orator, in words, which I reproduce here phonetically, as nearly as I can recall them, I have to remark that in appearance they resemble somewhat lines from Old English poetry.

> Wesjkiten fivilmestil puola
> eslamei sj ikfffnols. Wldibimned djus ksillsnz
> siemlineins il svid.
> Idith, sims, aimijoin lil
> altisslainilvan il a la Quelsmia is mis leneimoisq.
> Wfils sien a k sil jia.

145

With this recital the crowd broke into wild hozannas of praise and acclaim. Before their shouts had subsided the couple at last appeared from behind an immense black boulder at a distance from the Chief Priest Rothgar. His, the groom's, clothing apppeared of utmost elegance, consisting of lavish brocades that shimmered in the torchlight; silks of whitest Absenthe leaves adorned his throat, his cuffs and hands, and white feathers of the osprey festooned his legs. His small face was flat like the cut of half a melon, his big, mysterious Phanterican eyes peering and bold, the corrugated right left brain head shape was quite visible, and a smile struck like the cut of a cirass across his face-no teeth, pale lips, as things, set him apart as an object of bridal worship, beauty and adoration. His spouse-to-be showed a small ovular face, laced with beauty spots, carmine lips, a chignon dressed in the cold flames of neutron fire, her cheeks hollowed out, sucked in for the occasion. Upon the right hand of each there clung snugly a dueling glove of sheer cloth, black and sequeinned and dripping with ribbons, the better to be seen on the field. The Priest Wizard announced them to be the bride and groom, apparently a *fait accompli* at his word. Certain Indian tribes on the Great Plains had the same custom. *Bundling* in New England had produced similar results. And among the ancient Hebrews the practice was not uncommon. I should not have been surprised

They were to contest this day-society i a more apt word—in order to fulfill the vows of the official Phanterican marriage-that was to duel against the other until death should part them. The completely upside down nature of this custom seemed idiotic and perverse to me. Yet I was just the observing anthropologist. They would fight till death, live to fight, die to five and live in dying. These folk of the Phanterican civiliation—society is a more apt word—had worked out the anomalies of our ancient marriage to a tee. They had resolved the conundrum of hate within love-bonds, of silence before speaking, of physique communication, of survival through memory and that alone. Strange. Yet did we not play the legal game of reward the loser in our churches and court system?

The engagement, the demonstration of enduring love commenced with a sharp, clanging of of steel on steel, for it was now clear that they intended to duel. Their rapiers rang, their thrusts, parryings were skillful. Both the man and his wife—I use the terms loosely-had had pre-nuptial training for certain. They set their pace for almost an hour, a woman of great stamina, and he of manly persistence. Nothing I had seen in the canverns had left me so depressed as watching this nuptual duel on the public playing field, as it were. There being neither morality nor conscience among the Phantericans, this was sheer lethal rapier play, a utilitarian bout to eliminate the competitor, better still, the *antagonist.* Some animals and insects have a similar ritual, in which the female devours or kills the male, the male instinct to consume its offfepring harkening to cannibalism. But in this case there were no ofispring. The Wizard did not interfere; nothing intervened to separate them. I wanted to shout, to run the *short* few meters into the arena and stop this absurd match destined to end in consensual death. Or then, again, I wondered, was this like the mock drama—intended for show only?

The groom had cut his bride severely with the tip of his steel and she had thrust her rapier point into the flesh of one of his forearms. Each contestant bled profosely. He pursued her, backing her into a rock, addling her rapier point, swashing his blade with vicious thrusrts and parries, point two, point three, down point, nicely done! He danced on the meadow grass. She sank into the mud at the base rock. He then thrust he rapier home and killed her in an instant, withdrawing his steel and noting with aplomb its coating of blood. He then stooped to fasten her bonnet lest she catch a chill.

The bride was now a corpse, made so by her lover. I recalled that we had a folk song "Memphis Girl" in which her jealous lover kills her down by the river then, ringed with fire, he cannot sleep that night for the agony of his conscience. But, here there is no *conscience.* Right and wrong are mere obsolete inconveniences. This bride was placed upon a catafalque, by the upthrust application of a focalized electromagnetic field and made to turn slowly to allow the crowd see her beauty. All guests formed a single line and marched in a circle about the slain bride, tossing gold wafers at her, as was also their custom, to show the approval of the manner of her death rather than to acknowledge respect for her life. The winner stood idly by, stonyfaeed, leaning on his rapier, After this part of the nuptial ceremony was finished, the guests, some of them, climbing up filament ladders, reascended in their balloons into the night sky.

The chanting, ringaround celebrants scattered from the foot of the catafalqude, to their several directions while the torchbearers handed

147

up their neutron flames to each of the musicans crouched atop their separate rocks. And there they sat, like sconced candles in the night while all else turned to silhouette except for the lonely emblem of womanhood that lay upon the catafalque, suspended above the ground, the victim of her own deadly covenant with the groom. He had gone I know not where, like a prairie dog down into its hole in the ground. Oh, where was *Trovar,* the Greeter, I wondered.

The ceremony was over. I had seen it all—a nuptual murder—I doubted not its reality—and had not raised my hand to stop a thing. I could no longer be indifferent to the tragic custom of the Phantericans. Somehow, somewhere I would have to begin to act. 1 had delayed any outward show of violence on the belief that these folk, suspicious by nature, would only hide Doctor Kennison deeper from our eyes, My time-continuum would measure the distance between now and then. If he was not dead, I doubted that he was living a riotous life or enjoying the indulgences of Phanterican women. He was not a sensualist; he was a fighter, a survivor, an … optimist. We would find him.

"Let us try the work other venues down here, Barodin. One never knows … quite possbly they're using him to obliterate the concept of work by a system of rewards for sloth…. Er, Tashca, where, my good fellow, is the *Acadmey of Euphoric Science?*

"Follow me." His expression showed instant suspicion. "We were still captives, that I was certain of. And his facial expresion was a clue that we were onto something.

Chapter 17

Mendicants, Workers and Elitists

I interpolate from a Me speech Lejah gave aus at her Ice Museum, her, I say because the was guardian mistress, expounder, visionary of a sort and ... dangerous, I will tell you why later. Here, however is her version of the nemesis of work, the default of profit and the of the system of free enterprise as we know it. She proudly assertsed that profit was a vestage of the old capitalistic civilization, long ago vanished, purged, villified and excoriated. Why? we both asked outselves. Their answer : it was unfair, unfair to the Mendicants who had nothing of this world's goods, unfair to the haves who did not have enough and unfair to the Elites, who had screwed up things so royally nobody had sufficient profit to satisfy his yearnings and his needs. Profit was shattered as a concept by the eternal compromise of social largesse to the natives, and she assumed, condemned as well by the nations of the world, friend and foe alike. Yet the concept of my work earnings lingered for centuries, in the Phanterican frame of time. The old communist creed of to each according to his ability, to all according to their need, had nothing whatsoever to do with Phanterican wisdom. since we had, to all intents and purposes, expunged labor from out culture. The Vestra, a Russian merchantman had sunk off the Keyes and the Phantericans had learned much about Lenin and Stalin from her captaina land the few sseamen who were saved from the wreck.

But to go on. The Phantericans took that notion and appeared to make something of it. Profit was what workers earmed by their sweat, over and above what money was needed for reinvestment or—to keep the company in business or to run the machinery, etc. The second half of the equation was eonsummerism, but since Phantericans produced little in the way of manufactures, and since their omnipotent Government took care of all their needs, both profit and consumption were excised from the equation and the natives were left with contributing for the good of all, a refined system of volunteerism in which profit was an obsoletism that attracted an odium of disdain and repugnance whenever mentioned. And consumption was a matter of simple Government supply and demand. The Elites never understood this relationship, but what did it matter at this late date? There indeed appeared to be a religiosity to this volunteerism.

Profit, the average Sycophants believed, goaded men's primitive natures to commit heinous acts of deprivation and naked greed. Penalty money was the only near cousin to ancient profits-that is, money extracted from remnants of the olden marketplace encounters. Their Great Wizard thought it beneficial if the people had some means to disperse their personal goods and display their pride, for which the holy, omnipotent central governemnt designed a recrudescence of the marketplace that fitted the purpose admirably. Phantericans were bonded to plea for entitlements as their due. And so away with work for profit to consume! False and injurious thoughts in the courtroom never did catch on as fund raisers. The adversary system and the open marketplace were too closely allied to fool some Sycophants as to their synergistic relationship.

Do not be deceived, however, Lejay droned in her high-pitched little voice. Despite its immense wealth and boasting of the existence of Mendicants-a proud admission of superiority-this rough side of life furnished the ballast to Phanterican purity of motive. These Mendicants lived in cave nitches, wore copper bells slung about their necks and begged alms for the poor. Some Mendicants acquired great wealth by begging, although a bowl of porridge and a cup of tea appeared to be their constituted earhly richess.

Begging enjoined its own industry and frugality to triumph—the standard-bearers for true wealth, yet paradoxically the sustenance of the Wayfarer. She would point frequently to the hanging corpses to emphasize her polemical issues. Only they, the wayfaring Mendicants in all of Phanterica, were exempt from the duty to contribute a lock of hair and an ounce of salt to the Central Government treasury. With these humble gifts the Elitists retired ancient debts owed by societies past in their wealth of hogs, horses and perishables. The GFreat Wizard literallyl wrote off draconian devrts owed by countries that had lost ships and airplanes in the Bermuda Triangle, keeping in mind the Phanteican obsession to salvege what they could of life, including … need I mention it here? rats. Millions and millions of them that proliferated in the rocks and folage above the complex tunnels system of the Domain.

The Great Wizard had, however, to set an example, and so he hired ropers to fashion the hair of contributions into silken fibres, strands made into clothes to adorn the Elite in Governmet: voila, hair shirts, symbols of humility. The attitude was that physical work was onerous and ought to be abolished in favor of play. Children were, a millinium ago, taught this social adjustment in their classrooms, yet old ideas die hard. Babies were pledged in advance of puberty. Upon arriving at that age when conception was possible the female child was obligated to work for three years at harvesting moss and rock lichens, a staple among Phantericans, to pay off her accumulated indebtedness to the benevolent Government—a debt imposed upon her for being female. The male child of five years had the option of becoming a "warrior" or a breeder stud. Many chose the latter, fearing death and therefore chosing love instead of war. An entire generation had once feasted on that ergonomic idea. As for war perse, combat consisted in fighting the elements in shipwreck storms and invasive alien presences, like Doctors Barodin and Conway.

"You think your society was so noble, enlightened and earnest? Let me show you the true foundation of your false concept of-compensation." I noticed that in their time-warp, our civilization was always referred to in the past tense.

"Compensation-many things we did had no price tag."

"You see, already money comes into play. We here in Phanterica have enobled the idea that compensation can be noble and enduring without the use of money."

"It's always involved," I said, "always, even when motives are pure. It taints everything for good or bad."

"We here told that gold is a fancy of the imagination. It embellishes reason with reward. It moves juries to vote a certain way, even when against the truth. It prompts the shakers and movers of your society to act,"

"Thats going a little far, in my friend," I said.

"There's nothing wrong with bargaining." Barodin put in.

"Ah, my Alien Intrude barter is the spirit of a bargain."

"Just so long as both parties agree," I said.

"You've hit it!—all agreements fit into three categories: political, social, or religious."

"I suppose when satan had to depart from heaven, that was an agreement."

"Not if force was used. Force nullifies the idea of compact."

"Then your natives here make no compacts."

"Have you seen any acts of violence? No, because there's nothing that the Government can't achieve or enforce for them. It is their father guide, you must have learned by this time."

"I have, but as to … gold, the manufacturing.…"

"Say no more. Come. Follow me and you will see a revelaion, Alien Voyagers."

We fell behind and I whispered to Barodin that it seemed to me we were being indoctrinated by the ruse of informing us as tourists. All of these novelties of life were beside the point, the urgency of our mission, to find our friend. Rothgar, Tashca and Catarlip were exploiting our naivete, not to mention her."

"Her …?"

"Lejah, the Ice Lady."

"Is this the precious thing you look for?" I asked Catarlip.

"Water," he replied with dry acrimony in his voice. We had arrived at … at … where were we exactly? II asked Barodin. He merelyl shrugged his shoulder.

"Water!" I exploded. I heard the wild and vicious river a short distance away. It roared deafeningly.

""Hear it!" I pointed at the torrent, "Over there." The water issued from a layer of rock high above, a slit that gave freedom to the water table.

"Water is sacred." said Catarlip, the keeper of the Omens, Water Omens. He smiled. A drop of water clung to his beard, his eyes probed my thoughts. "So you think we have no religion! Fools! We worship water. It gives life, it covers wrong, it glorifies the skies, it cleanses thought."

"But ... you do not drink it." I said.

"It will poison strangers but not our people."

He walked toward the torrent He reached out and clasped spray in his fingers and dropped it into a wooden cup." "Nature responds to those who love her," he said.

"Perhaps—the river. But ... can you not dig a well?"

The Keeper's whole physique took on a snakelike appaearance, an apparition of a hidden spirit. His laughter drowned out the roar of the river. He stooped down and scooped up a handful of mud. With this he fashioned a small image, kissed it, pressed into its clay an object from his pocket to give it eyes and flung the icon into the river. "We must take care to show our respect," he said.

"Blazing thrusts of spearmight and paindeath await him who injures the earth."

""How in blazes can you injure the earth when you dig for watrer?" Barodin asked, whose geophysicist training had familiarized him with not just the hydrological cycle but the finer points of origin, dispersion, migration and transcendant capacity.

"Wew are commanded by the mountain and forect worshippers never to harm the earth. When you dig, you injure the soil. We pay homage to it."

Catarlip moved a small boulder. From its dark mold he picked up a salamander amd blew activity into it, so that it seemed to glow as if afire. "All life, even what we do not see is sacred," he said to lus compatriots.

"Mother earth," astute Barodin said, interpreting rightly the Keeper's words.

A great rumble suddenly occurred as a rock slide broke free from a crevasse in the ceiling schist, and there stormed, like an advancing cavalry a troop of Sycophants, dressed in hunter's green, to swoop down upon us and surround us, their fish-tail whips, their glowing green shirts and obsidion belt knives all visible in the murk as they milled about usthreateningly on their albino horses. Their leader held a brief talk with Catarlip. It was perfectly obvious that our lives were in eminent danger.

Catarlip informed then that we were aliens and they were not to avenge theimselves on us for our ignorance of their ways.

"We came not to steal or deprecate your land but to find a friend," I spoke out in our defense. We certainly did wish to become corpses in Lejah's Ice Museum.

"I understand."

"Do not be scornful of the earth. It has its defenders."

"We are not violent," Barodin said.

"You migrant idiots speak nonsense. The earth hates Mankind's violence. She has her own kinds of violence."

"Men of violence seldom use their reason," said Catarlip, as if voicing an Omen under his care.

"Your armies have destroyed our mother earth's bounteous goods many times over."

"That could not be helped. " Barodin replied. "We bled just as the earth bled."

"You remain here—in our Domain-by our permission only. Your doctor friend Kennison stays by his choice."

"By your clever plot … your deceptive ploys."

"You accuse us of deception, Galway. Then why do you not leave? Go!"

"Not until we find our friend."

"He is in hiding."

"His molecules have been transposed," said Barodin in jest. I was angry with Catarlip's refusal and his reply.

"Time travels in an arc, the continuum is not a straight line. Your Einstein realized that We have put Kennison on a journey of disco very. He will return when the time is right for him to do so."

"What in the devil does that mean, Catarlip … that Kennison is running in a squirrel wheel?"

"That he is working in our petrological laboratory at the present time—to find why time has no essence though it is equal to matter. Since matter has suststance, it also represents time existence. Oh, but you do not understand these things. Nor do the rocks yield up their secret of the ionic encapsulation of human speech waves within the stone grain molecules … t though that is his quest … to find the answers to such questions your science is mute about. If sound can shatter rock … well, why hay mom?"

"You sell us short, Catarlip …"

"Sell you short..! Impossible!"

"Underestimate our comprehension. We may resort to …"

"Not to violence, Men Ones. For that will mean your deaths by introduction of genetic chaos."

"Cancer? Hardly," I plead, this time putting on an act. Catarah came over to where I knelt, still, and pressed his cold, flaky leathery palm against my face. Remember that the Sycophants in their checked fury still milled around us with threatening squeeks and great barbaric arms upraised with fishtail swatters held aloft, threateningly.

"I am real Do not attempt to fool me, Alien Ones. We have observed your science. The stone gods watch over us. Suddenly a shaft of sunlight, like a facet that catches vargrant light, flashed cinamon, yellow and cyan* And just as suddenly the rocks above us split and through the dust there descended a second cadre of armed men, with neither guns, spears nor arrows in their hands but with strange angular, global instruments that—I came to discover—measured our lives in nanoseconds. They showed their delight by extinguishsing the linear vitality of one of their kind, a Sycophant, who had come too close. They then, by manipulating this strange triangle-octagon-rectangle geogetric instrument of bronze, superintended by a ballof fire, they were able to restore a lost one to life, all this before our eyes. Catarlip waved away the first cadre in the irridescent green shirts and astride the snorting albino horses. The atmosphere had changed in our favor. We were not going to be flung into oblivion by some sort of Mongol hord.

"It appears you do have a religion-giver and taker of life? No?" I ventured.

"Our gods are not anthropnterphic, being of stone, yet alive. You do not know that, like your God, we can elecrtomagnetically rearrange the atomic structure of molecules for recombination of disparate elements into whatever we envison."

I looked at Barodin "Pure elementary chemictry," I said to him.

"Pure force," he replied.

"Our control of power and of superforce, a boiling energy confined by Rothgar's magnificent will, can be used for our people in altering completely what our physical world requires, We hold your lost survivors in our captivity solely for our use."

I was seduced by sheer curiosity, conned into going further with these creatures, like a band of brigands who had vandalized our culture, our science. We were considered the Mendicants.

The Sycophants stopped. A snake coiled around my body and neck. I panicked. Tascha laughed, as did the others, Catarlip pulled the snake from me. "Do you not understand how we control all life down here? I am Keeper of the Omens, and our sacred tithe is: "Once created, never destroyed, only changed. We forsee great trouble for you, disaster to your people. Beware your lust to worship security, since you trust not your capacitys to foil danger."

"Do you understand what this guy's talking about?" Barodin asked.

"I'm trying my hardest."

A pool of water suddenlly opened up near to us. Catarlip reached out and with one finder touched the pool in its mud with his bony finger. The water, limpid, brackish lin the dark, opened up like an eddy. A maelstrom of mists shone like gossamer before us, reaching back through the forest glades elsewhere in the Domain. Catarlip led and we followed, having put aside our quarrel, as the cadre of Magiciaiis disappeared through a rock cleft. The mists were circular, swirling like churning seafoam on breaker heads. Each foot I put down impressed itself into the soft snowthat clung to the misty walls of the coil of water.

"You lead us into a trap," saidying to make myself heard above the sound of the churning water,

"You perhaps are more of a fool than I thought," said Catarlip

"And I also see that you prefer your sort of death ... the strangulation of the eonselience."

The Keeper of the Omens sat on a boll of water and thought "Conscience? What is that?" he enquired. "Is it a sort of ... science?

The Sycophants babbled among themselves. We constantly felt that our lives were threatened, but I were too far into Phanteriea to effectively escape. In fact, we had no sense of direction or distance; they had been removed from our minds. All of this magic show, this fury of warrior display and impressive might had never really let up.

The air grew fetid, stiffling, the blue haze remained like a sworl of mist in a dream vision, spiraling downward. The way had closed in behind us. We were going to drown like two rats, suffocating to death by the cutoff of air? I could think of a thousand ways we should go to our deaths. But the Phantericans obviously wanted us to see something that lay ahead. We had to adopt the submissive way of the Phantericans or we might perish. Then I realized that a powerful image had intruded into our air space: Rothgar, the Great One.

"You have evaded death," Tashca said to us, we having left the Chamber of Omens behind ... or was it above us? Yet were we not entrapped by forces outside our control, forces of nature, energy, time, mass? As I looked around me, staying close by Barodin, we both realized that we had crossed the river—beneath its savage waters. I wondered again what fate might have overcome Kennison I thought we must linger. What was his fate?—a question that kept crossing my mind again and again until it had become my obsession,

"I read your thoughts," said Catarlip, Fate is your answer to the unknown. Science is ours. Here in Phanteriea, knowledge replaces religion, reason makes mind the only life, doubt is antequated, faith is a chimera, and Ttruth is one of life's great variables. Hedonism has much to recommend it. Carnality has much also to recommend it; it is good for the soul. Your doctor frilend clung to his old ways for so long; in his case their destruction was slow. Then our familiar guide and informe, Tashca, transmogrified himself and become, invisibly, apart of the surrounding rocks.

"I see you entertain a reasonable doubt as to the existence of the demons." I felt Catariip's his cold fingers on my forehead.

I replied, "Weave your web of suppositions."

"Your old methodology of a reasonable doubt is a fantasy. It does not bring reason into the picture at all but simply uses the word to destroy the opposition. If a doubt does exist, that doubt cannot be reasonable, since dubious reason is of no value at all. We have an omen: Doubt will prove your peril, denial of Truth your destiny and faith your destruction. These things always come to pass. That is, as you call it, an oxymoron. But; enough. You want to see your doctor. He labors ... forgive me the use of an archaism. He is a good Phanterican. We appreiate his brilliant mind."

As he spoke through the ages, the pain and torture of suffering, a voice of deep gutteral tones, the voice of the tomb, it entoned: "Power ... Wayfarere ... power ... suffer for power, seize power. It consoles, it redeems ... " The voice trailed off as into the distance. I and Dr. Barodin were astounded, stunned by this display of Medieval charisma, all the while Medieval armor, as if borne on the motes of the dust appeared and vanished before our eyes-chimera, hallucinations of the imagination. These barbarians had proved themselves to be of scientific enlightenment although of barbaric intent, decked out in pagan regalia., the true society of utility and obedience.

A few meters in front of me, in a pool of light as a spotlight in the theatre, there was outlined the form of a gargantuan man The light fell on his face. He spoke:

"You are welcome to my place of ... Power. It was Rothgar, the Great, none other could be so terrible. His face was shriveled, his flesh ashen, his v oice monotonal as if in a chant. I do not hide it. Be seated.". He jingled a small bell at his belt and a Sycophant entered with an air of obeisance and set before us a chalice of wine. The Gargantuan offered it to us. I sipped. Our host, for so he was, then lighted three slender tapers that stood on an ornate mahogany table-which I had completely overlooked in the shadows. "I seldom see guests from outside Phanteriea," he began, like one of the ancient monastic gerus, a Dalhi Lama.

"Outside ... how did you know?" He regarded me with a skeptical and piercing gaze that suggested a subtle disdain, that I, a scientist, should ask such a question.

"Power is legion ... yes, the very words power and legion ignite passion in me!" He hovered one hand over a candle flame. I smelted the burning of flesh. "Have you heard of legion power? "Of the angels."

"Power of mind over the flesh is but one sort." He examined his scorched hand. "This ... this is nothing compared to death by the hand of Power that is foe to mercy."

"I know of powers that physicists work with."

"Yes, Kennison is working in that area this minute ... speculation, the monent of enquiry, the absence of presumptuousness. Oh, these others-the believers in power are so presumptuousin our laboratory we work with changes in the constituent temperatures of minerals, metals and elements generally. Did you know that temperature has a dimension in its energy that can be measured in linear metres ... rather like expansion ami contractionor ... let us say ... the time interval between ignition and feeling. Energy in transit requires time to traverse distance, you realize ... or do you ... Alien Novitiates?

"No, but I can imagine it thus."

"You can imagine nothing! Confess it! I covet that core of blue heat ... my soul's light, the ambition of my power, the nexus of ambition-power."

This short oracular outburst, this reaching out toward power of various sorts amused me at first—until I saw how deadly serious he was about Power.

He picked up a second candle candle from its holder and, waving it in the air circumscribing half a circle several times, he clasped it to him repeating the gesture like a priest blessing the atmosphere and the flame.

"This ... flame ... purifies the environment ... power ... the power of flame to purge, cleanse, sanctify and sanitize ... the power of heat to transform," he finished with a slight hint of laughter, returning the candle to its holder on the table. As if returning from a distant trance, he then fixed his gaze upon both of us.

"Your corrupt civilization rarely accepted challenges to ambitous power, only to neglect it ... power that which mollifies and pacifies. So oppposite to what I love!" Catarlip walked away, paced across the polished travertine floor of his chamber, flinging his arms upward toward the mask of the Great RothgarWizard. For that was he. "Oh to wield power by word, by edict, by emotion! It's not the times that make the man. He achieves greatness by the power that he finds." He was in a mood for tyranny and inwardly I cringed. "Create fear and attain to power! Generate anger and exploit power. Cultivate love and express power." There was nothing human about his oracular tirade, but his words ami he were things to be feared as evil. I detest the word but still I luse it because it fits the dimensions of this Priest's words and his spirit of wrath.

He jingled the bell on his buckler and again the Sycophant entered who, as if on cue, placed a large book on the table from a wooden dolly. The cover was inlain with mother of pearl that shone in a ring of radiance around the volume.

"This is our Code of Phanterican Power, the distillation of eons of wisdom into one small book."
"I am anxious to know what it is ... this power you speak of." "Fear, anger, love are the true sources of power The man who sees this power must interpose himself between its source and its objective to become power itself, incarnate. Fear, anger love—each speaks

with a distinct voice borne partly from heridity and partly from the environment. The seeker after powr must never evade the bloody, whitehot, piercing centrism … his might, his role." He went on.

"Power is valorous. There is more science in one hour of sustained battle than in a fortnigfht's struggle with test tubes.

By this time it appeared to me that he deeply desired to don his full armor and engage me in some sort of sword combat—which would have ended my life at the hand of a barbarian.

"Power is useless unless it has a purpose. Power for show is vainglorious." I hopes my simple words would have an effect on his mesmerized mind.

"I see you are a natural-born mocker, Alien. There is in your society the decay of pride, its inability to adapt to change, to mutate its own species, to invest in new solutions."

"You should travel to my country."

"Power is the confirmation of history …"

"Yet it is the denial of progress. In excess it impedes freedom"

All the time while speaking his aides were suiting him up in a shining coat of mail and solid armor. And now, "Oh, gods of stone, cut off by Hehdtian blackbearded monsters, demons from hell. Do you see afar … they ride out in clouds of dust, boiling hell with blood and knives within churning wheels of cutting steel. Let us go … lances ready, have only one thrust to do our duty …!" With these words and folly suited up in Medieval armor, Rothgar in his madness sped from the stone Chamber of Power, leaving myself and Barodin to wonder at our own sanity. Catarlip, Tashca, who had returned, the aides and others stared off into the distance darkness with the expressive hauteur of pride on their countenances. We were closer than we thought to finding Doctor Kennison.

Chapter 18

Revolt of the Barbarians ... and Escape

I and Barodin were unexpectedly caught up in the fervor of revolt that a massive contingent of the Barbarians had begun with steel and savage venom We had no idea of how many ofl the giants Sycophants were up in arms, literally. We had intended, foremost, to pay a visit to the Petrology Laboratory where I, for one, mused on an intuition that Kennison might be there. As a geophysicist, he knew a great deal about rocks. As a human being, he would seek protection in the sanctuary most familiar to him, which was the laboratory. Furthermore, relative to petrological crystal experimentation, in the back of my mind was the notion that sound waves could be trapped and encapsulated within the ionic crystal structures of perhaps certain rocks. Varietiesof metamorphic strata would be the best contender for this type of solund wave recording. Or was I losing my mind, my perspective? ... to think that such a phenomenon could actually occur? The notion was so farfetched, so absurd that the expected answer was not possible. Yet, the luminiscent mind of Kennison would find an answer if anyone could.

But now this revolt of the Barbarians against whom" I had not the vagueist notion—perfhaps against Rothgar, the Wizard, or their omniscient Government, or he deprivations of their lives in these rocky burrows on Island 12386, my numbering. We had no option to flee, since our way was blocked by the Barbarians. All around us we heard the hot cries of the enlightened savages. My sword ... shield! Slash, clang … again I strike bloody blows for the Wizard and Phanterica hold on there … parry the thrust, you bastards … doubt the short and fear the raised club…. slash.., slash, slash … by the stone gods of the ways, keep clear or I'll turn you into a plow share, I promise … fbr me and great Rothgar … Thus did the bloody battle wage on and we were without either armor or weapon in this violent requiem to the grave. Tashca had deceived us. The benign appearance of these Visgoth-like giants, with all their immense strength and their profound enlightenment, frightened even the soul of the best of warriors. Numberless women and wives and babes were caught up in the general ferment of revolt, but neither I nor Doctor Barodin could figure out what they were revolting against, since their ways of life had always been so peaceful Or had we mised the slumbering rage of some prehistoric mutation of animal species fear? We were, somehow, as scientist Aliens, the painbearers, but not the combatants with the savage sword. Remarkably, too, as an anthropologist I found it amazing that their weaponry was 3.000 or more years out of date. There apparently lurked wsithin their genes an obsolete blood strain that had led them to this impasse, but was it against an oppressive leader for their personal freedoms? None of the Barbarians we had seen appeared to dwell with the spirits of rash hatred or revolutionary angst. Happiness, as I had earlier found, was endemic among the people of Phanterica.

Noble sword, congruous destiny, maldictive reply, kindly defender were phrases that came to mind. In this particular arena, where we had inadvertently found ourselves-we had no map of the tunneling in Phnterica-the combat arms, shield, spears, maces and the like affixed to one wall, the large figures sof the Madona holding her babe, the crucifix of the Hospitaliers of France, the stone catafalque of several dead leaders of the Phanterican State, the Code Book that Rothgar had read from and, most singular, an a carving of the crucified Christ on the Cross in solid gold, crown of thorns, body sunken and dead, side pouring real blood … this among these Barbarians, a prize of battle … I sensed a strange demonic power in here. I did not understand it or my sensation. As I was reflecting amidst the turmoil … a capacity most scientists possess … I felt the wind of a sword swish over my head.

A great Barbarian accosted me. "Do you go or do you stay?" He raised a mailed fist and shook it in my face. Creatures of Enlightenment were they! victims of the casuistry of false premises … men are good and time cures all ills. We fled, picking our through the entwined, writhing mass of combattant forms if the slain in the semi-darkness. At the tunnel entrfence a giant of a man with a sword in his hand, poised as if the executioner with the guillotine knife ready to strike, let us pass, this to my great surprise. I thought we wore gonners for a moment What, I mused, if Kennison were in there and flailing away as one of the captive warriors. It would have been so out of keeping for him.

A strange voice said to us, "Come to the rookery!" Of course,I thought, he meant the slum of some description, but instead it was more like a situation room, with a cadre of four or five giants pouring over their maps of Phanterica. A first glance at the map suggested the tunneling in an underground mine-which much of this domain was. Again I—we—could tear the boom of storm seas against the rocks above our heads. We were out of danger temporarily. Here was where the money, so-called, was minted. Over by an immense hearth a Barbarian ladled liquid gold into button molds for the wafers used by Phantericans as coinage. This multipurpose room was alive with the tension of the rebellion. A laboratory aide with bleached skin and almost sightless pink eyes directed our attention to the map table with his pointer of elephant ivory.

"You will not be able to leave our Domain without help."

"We do not intend to leave ... just yet. We are searching for a friend who was lost some years ago here lin Phanterica. We hope to find him."

"Phanterica is now is a state of turmoil. I doubt you will be able to find him under these circumstances."

"We will never give up trying," I said.

"As you wish. But just remember that we cannot help you as we would ... like to."

"Where is the main laboratory?" Barodin asked.

"Don't expect to find it without ... assistance."

At that precise moment I heard the shouts and screams of what sounded like a thousand children, their tiny fists pounding on the door to the Situation Room. "What ... what is that?" I asked the Barbarian at the map table.

"Those are our children. They too are in revolt."

"But why?" I asked though I knew all too well why—a perception of maldictive parental constraints-but I had not anticipated their full-scale rebellion.

"Children in Phanterica are bred for artificial purposes, since they have proof through pornographic films of their useful existence." I heard whimpering, then crying, sobbing, as some of the children were led away. "You must remember that they go to their deaths, their sacrifical deaths."

"Sacrificial …!" I was astounded, bemaused, totally taken by surprise.

"But why are they sacrificed?" Barodin asked.

"They ensure the longevity of our people by surrenering up their own lives."

His explanation seemed incomprhensible to me, a blatant contradiction in purposeful procration. "They do not leave us either helter-skelter, but must be slain when the moon and stars are positioned just right."

"My God! Infanticide … but why, why?" Barodin cried.

"Female children, breeders only, then … death." I was speechless.

"And cripples whose defects are not innate, they too breed warriors, scientists, protectors … We sort them out later in our breeding program, when they manifest their true natures."

"And how is that … done?" I enquired, intimidated by the montrorous linhumane implications of the Phanterican program.

"Astrology!" the interpreter said."Would you care to watch a filming?" he asked. I refused as did the Doctor. "If you succeed in leaving us, that is only because one of the children, chosen by the roll of the blessed dice in conjunction with astrological readings will be sacrificed to bless your departure."

Again, I was dumb founded. I tried to make it clear that we would not leave without Kennison, whatever necromancy was sinvolved. "We are … patient … searchers," I told the Barbarian. Tgebm when the idea of our rescue came to me, I thought to ask, "How is it that Phanterica is never seen from the air."

"Simple, " said our soul Interpreter, who was also our map guide. "As a stick is seen to bead when emersed in a jar of water, so our island disappears by such tending of the sun's light by prisms located strategically around its perimeter.

I gasped, "Impossible!" And yet it had to be. The prisms bend image of the island into invisibility* My scientific thoughts were thrown out of content when they were abruptly brought up by a new horrific experience. As soon as we had left the Situation Room and the manufectory of gold wafers, I was sorry for our decision. For roaming the corridor like beasts suddenly released from their cages were hundreds of Gargoyles in rebelliuon. It was they who had started the mass revolt. Of that I was certain. Their ugliness and their perverse ways could lead them to act no differently. It was as if all of Christendom lhd been rolled back to the Middle Ages and these fiends of false lthirst for truth, these demons sof the deliberate lie of sanctuary were let loose upon lus by ... by Rothgar? My mind reeled with their sudden mad attack, as alien representatives of the Dark Ages. They foamed with sensate hatred of B arbarilaa enlightenment, as I had observed it to be ... at timems. Gargoyes, ex cathedra, as it were.

Gargoyles. They mocked at modesty, so enthralled were they with their black robes of power-angst under a mysterious light that shone from nearby rocks. I espied, dressed in britches, a female Phanterican, having her long golden hair put to the scissors, the tresses falling upon the wine-colored rag in tangled beauty. Her hands were stretched out, fingers ornamented with precious stones; the long, delicate-featured face looking merely sad. From time to time she would look at herself in a hand mirror.

"She is beautifull-4he Wizard's wife, Lejah, who promised her people she would cut her long golden hair when her husband began to relent of his control over the Sycophants. But since he has not done so, she cuts her golden hair anyway out of homage to his lying promise."

It was the voice again of Tashca who was speaking. Where had he been, come now, come then?

"She is exercising a rite to homage," he explained.

"We do not care much for this ... display."

"Oh, but you must realize. This is her true angst, since she wills to power over the domain co-equal to Rothgar's"

"He risists."

"You have noticed ... and you are right, Intruder Aliens."

I marveled at the strange custom, te exchange of values, freedom for the Sycophants or death to the beauty of the tyrant's wife. I heard the loud, boisterous giggling among Gargoyles nearby. They cursed amongst themselves, they growled their displeasure, contending against Barbarian mockeries. Their gutteral shrieks were wild and untamed, Outbursts came like piercing and ominous threats to our ears. Their mouths spewed water, as of old, though they were venomous, beasts of the jungle who were in love with violence and death. They were unspeakably ugly to me.

"What are they but Gargoyles."

"Demons," Tashca replied.

"They are ghastly! But why are they here?"

"They will tlry to tempt you to remain here, in Phanterica, to keep them company."

"I am mad."

"Not quite yet, Doctor," said Tashca. I was trying to grasp the significance of their being here, like great leeches risen from out of the mud. They continued to watch and to growl and shriek from time to time. "But what persuasion do they put forth? I am here ... that is, I remain here with my good friend Dr. Barodin, until we locate him."

"They known all about him. They are familiar with his purpose here in their domain."

I watched them admiring their owns flesh. They poured libations onto the floor that became brackish yellow water, casting back broken bronze reflections. Their eyes were of stone, their faces macabre, ears batlike, huge vacant eyes, fanged lower jaws on one and grinning stone teeth in another, representing neither animals nor humans but demons They leaped down, spraying us with their smelly splash from the bracksh pools. They seemed to beckon us to join in their frolic.

"If you do not run and they find cause to trust you, they will speak."

"You come and stay with us. We will give you happiness," said one with a snicker and a splash of water from the pool. The snout of one was fixed in a broad grin, another used his fingers to pull Ms fat lips apart, yet another with a lolling tongue seemed to mimic evil approbation. I turned my back on them and ould hear their spashing about, muffling their murmurs. Both the living and the dead seemed transfixed on their stony faces, preferring a bleeding orgy of perverse pleasure to silent dark spirit-indoctrination. One sang then whispered, than sang again into my ear. Perhaps that was to relax my suspicion. A little farther on we came to a sunken pool into which a strange hidden irridescent light played, revealing, strewn across the bottom, the jewels of the ages, like a fantasy of wealth none of our world knew. I stopped to read a sign in the exotic Phanterican tongue, translated herewith:

These treasures are thrice blest
by you, the gods and all behest.
Keep none for your vacant use
but cache all for man's abuse.
It's yours if you'll deny your soul.
Come, rake the heavens like a cleansed
bowl.
Forsake banile trust, reasoned jest,
Induloe your heart at your own best.
With wealth, richess and sacred gold
you create life, you purse death
foretold.

"The are putting on their best show, to entice you to become like they, rich beyond measure and with access to the wonders of science- which you have already tasted."

I could never ever become confidential with these Sycophant Barbarians and, most especially, since they counted amongst their familirs the ugly Gargoyles-tempters of the Middle Ages, they that drink water and invite us to go refresh and share in life's ugly tragedies. Yet they had delivered their enchanting invitatioa Strangefy, I fell into a mood, sensing time's remove and a fading consciousness. Had not Barodin caught me I should have struck my head upon a nearby rock outcropping. The environment was indieed a hostile one, made for spelunkers and demllons. In my twilight of consciousness, I felt that I was being led down to the chamber pool of bejeweled water. A dream came to me awhile I floated supine on the water.

As a soul I struggled upward, like floating to the surface, my head helmeted, the cask overlain with lavish silver and gold. My face glowed with surprise, jubilation and eternal joy. My eyes roved greedify to find where my body lay. Finding it separated, my head remained to itself, then found the solid agate of my body's torso, bleached to purity white by the waters of the pool My feet remained attached, encased in boots of rich tigre skin, tied with the sinews of an alephant's skin and its toes shorned, the heels sheathed in horn of animal hooves.

I am attired but cannot describe in what, yet I overlook my vast treasure atop a rock, which metamorphoses into the steeple of an ancient cathedral. I raise a chalice, give a benediction and drink heavy draughts of the sacramental wine. I them take on the figure, the stature, the power of the subdued Christ who, I am led by the chorester to believe, is myself. My reasoning is chimerical, maddraingly random and jingling.

The Chorester is dressed in one of the Biblical cloaks depicted In Da Vinci's Last Supper. He scrapes up all the jewels on the bottom of the pool, entoning his blessings, while I, immobilized by my dream of perfidity, await the next command.

I am an opiate to my own senses, having been tempted for the time being. At least my lown soul to this vision of instant richess. I wait. The angels cut off my legs and I can then disappear beneath the surface of the pool. The watser now churns furiously. My severed head rejoins my body and the full corpse drifts away whilel, in my reasonig, remain floating atop the pool water, the senstenee of death having been delivered. I awake.

I first notice the Chorester, fluting on the edge of the pool. Rats that were peeking from the cracks vanish with his notes. He puts down his instrument and picks up a book, whose words appear on the outside as well as on the insidse.

Pearls of wisdom, jewels of intelligence,
topaz of fine manners and agate of
trust, These are yours if you'll stay, but go
and you will rot away, decay into
Waters of oblivion. Feath and sranguktion,
make the soul dance wiith death's
agony.

The Choristser flutist closed his book. The waters churned, and he was gone below, as if diving for great clamls or abalone or pearls. What was I to make of both the dream and the words from the book that Chorester read. And who was he, anyway? The book seemed to point to the future in some strange way. Sycophants, I knew, clung to a strange reverence for the flesh, dead or alive. When one departed this domain, he was suspended by magnetic repulsion while wierd music and flickering lights played upon his revered body. Some Indian tribes practiced the same ritual, only they used poles to lsuspen the corpse.

The Book simply stated that reverence in realistic terms There was also a passage, which I later remembered, that said that the deceased might be used in future experiments. By a method of chromosomatic fission, scientists might supply a deficiency, say, in longivity or disease resistance, by cloning the deceased, who would then be of help to meet certain societal needs. The freezer bodies were one source, but they were kept for information purposes. The cloning specimen, picketed in formaldyhyde, was a veritable DNA source. The salvation of all Phantericans, like the Shakers of old, was a total reliance on their autonomous preservation—although, unlike the Shakers, they did practice sex. They were, indeed, a colony. Phantericans made it their custom to turn their eyes skyward as the spirit of the deceased hovered in the air. The energy of suspension was slowly reduced and the body, loaded into a small skiff, was borne seaward by twenty of his chosen friends as oarsmen, a practice that harkened back to knighthood when the afterlife was thought to lie beyond the waters of a river or a lake. As an anthropologist I make note of these practices.

But back to our revolt of the Barbarians. I had twice been attacked white in the vicinity of the diamond pool, but was saved by the dissolution of the swords by some strange energy of fragmentation, in which the bonded molecules in the chystals of the steel simply vanished, transmuted, into the air as if gas. Yet the savages wsith great glee and babbling amongst themselves had thrown me into the the Gargoyles pool of acred reflections and covert wealth where I gurggled and tried to climb out Tashsa had intervened at just the right instant to protect me. Enduring the pool slime, he extended the shank bone of a great prehistoric beast for me to take hold of and hauled me forth to stand dripping in slime of good, quite poisonous to lingest.

While I was ust emerging from the sunken pool I heard the fanged thunder of a horde of Barbarians, carrying torches and some wafting banners that said, Kill the Aliens. They flew down upon us like an avalanche of horse and human flesh. I and Barodin were not Medieval fighters. But we did have other world insigfht We clasped an armflul sinuous spider threads from a nearby weaver of webbing, some eight or ten of these, and flung them at the legs of the horses. We succeeded in thereby tripping them up. I and Borodin each of us then seized a Claymore-like broadsword and commenced to swinging into the marauders, here and there lopping off a head or disemboweling one of the Barbarians. Sheer Luck! … and their clumsiness due to their size. I decapitated two of the Heathens before I was struck in the foot Barodin slew one one, but our resistance slacked off with the sound of their Masters voice and a trumpet call from afar that instantly turned them around. We apparently were but small game, actually.

No sooner had the Barbarians, not defeated but obeying their commander Rothgar, left us than we heard wild screeching. The shrieks came from the stony throats of the Gargoyles, who were on the march again, to destroy as many Barbarians as they could find who were drinking Phanterica's water.

"Devils at play-it's them again," Barodin exclaimed as he prepared to defend himself with Slaymore steel which he had drawn froma its wedged thrust into a rock linl the battle for our lives … and lucky, too, since the Barbarian had lain his spiked fist into a piece of schilst, missing the doctor's head by ;inches. in the fury of their combat. While he began to swing at the ugly stone faces of the nearest Gargoyles, who spat out water at him, I was determined to show grit and pride in the face of these grinning, lascivious troublemakers, the Gargoyles. I simply removed from one pocket a comb and striking it on a nearbylrock convertsed its agnetic properties into a hand weapon, a harrow of pointed spikes and sharp rims that covered the fist. I began to lay about. Not a few retreated, since they feared losing face from a well placed blow. Hand blows being of no avail to dispel the ugly creatures, I picked up a spiked club, a Medieval monarch of battle, and began to swing it arosund my head when, just as suddenly as they had appeared, they departed from us, A voice, a trumpet call I did notl hear had called them to retreat. It was obvious that they were not pleased with us. Tuning back toward us, one, with a grunt, spat flame at me like a flame thrower. It just as instantly turned to a harmless treacle that lay bubbling on the ground.

"Those Gargoyles—what were they all" I askedwith little presence of mind.

"They gamble. They gamble your life against theirs." an Unidentfied Informant answered.

"How so. They must be mad," I said.

"They may be ugly, doctor, but they are the inspiration for the Barbarians, our citizens of Phanterica.""

In what way? I asked

"They bring up phantoms from hell. They conjure dark spirits to inspire the Sycophants. They manufacture—your word is create ... solopcisms-untruths that deny truths-all for the merriment of the Barbarians ... since happiness is their ultimate goal. If all this sounds ... perplexing to you, Alien Ones, remember that strangers from your world are just as perplexing." Tears shone on his cheeks. Our Unidentified Informant left us. His sadness baffled me. Perhaps he was one of the devious ones or, then again, a rebel seeking asylum ... somewhere.

The Barbarians made another attempt to intimidate us. They shouted and yelled as they charged our small company of two on their albino horses. Several swept past us, hoping to frighten us to run from them. But run—to where? I ask.

One dismounted and to my utter surprise, offered me Ms sabre. "Kill me," he said as if ordering a subaltern to perform murder in order to avoid disgrace in battle.

"Why?"

"Dere's one ting gratis yez ban gotta learn earned, floy, and tat's that life is force."

"Thanks for the info," I said, "I thought all the time it was energy."

"Force ... force is what makes the conony go round."

"I see in the instance of your people that force runs to rathlessness."

"Illusion."

Barodin saw my utter dismay at this odd conversation. Yet this time he did not come to my rescue. And why should he have? Before our very eyes, this Barbarian fighter metamsorphosed into a Medieval gentleman, wearing his armor still but attired like a diplomat in black bow toe. tails and spats over his burnished armor. When we arrived at the Petrological Laboratory—did I mention that our fortunes in finsing Kennison in a petrological lab were far better than a fruitless search of any other venue? we both stopped as if we had sprung a steel animal trap. A strange pungeance came to my nose-the scent of hot, nay of burning rocks. They emit a clean, piercing flat sort of odor … when not containing oil. As I rounded a corner, at which a group of tenchlician were assembling fragments of Venus Rocks-a sign informed me of this-I can upon a wierd-looking creature, not a giant of a man but, indeed, rather wizened. His face was dour, his body showed the long bowed looks of an enfeebled and decrepid man bent over his twork lab bench. And upon the top I saw the most amazing silght, a display of rock fragments placed upon a vibrating miniatlure platten which, like Mexican jumping beans, were, poppint qne moving about on the table as if a magnetic force was directing them from within—reminiscent of a show I played as a boy with a magnet and iron filings. As he watched, the grains, the particles of rock, were inscribing their random paths u;pon an adjacent motion drum. On a green screen before him waves, as sound waves or aurlicular pulses, smoved at criss-cross angles. He was attempting, I assumed, to record the sounds within the measured grains of rock whose crystals had received, ascrystatsets of old, radio waves of human voices of the ages.

I looked closer at the face, drawn, eyes dark withall and hollowed with hidden fear yet, as I watched, he projected an almost gentle look on his lips, as if he purred sover his experiment. His hands were bony, skeletal almost, yet upon one of them I spotted-my God! the ring of Westmont Science Academy, my old school. He did not look up at me; I spoke first.

"You arte … you are … " I ould searcefy get the name out Barodin came into my peripheral sight, I glanced at his face transfixed by alook of stonishment

Again, I said, You are … " I could was unable to finish.
"You are looking for me.?
"Doctor Kennison, I presume."
He did not move but, looking at the moving grains so frock and glancing at his graph recordiang of the sounds within their molecular structure, he said. "I am he, yes, I am Doctor Kennison."

I expected him to rise or turn to face me but he refused, instead keeping a steady eye on his experiment.

Another approach, the famoiliar one: "And you are recording … sound waves, inherent in,..

"Captured by the rocks over the ages, sound waves trapped and inert within the molecular structure of the rocks."

"Remarkable."

"Yes, isnt 't?" he replied The great voices, the magnificent sounds of nature, the words of civilizations past … I shall not die until I have completed my experiment."

"All there, in those grains of rock."

"Like the sands of the deserts of the world. The rocks are the true keepers of history, human history, Doctor Galway."

"You have been at this … experimemnt for quite some time.…"

"Thirty years to be exact I have already transcribed the voices of the rocks in my second volume. Scence is making history in this small experiment, Doctor."

For the first time he turned and looked up at hem. "Doctor. Galway … I should have associated your name with … the Blarney Stone. Galway.… " He lapsed into silence again and returned to concentrateon his experiment.

"We are leaving …"

"Leavmg … Phanterica?

"Yes."

"And I suppose you expect me to go with you, I am indebted to you for your patentee and courage in coming here, Dr. Galway, but …

Yes, Dr. Kennison.… " le reached up and back in a great and empty sigh and stretch, as if the weight of one thousand experiments rested on his mind, soul and frail body, Then … "I have taken an oath to Rothgar, the Great Wizard. I serve him and our Beneficient Holy Government." He paused. "My allegiance is not to Phanterica, my new land, Dr. Galway."

Barodin spoke up. "We could place you in the finest of laboratories in the States where you could continue your experiment with the very best of scientific equipment.

"This is sufficient," was all he said. From then on we could exact no more from our rescued victim. We realized that we would have to surrender up the remainder of our mission to fate. For now Knnislon was thoroughly captivated by his adopted Domain and enmeshed in an experiment which, to be quite candid, would bring only scoffing from scientists back home. Here he was content. We would leave him thus to remain contented and to seek whatever scientific answers he searched for and that would resolve his life, for he was no longer a young man. Taking a deep whiff of the odor of the hot rocks glowing red over the bunsen burner, and casting a last glance at Kennision, we turned to find our way out of the petrology laboratory.. Our mission was completed. But why, I wondered ... how had he come to this venue in his life? AH I could think of was that he had been kidnapped, perhaps sailing in too close to Phanterica. He was an avid fisherman at one time in his life and that zest had brought him to this fate. We would have to wend out way out at last. But along the way....

I heard from a distance a noise like a great choir. While my attention was diverted, the elegant knight disappeared. A teleological truth then struck line-that these Barbarians were the ambivalent creation of their central dictatorial Government, and that their bifurcated personalities were intentionally developed by centrist regulatory doctrine so as to facilitate their movement the more readily either to one side or the other of a political fray, a sleeping ideology or an actual combat. This deliberate political caprice represented the highest pinnacle of societal disinformation. In this manner they could accommodate the surprises and speculations of politics, which were mere pretense anyway in the totalitarian State of Phanterica.

But that singing—a tune I ought to have recognized—did sound so familiar. I listened more intently. I took a few steps only to find mnyself, alongside Barodin, inside a cathedral like room hewn from the petra schist, having a great high ceiling of rock with light transmitting sheets of stone exposed to the outer sky. Emvedded in the see[age stalagmites around the walls were thousands of skulls of former Sycophants, a sort of crypt in fact, and reminiscent of the ancient catacombs that the Christians had developed to evade Roman persecution.

As I expected, a choir of Barbarians, all of them attired like the elegant armored knight, were standing in ranks and weeping as they chanted—Rock of Ages—which was a comical parody on our circumstances. The choir must have numbered several thousand; they rang their ancient hymns from the rear of the great chamber. The entire room was enveloped in an enferno of cold flame, produced I know not how, but suggesting trial by fire of Phanterican faith in the Great Wizard Rothgar. Was this spectacle forty millions of light years from scientific actuality on earth? I tried without success to consult the time continuum of multiplanetary light years. The flames did not burn myself or Barodin, and I saw no angels walking about to protect us. Could it be that these Choiresters acknowledged suffering of any sort? What then had happened to the happiness creed? While they sang each man thrust a fragment of stalagmite into the air, a translucent icecicle, as a kind of salutation, turning then to embrace one another, again facing front to sxtend their rock salutation, as if they did, indeed, worship the very rocks from which they had carved their Domain. It then occcurred to me that these singers were cultural holdovers, anachronisms of another age, who sought immortality by praisisng death and extolling power-which they believed could ble transmuted into the after life. To the Phantericans, immortality represented the enthronement of death rather than the grappling with life. And they were holding up to us this miasma, this shsibboleth of faith, expecting that we would in time come to believe! Great Scott!-in what-immortality? I had long ago given up that empty hope.

I, we, stood at the back of what would have been a nave of a traditional cathedral when, with a magnificent, stirring, a rattling thunder of feathers-similar to s flight of the Pterodactyl fisher birds—their cloaks became as wings and, lifting off like angels, they arose from their places and flew to some other part of the domain. What I had just seen would defy common-sense description, yet I must record the spectacle.

Phantericans did not, however, believe in an afterlife, despite their show of religiosity. Was I to search for the grave instead of the living flesh of Doctor Kennison. A herd of Barbarians, Barbarian vandals, thundered through the chamber, which only moments ago had been their chamber of worship. They carried guttering torchels. I thought again of the laboratory, of the implements therein being so familiar to Kennison. I had a sudden impulse and desire to visit the main laboratory of Phanterica. By this tilme I was fairly confident of how to find my way in the maze of tunnels. It would have to be the Petrology Laboratory. The Interpreter in Medieval armor and wearing the elegant bow tie and gloves reappeared as a dort of usher walking before us. Once within the lab complex, I perceived the saffron smock

175

on the otherside of the shelving, loaded with retorts and other glassware. I had almost completely forgotten about Barodin, standing there beside me. So as not to ellicit surprise, I shuffled to the end of the laboratory lbench and glanced down the aisle. Busy measuring a crimson liquid into a test tube, my eyes fell upon the emaciated form of my friend Kennison, bent over his experiment and the bunsen burner flame!

"MyGod! It's him!"

Even in the thirty years of his absence, can this be? His hair was white, as I had expected, but his frame was so modified as to no longer resemble the body of an ordinary man but an exotic extrapolation of a man, down through evolutionary history. He had become a replica of physiological projection, in terms of the anthropologist, into a mutated fom of a Phantericaa He, the eminent Doctor Kennison, had become one of them—a Sycophant, a Phanterican. I was stricken with horror. My voice caught like a wood chip in my throat. I did not know if I should simply leave or acknowledge my presence and attempt to refer to our old friendship. He sensed that eyes were fixed upon him. He raised up. There were those immense, lambent Phanterican eyes, the blue veins so prominent in the parchment-like white skin, the tony fingers, the misshapened head and small feet.

"You recognize me, of course, Galway?"

"You remember my name...."

"Quite naturally," he answered with impatience. "You are puzzled and surprised by what you see."

"Yes. And I am not a little agitated."

"Agitated—for what reason are you agitated, Galway? You are a son of corruption. Here you see the true mutation of a stripped of his corruptibility, of his evil emanations, of a soul that held him back from utter exploration of space and creation of life."

"That was not the soul...."

"Conscience, damned conscience. That was it."

"I can't answer that for you, Mory."

"Nor have you forgotten my first name...."

The lean old figure next in words that were the last I should ever hear from him. He spoke as if into the bubbling retort over the burner flame. "You are corruption. Your civilization was corruption...."

"Then why do you cling to its idols, Kennison. I have seen them all, here in Phanterica.?

"Simply because the gods are with us, always. Those old insensate ways, those artifacts must also stay?" He spat out flame; his spittle flashed like particles of phosphorescence.

"Why must I stay? No, Kennison, you still cling to gods for surpport I, we here, must go."

He looked at me for a long minute and then he said something that I shall never forget. "In life's survival conflicts, mutations must be recaptulated, not to worship the corrupt past as you did in your insolence, but to provide us with a sense of unstoppable, unchangeable destiny and the absolute direction of our Phanterican history."

His words shot a thrill of horror through me. I had to run. I had to go. I turned and ran from the room, capsizing a barrel of heavy water in my flight. I felt that I was losing my mind, the whole purpose of my journey, my vagabondage was lost in the moment of time when I confronted the entire Phanerican destiny in one man. I felt that I was slipping into madness. I ran down the corridor, screaming aloud, oblivious to what lay before me, until my strength should give out. An intuition had pronqrted me many times at the start of my mission; it now seemed to direct my raging steps.

Just as we thought escape was within our graps I heard the mad laugfltfer and moans, then the wailing of of—Lejah. "I send you my sons," she cried. We heard the shrill squeekings of, my God, hordes, swarms, literally hundred of thousands of brown rats that had invaded our tunnel from the forest above. Rats! My God, Barodin, we'll be eaten alive!. They would trap us,? Barodin.

Not quite. He pulloed from his leather jerkin a flute-like instrument. "Salvage, old boy-from a member of the w4dding band. Ifigured I could do a better job than he. I saw the little animals peering with their shining black bulbous eyes at me, and how they reacted to the sound of this flute.

'Run, Barodin, I shouted.

Instead, htook up a position on a recomblent bouder and began to blow, but no sound clame forth from the insgtrument.

"They heard it-pitch is too high for lusl." The rats looked confused and ran about undin the light of the tunnel torches as if searching for something, while Barodin continued to blow. All I heard was his breath over the reed of the instlrument Within another halfg an hour and no more the last of the rats had disappeared into the cracks sof the nearbvy rocks, from whence they had first emerged.

"Thery cant stand the shrill pitch and so it hurts their little pink ears, and so they go," Barodin explained.

Barodin, are a veritable Modes driving the frogs back to the Nile, in this case the rats. Lets go, man. Lewt's get out of here. Kennision is bewsitched and we can't carry him out drugged."

"Maybve he'll improve their—science?" said Barodin.

"His passion-no matter where he is." We both knew, being slcientists, that this was a true statement of his dedication to hisart and discipline—which we shared with the prisoner—that Kennision would alchieve some degree of happiness where he worked in their laboratory,

I found the trunnel way that led to the entrance of the Phanterica complex. The beast was not there. I sprang depths sof the sea. I stumbled, I tripped and fell. Picking myself up, I ran on to what destination I was not certain. But intuition told me the way was right. Barodin, like a shadow, was not far behind me. I reached an outcropping on the eastern side—I presumed it was east by the surfs position—where I arrived by the impulse of terror.

A familar sight caused me to stop suddenly. A miracle! Was this, could it be? It was—Marco! This was an hallucination. I was out of my mind. I strapped off my shirt and waved it wildly, frantically, at the small craft I climbed atop a nearby rock and kept waving my shirt. A hatted figure aboard the boat waved back. Meantime Barodin had built a small fire of bark duff and dry reeds, fanning its smoke into the air with his hands. The moments seemed like forever, when the fisherman put a small skilff into the water from the stern ofl his trawler. I rushed to the water's edge with Barodin, fixated by the prow's cutting the inlet water until at last we heard the keel scrape on the beach sand.. We climbved in, embraced Marco joyously and asked why he had taken so long. We all laughed with the great relief of our tension, whereupon, removing my outer coat, I placed it in the bottom of the boat and promptly fell asleep, exhausted and in considerable pain from the damp, rheumatic conditions of the ordeal we had endured.

I did not regain consciousness until I awoke in a bed, in a familiar house. Dr. Grogan was bending over me, trying to get me to sip a little broth and bathing my fevered face and forehead with cool towels.

"You've been through a lot, obviously ... and away a long time, Galway."

"Too long ... too far ... " I could not think of anything else to say and dropped off again into a deep sleep.

"I awoke again in a delirium, shouting at the top of my voice, Where is God ... where is God! Doctor, where is God?" I tried to get up to put on my clothes but was hastily pushed back into the pillows.

"He is here ... if that's what you want, Doctor. Galway. We found you wandering along the shore."

"I was put ashsore, Doctor Grogan ... by a fisherman friend."

"I see. Well, suppose you rest a little longer." No sooner had he said that that I lapsed once again into a delirium. This time it lasted almost three days. When I awoke, medical doctors, three of them, were bending over me.

"We saw no reason to remove you to a hospsital. The delirium of a fever has strange hallucinatory manifestations ... other than that, all other diagnostic evidence is relatively normal"

"Hallucinations? What was I saying, what was I doing?'

You have sustained a severe trauma to your psyche. Amnesia ... our friends say you cannot accout for your absence."

I wish I could remember all that has happened to me, how I got here.

"Perhaps there will be no need to, Doctor Galway," said Dr.Grogan. "You see here ... here are notes, rather scrambled,..in your condition ... We found them in your pockets, notes that partially describe your adventure to ... Phanteriea?" The very sound of the word sent a convulsive shiver through my body. "This ... civilizationl that you visited: we should like to hear more about it."

"I'm not sure I'll be able to."

"The mind, even in its hallucinatory state, is highly retentive, Doctor Galway," said sone ofl the medical doctors. "But for now ... rest." All but Dr. Grogan left the room.

"Is this ... this adventure true? It can't be yet ... it is."

"I am no poet, Doctor Grogan, and scarcely a writer of stories. But all I have written in those notes and what I shall recount to you happened just as I relate it."

"Hold on. Let sme fetch my pad and pencil."

He was back in a moment, drew up a chair to my bed and to write down the adventure of my wandering in search of Kennison, which I have retold in these few pages. One day, believe or not believe, according to the impulses of one's own imagination, perhaps my experience will shatter some preconceptions of the scientific world. But that I endured these experinces I persosnally have not the slightest doubt and so affix my signature to these last words as a true and accurate testimony of my wanderings. Doctor Kennison was lost to another world,and insofar as I had discovered where he was, my mission I accounted a success. Friend Doctor Igmar Barodin was my witness to the truth of all the events that befell us both. After a full recovery, I would like to try to publish my memoirs.